"Imagine the earth 10,000 years hence; envision all the infinite possibilities ultra-evolution offers homo sapiens, and catapult into the world of Gordon R. Dickson's MUTANTS. . . . A well-known science fiction master, Dickson has wove eleven chilling stories of a brain-dominated superfuture into a shattering glimpse of man's possibilities."

—Baton Rouge *Morning Advocate*

"Vividly imaginative."

—*Book News*

"Sometimes comic . . . sometimes grim . . . but always thought-provoking."

—*Hartford Courant*

"To be topnotch, science fiction must have life and plausibility. MUTANTS has those characteristics."

—Washington *Star*

**GORDON R. DICKSON**

**has also written:**

**ANCIENT, MY ENEMY**

**NAKED TO THE STARS**

**HOUR OF THE HORDE**

**NONE BUT MAN**

**THE STAR ROAD**

**etc.**

# MUTANTS

*Gordon R. Dickson*

**DAW Books, Inc.**
Donald A. Wollheim, Publisher
1633 Broadway, New York, N.Y. 10019

"Warrior" and "Idiot Solvant" were first published
in *Analog Science Fiction-Science Fact*.

"Danger—Human!" and "By New Hearth Fires"
were first published in *Astounding Science Fiction*.

"Of the people," "Rehabilitated," "Listen," "Roofs
of Silver," "The Immortal," and "Miss Prinks"
were first published in *The Magazine of Fantasy
and Science Fiction*.

"Home from the Shore" was first published in
*Galaxy Magazine*.

FIRST DAW PRINTING, MARCH 1983

1  2  3  4  5  6  7  8  9

 DAW TRADEMARK REGISTERED
U.S. PAT. OFF. MARCA
REGISTRADA. HECHO EN U.S.A.

PRINTED IN U.S.A.

# CONTENTS

# INTRODUCTION

In the alchemical laboratory of the mind, we see the Alchemist, wrapped in a blue gown with the signs of the zodiac upon it; on his head a tall, conical cap covered with cabalistic symbols. He bends over the instruments of his craft on a long, dark table.

An experiment is in progress. Apparatus runs from one end of the table to the other. At the far end, flames flicker, licking upward, red and yellow and blue, around the blackened base of a retort in which something like green seawater bubbles. From the top of the retort, through a tube, passes off a mysterious gas of a red-blood color, twisting and turning, flowing through a number of vessels, from a first one shaped like an Egyptian pyramid, through shapes like galleons and cathedrals to others like tall, modern office buildings and—yes, even one like a space capsule seated atop a Saturn Five engine, ready for liftoff from Cape Kennedy.

But this is not the last vessel. The gas proceeds even from there, with many a strange twist and turn and weird flickerings of light, through further shapes hard to describe . . . until at last it distills into a large, bulbous, crystalline retort. In this retort, finally, we see the distillate toward which the Alchemist is working.

But what is it? For the distillate continually changes shape and form and color—now white, now black, now brown, now red, now yellow . . . and even, it seems, there are still other colors there, but changing too quickly for the eye to identify them. Now earth, now air, now fire, now water—the distillate seems to be all these in turn and all at once. But is there no way to separate and identify its parts?

Yes, as the Alchemist knows. One by one, he takes up a

row of test tubes and draws off into each a little of the distillate. In the test tubes the drawn-off vapors settle and resolve themselves, in each tube into a different form and shape. Here is one like a mighty, dark, and unconquerable man. And another like two children, so far developed over present-day man that there can be no understanding, no kindness between them and him. Here is another man, human still in form, but one who has turned his back on the land, in response to the ancient, irresistible call of that sea from which the fluid was drawn in the Alchemist's first retort—that seawater which is still almost identical with the blood in human veins. And *here*, and *here*, and *here* . . . are other possibilities, in all, eleven in number. No two are alike; but each one is a living fraction of that distillate called HUMAN, which the Alchemist has obtained.

But . . . now, the Alchemist has used up all his test tubes and still the distillate has not visibly diminished in the final retort. He has taken out eleven possible human variants; and still the mass called HUMAN in its potential seems hardly to have been touched. The conclusion is inescapable. Not in his lifetime, or in the lifetime of a thousand Alchemists, can all the different possibilities of the distillate be drawn off and identified.

Under the blue gown with the stars and planets and moons depicted upon it, the Alchemist's shoulders sag with defeat. The task he has begun is beyond his powers; as impossible as pacing off the vast boundaries of the galaxy, step by slow step. But then, he brightens.

For, if nothing else, he still has his eleven separate forms— to be examined, to be savored, to be known. Turning his back firmly on the limitless unresolved possibilities of the distillate, he picks up a magnifying glass and reaches for the first of the mutant possibilities he has decanted.

It is the test tube holding the shape of the dark and mighty man. . . .

# WARRIOR

The spaceliner coming in from New Earth and Freiland, worlds under the Sirian sun, was delayed in its landing by traffic at the spaceport in Long Island Sound. The two police lieutenants, waiting on the bare concrete beyond the shelter of the Terminal buildings, turned up the collars of their cloaks against the hissing sleet, in this unweatherproofed area. The sleet was turning into tiny hailstones that bit and stung all exposed areas of skin. The gray November sky poured them down without pause or mercy; the vast, reaching surface of concrete seemed to dance with their white multitudes.

"Here it comes now," said Tyburn, the Manhattan Complex police lieutenant, risking a glance up into the hailstorm. "Let me do the talking when we take him in."

"Fine by me," answered Breagan, the spaceport officer, "I'm only here to introduce you—and because it's my bailiwick. You can have Kenebuck, with his hood connections, and his millions. If it were up to me, I'd let the soldier get him."

"It's him," said Tyburn, "who's likely to get the soldier—and that's why I'm here. You ought to know that."

The great mass of the interstellar ship settled like a cautious mountain to the concrete two hundred yards off. It protruded a landing stair near its base like a metal leg, and the passengers began to disembark. The two policemen spotted their man immediately in the crowd.

"He's big," said Breagan, with the judicious appraisal of

9

someone safely on the sidelines, as the two of them moved forward.

"They're all big, these professional military men off the Dorsai world," answered Tyburn a little irritably, shrugging his shoulders against the cold, under his cloak. "They breed themselves that way."

"I know they're big," said Breagan. "This one's bigger."

The first wave of passengers was rolling toward them now, their quarry among the mass. Tyburn and Breagan moved forward to meet him. When they got close they could see, even through the hissing sleet, every line of his dark, unchanging face looming above the lesser heights of the people around him, his military erectness molding the civilian clothes he wore until they might as well have been a uniform. Tyburn found himself staring fixedly at the tall figure as it came toward him. He had met such professional soldiers from the Dorsai before, and the stamp of their breeding had always been plain on them. But this man was somehow more so, even than the others Tyburn had seen. In some way he seemed to be the spirit of the Dorsai, incarnate.

He was one of twin brothers, Tyburn remembered now from the dossier back at his office. Ian and Kensie were their names, of the Graeme family at Foralie, on the Dorsai. And the report was that Kensie had two men's likability, while his brother Ian, now approaching Tyburn, had a double portion of grim shadow and solitary darkness.

Staring at the man coming toward him, Tyburn could believe the dossier now. For a moment, even, with the sleet and the cold taking possession of him, he found himself believing in the old saying that, if the born soldiers of the Dorsai ever cared to pull back to their own small, rocky world and challenge the rest of humanity, not all the thirteen other inhabited planets could stand against them. Once Tyburn had laughed at that idea. Now, watching Ian approach, he could not laugh. A man like this would live for different reasons from those of ordinary men—and die for different reasons.

Tyburn shook off the wild notion. The figure coming toward him, he reminded himself sharply, was a professional military man—nothing more.

Ian was almost to them now. The two policemen moved in through the crowd and intercepted him.

"Commandant Ian Graeme?" said Breagan. "I'm Kaj Breagan of the spaceport police. This is Lieutenant Walter Tyburn

10

of the Manhattan Complex Force. I wonder if you could give us a few minutes of your time?"

Ian Graeme nodded, almost indifferently. He turned and paced along with them, his longer stride making more leisurely work of their brisk walking, as they led him away from the route of the disembarking passengers and in through a blank metal door at one end of the Terminal, marked UNAUTHORIZED ENTRY PROHIBITED. Inside, they took an elevator tube up to the offices on the Terminal's top floor, and ended up in chairs around a desk in one of the offices.

All the way in, Ian had said nothing. He sat in his chair now with the same indifferent patience, gazing at Tyburn, behind the desk, and at Breagan, seated back against the wall at the desk's right side. Tyburn found himself staring back in fascination. Not at the granite face, but at the massive, powerful hands of the man, hanging idly between the chairarms that supported his forearms. Tyburn, with an effort, wrenched his gaze from those hands.

"Well, Commandant," he said, forcing himself at last to look up into the dark, unchanging features, "you're here on Earth for a visit, we understand."

"To see the next-of-kin of an officer of mine." Ian's voice, when he spoke at last, was almost mild compared to the rest of his appearance. It was a deep, calm voice, but lightless— like a voice that had long forgotten the need to be angry or threatening. Only . . . there was something sad about it, Tyburn thought.

"A James Kenebuck?" said Tyburn.

"That's right," answered the deep voice of Ian. "His younger brother, Brian Kenebuck, was on my staff in the recent campaign on Freiland. He died three months' back."

"Do you," said Tyburn, "always visit your deceased officers' next of kin?"

"When possible. Usually, of course, they died in line of duty."

"I see," said Tyburn. The office chair in which he sat seemed hard and uncomfortable underneath him. He shifted slightly. "You don't happen to be armed, do you, Commandant?"

Ian did not even smile.

"No," he said.

"Of course, of course," said Tyburn, uncomfortable. "Not that it makes any difference." He was looking again, in spite

11

of himself, at the two massive, relaxed hands opposite him. "Your . . . extremities by themselves are lethal weapons. We register professional karate and boxing experts here, you know—or did you know?"

Ian noddd.

"Yes," said Tyburn. He wet his lips, and then was furious with himself for doing so. Damn my orders, he thought suddenly and whitely, I don't have to sit here making a fool of myself in front of this man, no matter how many connections and millions Kenebuck owns.

"All right, look here, Commandant," he said, harshly, leaning forward. "We've had a communication from the Freiland-North Police about you. They suggest that you hold Kenebuck—James Kenebuck—responsible for his brother Brian's death."

Ian sat looking back at him without answering.

"Well," demanded Tyburn raggedly after a long moment, "do you?"

"Force-leader Brian Kenebuck," said Ian calmly, "led his Force, consisting of thirty-six men at the time, against orders farther than was wise into enemy perimeter. His Force was surrounded and badly shot up. Only he and four men returned to the lines. He was brought to trial in the field under the Mercenaries Code for deliberate mishandling of his troops under combat conditions. The four men who had returned with him testified against him. He was found guilty and I ordered him shot."

Ian stopped speaking. His voice had been perfectly even, but there was so much finality about the way he spoke that after he finished there was a pause in the room while Tyburn and Breagan stared at him as if they had both been tranced. Then the silence, echoing in Tyburn's ears, jolted him back to life.

"I don't see what all this has to do with James Kenebuck, then," said Tyburn. "Brian committed some . . . military crime, and was executed for it. You say you gave the order. If anyone's responsible for Brian Kenebuck's death, then, it seems to me it'd be you. Why connect it with someone who wasn't even there at the time, someone who was here on Earth all the while, James Kenebuck?"

"Brian," said Ian, "was his brother."

The emotionless statement was calm and coldly reasonable in the silent, brightly lit office. Tyburn found his open hands had shrunk themselves into fists on the desk top. He took a deep breath and began to speak in a flat, official tone.

"Commandant," he said, "I don't pretend to understand you. You're a man of the Dorsai, a product of one of the splinter cultures out among the stars. I'm just an old-fashioned Earthborn— But I'm a policeman in the Manhattan Complex and James Kenebuck is . . . well, he's a taxpayer in the Manhattan Complex."

He found he was talking without meeting Ian's eyes. He forced himself to look at them—they were dark, unmoving eyes.

"It's my duty to inform you," Tyburn went on, "that we've had intimations to the effect that you're to bring some retribution to James Kenebuck, because of Brian Kenebuck's death. These are only intimations, and as long as you don't break any laws here on Earth, you're free to go where you want and see who you like. But this *is Earth, Commandant*."

He paused, hoping that Ian would make some sound, some movement. But Ian only sat there, waiting.

"We don't have any Mercenaries Code here, Commandant," Tyburn went on harshly. "We haven't any feud-right, no *droit-de-main*. But we do have laws. Those laws say that though a man may be the worst murderer alive, until he's brought to book in our courts, under our process of laws, no one is allowed to harm a hair of his head. Now, I'm not here to argue whether this is the best way or not; just to tell you that that's the way things are." Tyburn stared fixedly into the dark eyes. "Now," he said, bluntly, "I know that if you're determined to try to kill Kenebuck without counting the cost, I can't prevent it."

He paused and waited again. But Ian still said nothing.

"I know," said Tyburn, "that you can walk up to him like any other citizen, and once you're within reach you can try to kill him with your bare hands before anyone can stop you. I can't stop you in that case. But what I can do is catch you afterwards, if you succeed, and see you convicted and executed for murder. And you *will* be caught and convicted, there's no doubt about it. You can't kill James Kenebuck the way someone like you would kill a man, and get away with it here on Earth—do you understand that, Commandant?"

"Yes," said Ian.

"All right," said Tyburn, letting out a deep breath. "Then

you understand. You're a sane man and a Dorsai professional. From what I've been able to learn about the Dorsai, it's one of your military tenets that part of a man's duty to himself is not to throw his life away in a hopeless cause. And this cause of yours to bring Kenebuck to justice for his brother's death is hopeless."

He stopped. Ian straightened in a movement preliminary to getting up.

"Wait a second," said Tyburn.

He had come to the hard part of the interview. He had prepared his speech for this moment and rehearsed it over and over again, but now he found himself without faith that it would convince Ian.

"One more word," said Tyburn. "You're a man of camps and battlefields, a man of the military; and you must be used to thinking of yourself as a pretty effective individual. But here, on Earth, those special skills of yours are mostly illegal. And without them you're ineffective and helpless. Kenebuck, on the other hand, is just the opposite. He's got money—millions. And he's got connections, some of them nasty. And he was born and raised here in Manhattan Complex." Tyburn stared emphatically at the tall, dark man, willing him to understand. "Do you follow me? If you, for example, should suddenly turn up dead here, we just might not be able to bring Kenebuck to book for it. Where we absolutely could, and would, bring you to book if the situation were reversed. Think about it."

He sat, still staring at Ian. But Ian's face showed no change, or sign that the message had gotten through to him.

"Thank you," Ian said. "If there's nothing more, I'll be going."

"There's nothing more," said Tyburn, defeated. He watched Ian leave. It was only when Ian was gone, and he turned back to Breagan that he recovered a little of his self-respect. For Breagan's face had paled.

Ian went down through the Terminal and took a cab into Manhattan Complex, to the John Adams Hotel. He registered for a room on the fourteenth floor of the transient section of that hotel and inquired about the location of James Kenebuck's suite in the resident section; then sent his card up to Kenebuck with a request to come by to see the millionaire. After that, he went on up to his own room, unpacked his lug-

14

gage, which had already been delivered from the spaceport, and took out a small, sealed package. Just at that moment there was a soft chiming sound and his card was returned to him from a delivery slot in the room wall. It fell into the salver below the slot and he picked it up. The penciled note read:

*Come on up. K*

He tucked the card and the package into a pocket and left his transient room. And Tyburn, who had followed him to the hotel, and who had been observing all of Ian's actions from the second of his arrival, through sensors placed in the walls and ceilings, half rose from his chair in the room of the empty suite directly above Kenebuck's, which had been quietly taken over as a police observation post. Then, helplessly, Tyburn swore and sat down again, to follow Ian's movements in the screen fed by the sensors. So far there was nothing the policeman could do legally—nothing but watch.

So he watched as Ian strode down the softly carpeted hallway to the elevator tube, rose in it to the eightieth floor and stepped out to face the heavy, transparent door sealing off the resident section of the hotel. He held up Kenebuck's card with its message to a concierge screen beside the door, and with a soft sigh of air the door slid back to let him through. He passed on in, found a second elevator tube, and took it up thirteen more stories. Black doors opened before him—and he stepped one step forward into a small foyer to find himself surrounded by three men.

They were big men—one, a lantern-jawed giant, was even bigger than Ian—and they were vicious. Tyburn, watching through the sensors in the foyer ceiling that had been secretly placed there by the police the day before, recognized all of them from his files. They were underworld muscle hired by Kenebuck at word of Ian's coming; all armed, and brutal, and hair-trigger—mad dogs of the lower city. After that first step into their midst, Ian stood still. And there followed a strange, unnatural cessation of movement in the room.

The three stood checked. They had been about to put their hands on Ian to search him for something, Tyburn saw, and probably to rough him up in the process. But something had stopped them, some abrupt change in the air around them. Tyburn, watching, felt the change as they did; but for a moment he felt it without understanding. Then understanding came to him.

The difference was in Ian, in the way he stood there. He was, saw Tyburn, simply . . . waiting. That same patient indifference Tyburn had seen upon him in the Terminal office was there again. In the split second of his single step into the room he had discovered the men, had measured them, and stopped. Now, he waited, in his turn, for one of them to make a move.

A sort of black lightning had entered the small foyer. It was abruptly obvious to the watching Tyburn, as to the three below, that the first of them to lay hands on Ian would be the first to find the hands of the Dorsai soldier upon him—and those hands were death.

For the first time in his life, Tyburn saw the personal power of the Dorsai fighting man, made plain without words. Ian needed no badge upon him, standing as he stood now, to warn that he was dangerous. The men about him were mad dogs, but, patently, Ian was a wolf. There was a difference with the three, which Tyburn now recognized for the first time. Dogs—even mad dogs—fight, and the losing dog, if he can, runs away. But no wolf runs. For a wolf wins every fight but one, and in that one he dies.

After a moment, when it was clear that none of the three would move, Ian stepped forward. He passed through them without even brushing against one of them to the inner door opposite, and opened it and went on through.

He stepped into a three-level living room stretching to a large, wide window, its glass rolled up, and black with the sleet-filled night. The living room was as large as a small suite in itself, and filled with people, men and women, richly dressed. They held cocktail glasses in their hands as they stood or sat, and talked. The atmosphere was heavy with the scents of alcohol and women's perfumes and cigarette smoke. It seemed that they paid no attention to his entrance, but their eyes followed him covertly once he had passed.

He walked forward through the crowd, picking his way to a figure before the dark window, the figure of a man almost as tall as himself, erect, athletic-looking with a handsome, sharp-cut face under whitish-blond hair that stared at Ian with a sort of incredulity as Ian approached.

"Graeme . . .?" said this man, as Ian stopped before him. His voice in this moment of off-guardedness betrayed its two levels, the semihoodlum whine and harshness underneath, the polite accents above. "My boys . . . you didn't"—he stumbled—"leave anything with them when you were coming in?"

"No," said Ian. "You're James Kenebuck, of course. You look like your brother." Kenebuck stared at him.

"Just a minute," he said. He set his glass down, turned and went quickly through the crowd and into the foyer, shutting the door behind him. In the hush of the room there was heard a short, unintelligible burst of sharp voices, then silence again. Kenebuck came back into the room, two spots of angry color high on his cheekbones. He came back to face Ian.

"Yes," he said, halting before Ian. "They were supposed to . . . tell me when you came in." He fell silent, evidently waiting for Ian to speak, but Ian merely stood, examining him, until the spots of color on Kenebuck's cheekbones flared again.

"Well?" he said, abruptly. "Well? You came here to see me about Brian, didn't you? What about Brian?" He added, before Ian could answer, in a tone suddenly brutal, "I know he was shot, so you don't have to break that news to me. I suppose you want to tell me he showed all sorts of noble guts . . . refused a blindfold and that sort of——"

"No," said Ian. "He didn't die nobly."

Kenebuck's tall, muscled body jerked a little at the words, almost as if the bullets of an invisible firing squad had poured into it.

"Well . . . that's fine!" he laughed, angrily. "You come light-years to see me and then you tell me that! I thought you liked him—liked Brian."

"Liked him? No," Ian shook his head. Kenebuck stiffened, his face for a moment caught in a gape of bewilderment. "As a matter of fact," went on Ian, "he was a glory-hunter. That made him a poor soldier and a worse officer. I'd have transferred him out of my command if I'd had time before the campaign on Freiland started. Because of him, we lost the lives of thirty-two men in his Force that night."

"Oh." Kenebuck pulled himself together, and looked sourly at Ian. "Those thirty-two men. You've got them on your conscience, is that it?"

"No," said Ian. There was no emphasis on the word as he said it, but somehow to Tyburn's ears above, the brief short negative dismissed Kenebuck's question with an abruptness like contempt. The spots of color on Kenebuck's cheeks flamed.

"You didn't like Brian and your conscience doesn't bother you—what're you here for, then?" he snapped.

"My duty brings me," said Ian.

"Duty?" Kenebuck's face stilled, and went rigid.

Ian reached slowly into his pocket as if he were surrendering a weapon under the guns of an enemy and did not want his move misinterpreted. He brought out the package from his pocket.

"I brought you Brian's personal effects," he said. He turned and laid the package on a table beside Kenebuck. Kenebuck stared down at the package and the color over his cheekbones faded until his face was nearly as pale as his hair. Then slowly, hesitantly, as if he were approaching a booby-trap, he reached out and gingerly picked it up. He held it and turned to Ian, staring into Ian's eyes almost demandingly.

"It's in here?" said Kenebuck, in a voice barely above a whisper, and with a strange emphasis.

"Brian's effects," said Ian, watching him.

"Yes . . . sure. All right," said Kenebuck. He was plainly trying to pull himself together, but his voice was still almost whispering. "I guess . . . that settles it."

"That settles it," said Ian. Their eyes held together. "Good-by," said Ian. He turned and walked back through the silent crowd and out of the living room. The three musclemen were no longer in the foyer. He took the elevator tube down and returned to his own hotel room.

Tyburn, who with a key to the service elevators, had not had to change tubes on the way down as Ian had, was waiting for him when Ian entered. Ian did not seem surprised to see Tyburn there, and only glanced casually at the policeman as he crossed to a decanter of Dorsai whisky that had since been delivered up to the room.

"That's that, then!" burst out Tyburn, in relief. "You got in to see him and he ended up letting you out. You can pack up and go now. It's over."

"No," said Ian. "Nothing's over yet." He poured a few inches of the pungent, dark whisky into a glass, and moved the decanter over another glass. "Drink?"

"I'm on duty," said Tyburn, sharply.

"There'll be a little wait," said Ian, calmly. He poured

18

some whisky into the other glass, took up both glasses, and stepped across the room to hand one to Tyburn. Tyburn found himself holding it. Ian had stepped on to stand before the wall-high window. Outside, night had fallen, but—faintly seen in the lights from the city levels below—the sleet here above the weather shield still beat like small, dark ghosts against the transparency.

"Hang it, man, what more do you want?" burst out Tyburn. "Can't you see it's you I'm trying to protect—as well as Kenebuck? I don't want *anyone* killed! If you stay around here now, you're asking for it. I keep telling you, here in Manhattan Complex you're the helpless one, not Kenebuck. Do you think he hasn't made plans to take care of you?"

"Not until he's sure," said Ian, turning from the ghost-sleet, beating like lost souls against the window glass, trying to get in.

"Sure about what? Look, Commandant," said Tyburn, trying to speak calmly, "half an hour after we hear from the Freiland-North Police about you, Kenebuck called my office to ask for police protection." He broke off, angrily. "Don't look at me like that! How do I know how he found out you were coming? I tell you he's rich, and he's got connections! But the point is, the police protection he's got is just a screen—an excuse—for whatever he's got planned for you on his own. You saw those hoods in the foyer!"

"Yes," said Ian, unemotionally.

"Well, think about it!" Tyburn glared at him. "Look, I don't hold any brief for James Kenebuck! All right—let me tell you about him! We knew he'd been trying to get rid of his brother since Brian was ten—but blast it, Commandant, Brian was no angel, either."

"I know," said Ian, seating himself in a chair opposite Tyburn.

"All right, you know! I'll tell you, anyway!" said Tyburn. "Their grandfather was a local kingpin—he was in every racket on the eastern seaboard. He was one of the mob, with millions he didn't dare count because of where they'd come from. In their father's time, those millions started to be fed into legitimate business. The third generation, James and Brian, didn't inherit anything that wasn't legitimate. Hell, we couldn't even make a jay-walking ticket stick against one of them, if we'd ever wanted to. James was twenty and Brian ten when their father died, and when he died the last bit of tattle-tale gray went out of the family linen. But they kept their hoodlum connections, Commandant!"

Ian sat, glass in hand, watching Tyburn almost curiously.

"Don't you get it?" snapped Tyburn. "I tell you that, on paper, in law, Kenebuck's twenty-four carat gilt-edge. But his family was hoodlum, he was raised like a hoodlum, and he thinks like a hood! He didn't want his young brother Brian around to share the crown prince position with him—so he set out to get rid of him. He couldn't just have him killed, so he set out to cut him down, show him up, break his spirit, until Brian took one chance too many trying to match up to his older brother, and killed himself off."

Ian slowly nodded.

"All right!" said Tyburn. "So Kenebuck finally succeeded. He chased Brian until the kid ran off and became a professional soldier—something Kenebuck wouldn't leave his wine, women, and song long enough to shine at. And he can shine at most things he really wants to shine at, Commandant. Under that hood attitude and all those millions he's got a good mind and a good body that he's made a hobby out of training. But, all right. So now it turns out Brian was still no good, and he took some soldiers along when he finally got around to doing what Kenebuck wanted, and getting himself killed. All right! But what can you do about it? What can anyone do about it, with all the connections, and all the money and all the law on Kenebuck's side of it? And, why should you think about doing something about it, anyway?"

"It's my duty," said Ian. He had swallowed half the whisky in his glass, absently, and now he turned the glass thoughtfully around, watching the brown liquor swirl under the forces of momentum and gravity. He looked up at Tyburn. "You know that, Lieutenant."

"Duty! Is duty that important?" demanded Tyburn. Ian gazed at him, then looked away, at the ghost-sleet beating vainly against the glass of the window that held it back in the outer dark.

"Nothing's more important than duty," said Ian, half to himself, his voice thoughtful and remote. "Mercenary troops have the right to care and protection from their own officers. When they don't get it, they're entitled to justice, so that the same thing is discouraged from happening again. That justice is a duty."

Tyburn blinked, and unexpectedly a wall seemed to go down in his mind.

"Justice for those thirty-two dead soldiers of Brian's!" he said, suddenly understanding. "That's what brought you here!"

"Yes." Ian nodded, and lifted his glass almost as if to the sleet-ghosts to drink the rest of his whisky.

"But," said Tyburn, staring at him, "you're trying to bring a civilian to justice. And Kenebuck has you out-gunned and out-maneuvered——"

The chiming of the communicator screen in one corner of the room interrupted him. Ian put down his empty glass, went over to the screen and depressed a stud. His wide shoulders and back hid the screen from Tyburn, but Tyburn heard his voice.

"Yes?"

The voice of James Kenebuck sounded in the hotel room.

"Graeme—listen!"

There was a pause.

"I'm listening," said Ian, calmly.

"I'm alone now," said the voice of Kenebuck. It was tight and harsh. "My guests have gone home. I was just looking through that package of Brian's things. . . ." He stopped speaking and the sentence seemed to Tyburn to dangle unfinished in the air of the room. Ian let it dangle for a long moment.

"Yes?" he said, finally.

"Maybe I was a little hasty . . ." said Kenebuck. But the tone of his voice did not match the words. The tone was savage. "Why don't you come up, now that I'm alone, and we'll . . . talk about Brian, after all?"

"I'll be up," said Ian.

He snapped off the screen and turned around.

"Wait!" said Tyburn, starting up out of his chair. "You can't go up there!"

"Can't?" Ian looked at him. "I've been invited, Lieutenant."

The words were like a damp towel slapping Tyburn in the face, waking him up.

"That's right. . . ." He stared at Ian. "Why? Why'd he invite you back?"

"He's had time," said Ian, "to be alone. And to look at that package of Brian's."

"But—" Tyburn scowled. "There was nothing important in

21

that package. A watch, a wallet, a passport, some other papers . . . Customs gave us a list. There wasn't anything unusual there."

"Yes," said Ian. "And that's why he wants to see me again."

"But what does he want?"

"He wants me," said Ian. He met the puzzlement of Tyburn's gaze. "He was always jealous of Brian," Ian explained, almost gently. "He was afraid Brian would grow up to outdo him in things. That's why he tried to break Brian, even to kill him. But now Brian's come back to face him."

"Brian . . .?"

"In me," said Ian. He turned toward the hotel door.

Tyburn watched him turn, then suddenly, like a man coming out of a daze, he took three hurried strides after him as Ian opened the door.

"Wait!" snapped Tyburn. "He won't be alone up there! He'll have hoods covering you through the walls. He'll definitely have traps set for you——"

Easily, Ian lifted the policeman's grip from his arm.

"I know," he said. And went.

Tyburn was left in the open doorway staring after him. As Ian stepped into the elevator tube, the policeman moved. He ran for the service elevator that would take him back to the police observation post above the sensors in the ceiling of Kenebuck's living room.

When Ian stepped into the foyer the second time, it was empty. He went to the door to the living room of Kenebuck's suite, found it ajar, and stepped through it. Within the room was empty, with glasses and overflowing ashtrays still on the tables; the lights had been lowered. Kenebuck rose from a chair with its back to the far, large window at the end of the room. Ian walked toward him and stopped when they were little more than an arm's length apart.

Kenebuck stood for a second staring at him, the skin of his face tight. Then he made a short almost angry gesture with his right hand. The gesture gave away the fact that he had been drinking.

"Sit down!" he said. Ian took a comfortable chair and Kenebuck sat down in the one from which he had just risen. "Drink?" said Kenebuck. There was a decanter and glasses on the table beside and between them. Ian shook his head. Kenebuck poured part of a glass for himself.

"That package of Brian's things," he said, abruptly, the whites of his eyes glinting as he glanced up under his lids at Ian, "there was just personal stuff. Nothing else in it!"

"What else did you expect would be in it?" asked Ian, calmly.

Kenebuck's hands clenched suddenly on the glass. He stared at Ian, and then burst out into a laugh that rang a little wildly against the emptiness of the large room.

"No, no—" said Kenebuck, loudly. "I'm asking the questions, Graeme. I'll ask them! What made you come all the way here to see me, anyway?"

"My duty," said Ian.

"Duty? Duty to whom—Brian?" Kenebuck looked as if he would laugh again, then thought better of it. There was the white, wild flash of his eyes again. "What was something like Brian to you? You said you didn't even like him."

"That was beside the point," said Ian, quietly. "He was one of my officers."

"One of your officers! He was my brother! That's more than being one of your officers!"

"Not," answered Ian in the same voice, "where justice is concerned."

"Justice?" Kenebuck laughed. "Justice for Brian? Is that it?"

"And for thirty-two enlisted men."

"Oh—" Kenebuck snorted laughingly. "Thirty-two men . . . those thirty-two men!" He shook his head. "I never knew your thirty-two men, Graeme, so you can't blame me for them. That was Brian's fault; him and his idea—what was the charge they tried him on? Oh, yes, that he and his thirty-two or thirty-six men could raid enemy headquarters and come back with the enemy commandant. Come back . . . covered with glory." Kenebuck laughed again. "But it didn't work. Not my fault."

"Brian did it," said Ian, "to show you. You were what made him do it."

"Me? Could I help it if he never could match up to me?" Kenebuck stared down at his glass and took a quick swallow from it, then went back to cuddling it in his hands. He smiled a little to himself. "Never could even *catch* up to me." He looked whitely across at Ian. "I'm just a better man, Graeme. You better remember that."

Ian said nothing. Kenebuck continued to stare at him, and slowly Kenebuck's face grew more savage.

"Don't believe me, do you?" said Kenebuck, softly. "You better believe me. I'm not Brian, and I'm not bothered by Dorsais. You're here, and I'm facing you—alone."

"Alone?" said Ian. For the first time Tyburn, above the ceiling over the heads of the two men, listening and watching through hidden sensors, thought he heard a hint of emotion—contempt—in Ian's voice. Or had he imagined it?

"Alone—well!" James Kenebuck laughed again, but a little cautiously. "I'm a civilized man, not a hick frontiersman. But I don't have to be a fool. Yes, I've got men covering you from behind the walls of the room here. I'd be stupid not to. And I've got this. . . ." He whistled, and something about the size of a small dog, but made of smooth, black metal, slipped out from behind a sofa nearby and slid on an aircushion over the carpeting to their feet.

Ian looked down. It was a sort of satchel with an orifice in the top from which two metallic tentacles protruded slightly.

Ian nodded slightly.

"A medical mech," he said.

"Yes," said Kenebuck, "cued to respond to the heartbeats of anyone in the room with it. So you see, it wouldn't do you any good, even if you somehow knew where all my guards were and beat them to the draw. Even if you killed me, this could get to me in time to keep it from being permanent. So, I'm unkillable. Give up!" He laughed and kicked at the mech. "Get back," he said to it. It slid back behind the sofa.

"So you see . . ." he said. "Just sensible precautions. There's no trick to it. You're a military man—and what's that mean? Superior strength. Superior tactics. That's all. So I outpower your strength, outnumber you, make your tactics useless—and what are you? Nothing." He put his glass carefully aside on the table with the decanter. "But I'm not Brian. I'm not afraid of you. I could do without these things if I wanted to."

Ian sat watching him. On the floor above, Tyburn had stiffened.

"Could you?" asked Ian.

Kenebuck stared at him. The white face of the millionaire

contorted. Blood surged up into it, darkening it. His eyes flashed whitely.

"What're you trying to do—test me?" he shouted suddenly. He jumped to his feet and stood over Ian, waving his arms furiously. It was, recognized Tyburn overhead, the calculated, self-induced hysterical rage of the hoodlum world. But how would Ian Graeme below know that? Suddenly Kenebuck was screaming. "You want to try me out? You think I won't face you? You think I'll back down like that brother of mine, that—" he broke into a flood of obscenity in which the name of Brian was freely mixed. Abruptly, he whirled about to the walls of the room, yelling at them. "Get out of there! All right, out! Do you hear me? All of you! Out——"

Panels slid back, bookcases swung aside and four men stepped into the room. Three were those who had been in the foyer earlier when Ian had entered for the first time. The other was of the same type.

"Out!" screamed Kenebuck at them. "Everybody out. Outside, and lock the door behind you. I'll show this Dorsai, this—" almost foaming at the mouth, he lapsed into obscenity again.

Overhead, above the ceiling, Tyburn found himself gripping the edge of the table below the observation screen so hard his fingers ached.

"It's a trick!" he muttered between his teeth to the unhearing Ian. "He planned it this way! Can't you see that?"

"Graeme armed?" inquired the police sensor technician at Tyburn's right. Tyburn jerked his head around momentarily to stare at the technician.

"No," said Tyburn. "Why?"

"Kenebuck is." The technician reached over and tapped the screen, just below the left shoulder of Kenebuck's jacket image. "Slug-thrower."

Tyburn made a fist of his aching right fingers and softly pounded the table before the screen in frustration.

"All right!" Kenebuck was shouting below, turning back to the still-seated form of Ian, and spreading his arms wide. "Now's your chance. Jump me! The door's locked. You think there's anyone else near to help me? Look!" He turned and took five steps to the wide, knee-high to ceiling window behind him, punched the control button and watched as it swung wide. A few of the whirling sleet-ghosts outside drove from out of ninety stories of vacancy into the opening—and

25

fell dead in little drops of moisture on the window sill as the automatic weather shield behind the glass blocked them out.

He stalked back to Ian, who had neither moved nor changed expression through all this. Slowly, Kenebuck sank back down into his chair, his back to the night, the blocked-out cold, and the sleet.

"What's the matter?" he asked, slowly, acidly. "You don't do anything? Maybe *you* don't have the nerve, Graeme?"

"We were talking about Brian," said Ian.

"Yes, Brian . . ." Kenebuck said, quite slowly. "He had a big head. He wanted to be like me, but no matter how he tried—how I tried to help him—he couldn't make it." He stared at Ian. "That's just the way he decided to go into enemy lines when there wasn't a chance in the world. That's the was he was—a loser."

"With help," said Ian.

"What? What's that you're saying?" Kenebuck jerked upright in his chair.

"You helped him lose," Ian's voice was matter of fact. "From the time he was a young boy, you built him up to want to be like you—to take long chances and win. Only your chances were always safe bets, and his were as unsafe as you could make them."

Kenebuck drew in an audible, hissing breath.

"You've got a big mouth, Graeme!" he said, in a low, slow voice.

"You wanted," said Ian, almost conversationally, "to have him kill himself off. But he never quite did. And each time he came back for more, because he had it stuck into his mind, carved into his mind, that he wanted to impress you—even though by the time he was grown, he saw what you were up to. He knew, but he still wanted to make you admit that he wasn't a loser. You'd twisted him that way while he was growing up, and that was the way he grew."

"Go on," hissed Kenebuck. "Go on, big mouth."

"So, he went off-Earth and became a professional soldier," went on Ian, steadily and calmly, "not because he was drafted like someone from Newton, or a born professional from the Dorsai, or hungry like one of the ex-miners from Coby, but to show you you were wrong about him. He found one place where you couldn't compete with him, and he must have started writing back to you to tell you about it—half rubbing it in, half asking for the pat on the back you never gave him."

Kenebuck sat in the chair and breathed. His eyes were all one glitter.

"But you didn't answer his letters," said Ian. "I suppose you thought that'd finally make him desperate enough to do something fatal. But he didn't. Instead he succeeded. He went up through the ranks. Finally, he got his commission and made Force-Leader, and you began to be worried. It wouldn't be long, if he kept on going up, before he'd be above the field officer grades, and out of most of the actual fighting."

Kenebuck sat perfectly still, leaning forward a little. He looked almost as if he were praying, or putting all the force of his mind to willing that Ian finish what he had started to say.

"And so," said Ian, "on his twenty-third birthday—which was the day before the night on which he led his men against orders into the enemy area—you saw that he got this birthday card. . . ." He reached into a side pocket of his civilian jacket and took out a white, folded card that showed signs of having been savagely crumpled but was now smoothed out again. Ian opened it and laid it beside the decanter on the table between their chairs, the sketch and legend facing Kenebuck. Kenebuck's eyes dropped to look at it.

The sketch was a crude outline of a rabbit, with a combat rifle and battle helmet discarded at its feet, engaged in painting a broad yellow stripe down the center of its own back. Underneath this picture was printed in block letters the question, "WHY FIGHT IT?"

Kenebuck's face slowly rose from the sketch to face Ian, and the millionaire's mouth stretched at the corners, and went on stretching into a ghastly version of a smile.

"Was that all . . .?" whispered Kenebuck.

"Not all," said Ian. "Along with it, glued to the paper by the rabbit, there was this. . . ."

He reached almost casually into his pocket.

"No, you don't!" screamed Kenebuck, triumphantly. Suddenly he was on his feet, jumping behind his chair, backing away toward the darkness of the window behind him. He reached into his jacket and his hand came out holding the slug-thrower, which cracked loudly in the room. Ian had not moved, and his body jerked to the heavy impact of the slug.

Suddenly, Ian had come to life. After being hammered by

a slug, the shock of which should have immobilized an ordinary man, he was out of the chair on his feet and moving forward. Kenebuck screamed again—this time with pure terror—and began to back away, firing as he went.

"Die, you—! Die!" he screamed. But the towering Dorsai figure came on. Twice it was hit and spun clear around by the heavy slugs, but like a football fullback shaking off the assaults of tacklers it plunged on, with great strides narrowing the distance between it and the retreating Kenebuck.

Still screaming, Kenebuck came up with the back of his knees against the low sill of the open window. For a second his face distorted itself out of all human shape in a grimace of its terror. He looked, to right and to left, but there was no place left to run. He had been pulling the trigger of his slug-thrower all this time, but now the firing pin clicked at last upon an empty chamber. Gibbering, he threw the weapon at Ian, and it flew wide of the driving figure of the Dorsai, now almost upon him, great hands outstretched.

Kenebuck jerked his head away from what was rushing toward him. Then, with a howl like a beaten dog, he turned and flung himself through the window before those hands could touch him, into ninety-odd stories of unsupported space. And his howl carried away down into silence.

Ian halted. For a second he stood before the window, his right hand still clenched about whatever it was he had pulled from his pocket. Then, like a toppling tree, he fell.

As Tyburn and the technician with him finished burning through the ceiling above and came dropping through the charred opening into the room, they almost landed on the small object that had come rolling from Ian's now-lax hand. An object that was really two objects glued together—a small paintbrush and a transparent tube of glaringly yellow paint.

"I hope you realize, though," said Tyburn, two weeks later on an icy, bright December day as he and the recovered Ian stood just inside the Terminal waiting for the boarding signal from the spaceliner about to take off for the Sirian worlds, "what a chance you took with Kenebuck. It was just luck it worked out for you the way it did."

"No," said Ian. He was as apparently emotionless as ever; a little more gaunt from his stay in the Manhattan hospital, but he had mended with the swiftness of his Dorsai constitution. "There was no luck. It all happened the way I planned it."

Tyburn gazed in astonishment.

"Why," he said, "if Kenebuck hadn't had to send his hoods out of the room to make it seem necessary for him to shoot you himself when you put your hand into your pocket that second time . . . or if you hadn't had the card in the first place—" He broke off, suddenly thoughtful. "You mean . . .?" he stared at Ian. "Having the card, you planned to have Kenebuck get you alone . . .?"

"It was a form of personal combat," said Ian. "And personal combat is my business. You assumed that Kenebuck was strongly entrenched, facing my attack. But it was the other way around."

"But you had to come to him. . . ."

"I had to appear to come to him," said Ian, almost coldly, "otherwise he wouldn't have believed that he had to kill me—before I killed him. By his decision to kill me, he put himself in the attacking position."

"But he had all the advantages!" said Tyburn, his head whirling. "You had to fight on his ground, here where he was strong——"

"No," said Ian. "You're confusing the attack position with the defensive one. By coming here, I put Kenebuck in the position of finding out whether I actually had the birthday card and the knowledge of why Brian had gone against orders into enemy territory that night. Kenebuck planned to have his men in the foyer shake me down for the card—but they lost their nerve."

"I remember," murmured Tyburn.

"Then, when I handed him the package, he was sure the card was in it. But it wasn't," went on Ian. "He saw his only choice was to give me a situation where I might feel it was safe to admit having the card and the knowledge. He had to know about that, because Brian had called his bluff by going out and risking his neck after getting the card. The fact Brian was tried and executed later made no difference to Kenebuck. That was a matter of law—something apart from hoodlum guts, or lack of guts. If no one knew that Brian was braver than his older brother, that was all right; but if I knew, he could only save face under his own standards by killing me."

"He almost did," said Tyburn. "Any one of those slugs——"

"There was the medical mech," said Ian, calmly. "A man like Kenebuck would be bound to have something like that around to play safe—just as he would be bound to set an amateur's trap." The boarding horn of the spaceliner sounded. Ian picked up his luggage bag. "Good-by," he said, offering his hand to Tyburn.

"Good-by," he muttered. "So you were just going along with Kenebuck's trap, all of it. I can't believe it. . . ." He released Ian's hand and watched as the big man swung around and took the first two strides away toward the bulk of the ship shining in the winter sunlight. Then, suddenly, the numbness broke clear from Tyburn's mind. He ran after Ian and caught at his arm. Ian stopped and swung half around, frowning slightly.

"I can't believe it!" cried Tyburn. "You mean you went up there, *knowing* Kenebuck was going to pump you full of slugs and maybe kill you—all just to square things for thirty-two enlisted soldiers under the command of a man you didn't even like? I don't believe it—you can't be that cold-blooded! I don't care how much of a man of the military you are!"

Ian looked down at him. And it seemed to Tyburn that the Dorsai face had gone away from him, somehow as remote and stony as a face carved high up on some icy mountaintop.

"But I'm not just a man of the military," Ian said. "That was the mistake Kenebuck made, too. That was why he thought that stripped of military elements, I'd be easy to kill."

Tyburn, looking at him, felt a chill run down his spine as cold as wind off a glacier.

"Then, in heaven's name," cried Tyburn, "what are you?"

Ian looked from his far distance down into Tyburn's eyes and the sadness rang as clear in his voice finally, as iron-shod heels on barren rock.

"I am a man of war," said Ian, softly.

With that, he turned and went on, and Tyburn saw him black against the winter-bright sky, looming over all the other departing passengers, on his way to board the spaceship.

# OF THE PEOPLE

But you know, I could sense it coming a long time off. It was a little extra time taken in drinking a cup of coffee, it was lingering over the magazines in a drugstore as I picked out a handful. It was a girl I looked at twice as I ran out and down the steps of a library.

And it wasn't any good and I knew it. But it kept coming and it kept coming, and one night I stayed working at the design of a power cruiser until it was finished, before I finally knocked off for supper. Then, after I'd eaten, I looked ahead down twelve dark hours to daylight, and I knew I'd had it.

So I got up and I walked out of the apartment. I left my glass half full and the record player I had built playing the music I had written to the pictures I had painted. Left the organ and the typewriter, left the darkroom and the lab. Left the jammed-full filing cabinets. Took the elevator and told the elevator boy to head for the ground floor. Walked out into the deep snow.

"You going out in January without an overcoat, Mr. Crossman?" asked the doorman.

"Don't need a coat," I told him. "Never no more, no coats."

"Don't you want me to phone the garage for your car, then?"

"Don't need a car."

I left him and I set out walking. After a while it began to snow, but not on me. And after a little more while people started to stare, so I flagged down a cab.

"Get out and give me the keys," I told the driver.

"You drunk?" he said.

"It's all right, son," I said. "I own the company. But you'll get out nonetheless and give me the keys." He got out and gave me the keys and I left him standing there.

I got in the cab and drove it off through the night-lit downtown streets, and I kissed the city good-by as I went. I blew a kiss to the grain exchange and a kiss to the stockyards. And a kiss to every one of the fourteen offices in the city that knew me each under a different title as head of a different business. You've got to get along without me now, city and people, I said, because I'm not coming back, no more, no more.

I drove out of downtown and out past Longview Acres and past Manor Acres and past Sherman Hills and I blew them all a kiss, too. Enjoy your homes, you people, I told them, because they're good homes—not the best I could have done you by a damn sight, but better than you'll see elsewhere in a long time, and your money's worth. Enjoy your homes and don't remember me.

I drove out to the airport and there I left the cab. It was a good airport. I'd laid it out myself and I knew. It was a good airport and I got eighteen days of good hard work out of the job. I got myself so lovely and tired doing it I was able to go out to the bars and sit there having half a dozen drinks—before the urge to talk to the people around me became unbearable and I had to get up and go home.

There were planes on the field. A good handful of them. I went in and talked to one of the clerks.

"Mr. Crossman!" he said, when he saw me.

"Get me a plane," I said. "Get me a plane headed east and then forget I was in tonight."

He did; and I went. I flew to New York and changed planes and flew to London; and changed again and came in by jet to Bombay.

By the time I reached Bombay, my mind was made up for good, and I went through the city as if it were a dream of buildings and people and no more. I went through the town and out of the town and I hit the road north, walking. And as I walked, I took off my coat and my tie. And I opened my collar to the open air and I started my trek.

I was six weeks walking it. I remember little bits and pieces of things along the way—mainly faces, and mainly the faces of the children, for they aren't afraid when they're young. They'd come up to me and run alongside, trying to match the strides I'd take, and after a while they'd get tired and drop back—but there were always others along the way. And there were adults, too, men and women, but when they got close they'd take one look at my face and go away again. There was only one who spoke to me in all that trip, and that was a tall, dark brown man in some kind of uniform. He spoke to me in English and I answered him in dialect. He was scared to the marrow of his bones, for after he spoke I could hear the little grinding of his teeth in the silence as he tried to keep them from chattering. But I answered him kindly, and told him I had business in the north that was nobody's business but my own. And when he still would not move—he was well over six feet and nearly as tall as I—I opened my right hand beneath his nose and showed him himself, small and weak as a caterpillar in the palm of it. And he fell out of my path as if his legs had all the strength gone out of them, and I went on.

I was six weeks walking it. And when I came to the hills, my beard was grown out and my pants and my shirt were in tatters. Also, by this time, the word had gone ahead of me. Not the official word, but the little words of little people, running from mouth to mouth. They knew I was coming and they knew where I was headed—to see the old man up beyond Mutteeanee Pass, the white-bearded, holy man of the village between two peaks.

He was sitting on his rock out on the hillside, with his blind eyes following the sun and the beard running white and old between his thin knees and down to the brown earth.

I sat down on a smaller rock before him and caught my breath.

"Well, Erik," I said. "I've come."

"I'm aware you have, Sam."

"By foot," I said. "By car and plane, too, but mostly by foot, as time goes. All the way from the lowlands by foot, Erik. And that's the last I do for any of them."

"For them, Sam?"

"For me, then."

"Not for you, either, Sam," he said. And then he sighed. "Go back, Sam," he said.

"Go back!" I echoed. "Go back to hell again? No thank you, Erik."

"You faltered," he said. "You weakened. You began to

33

slow down, to look around. There was no need to, Sam. If you hadn't started to slacken off, you would have been all right."

"All right? Do you call the kind of life I lead, that? What do you use for a heart, Erik?"

"A heart?" And with that he lowered his blind old eyes from the sun and turned them right on me. "Do you accuse me, Sam?"

"With you it's choice," I said. "You can go."

"No," he shook his head. "I'm bound by choice, just as you are bound by the greater strength in me. Go back, Sam."

"Why?" I cried. And I pounded my chest like a crazy man. "Why me? Why can others go and I have to stay? There's no end to the universe. I don't ask for company. I'll find some lost hole somewhere and bury myself. Anywhere, just so I'm away."

"Would you, Sam?" he asked. And at that, there was pity in his voice. When I did not answer, he went on, gently. "You see, Sam, that's exactly why I can't let you go. You're capable of deluding yourself, of telling yourself that you'll do what we both know you will not, cannot do. So you must stay."

"No," I said. "All right." I got up and turned to go. "I came to you first and gave you your chance. But now I'll go on my own, and I'll get off somehow."

"Sam, come back," he said. And abruptly, my legs were mine no longer.

"Sit down again," he said. "And listen for a minute."

My traitorous legs took me back, and I sat.

"Sam," he said, "you know the old story. Now and then, at rare intervals, one like us will be born. Nearly always, when they are grown, they leave. Only a few stay. But only once in thousands of years does one like yourself appear who must be chained against his will to our world."

"Erik," I said, between my teeth. "Don't sympathize."

"I'm not sympathizing, Sam," he said. "As you said yourself, there is no end to the universe, but I have seen it all and there is no place in it for you. For the others that have gone out, there are places that are no places. They sup at alien tables, Sam, but always and forever as a guest. They left themselves behind when they went and they don't belong any longer to our Earth."

He stopped for a moment, and I knew what was coming.

"But you, Sam," he said, and I heard his voice with my head bowed, staring at the brown dirt. He spoke tenderly. "Poor Sam. You'd never be able to leave the Earth behind. You're one of us, but the living cord binds you to the others. Never a man speaks to you, but your hands yearn towards him in friendship. Never a woman smiles your way, but love warms that frozen heart of yours. You can't leave them, Sam. If you went out now, you'd come back, in time, and try to take them with you. You'd hurry them on before they are ripe. And there's no place out there in the universe for them—yet."

I tried to move, but could not. Tried to lift my face to his, but I could not.

"Poor Sam," he said, "trapped by a common heart that chains the lightning of his brain. Go back, Sam. Go back to your cities and your people. Go back to a thousand little jobs, and the work that is no greater than theirs, but many times as much so that it drives you without a pause twenty, twenty-two hours a day. Go back, Sam, to your designing and your painting, to your music and your business, to your engineering and your landscaping, and all the other things. Go back and keep busy, so busy your brain fogs and you sleep without dreaming. And wait. Wait for the necessary years to pass until they grow and change and at last come to their destiny.

"When that time comes, Sam, they will go out. And you will go with them, blood of their blood, flesh of their flesh, kin and comrade to them all. You will be happier than any of us have ever been, when that time comes. But the years have still to pass, and now you must go back. Go back, Sam. Go back, go back, go back."

And so I have come back. O people that I hate and love!

# DANGER—HUMAN!

The spaceboat came down in the silence of perfect working order—down through the cool, dark night of a New Hampshire late spring. There was hardly any moon, and the path emerging from the clump of conifers and snaking its way across the dim pasture looked like a long strip of pale cloth, carelessly dropped and forgotten there.

The two aliens checked the boat and stopped it, hovering, some fifty feet above the pasture, all but invisible against the low-lying clouds. Then they set themselves to wait, their woolly, bearlike forms settled on haunches, their uniform belts glinting a little in the shielded light from the instrument panel, talking now and then in desultory murmurs.

"It's not a bad place," said the one of junior rank, looking down at the earth below.

"Why should it be?" answered the senior.

The junior did not answer. He shifted on his haunches.

"The babies are due soon," he said. "I just got a message."

"How many?" asked the senior.

"Three, the doctor thinks. That's not bad for a first birthing."

"My wife only had two."

"I know. You told me."

They fell silent for a few seconds. The spaceboat rocked almost imperceptibly in the waters of night.

"Look—" said the junior, suddenly. "Here it comes, right on schedule."

The senior glanced overside. Down below, a tall, dark form had emerged from the trees and was coming out along the path. A little beam of light shone before it, terminating in a blob of illumination that danced along the path ahead, lighting its way. The senior stiffened.

"Take controls," he said. The casualness had gone out of his voice. It had become crisp, impersonal.

"Controls," answered the other, in the same emotionless voice.

"Take her down."

"Down it is."

The spaceboat dropped groundward. There was an odd sort of soundless, lightless explosion—it was as if a concussive wave had passed, robbed of all effects but one. The figure dropped, the light rolling from its grasp and losing its glow in a tangle of short grass. The spaceboat landed and the two aliens got out.

In the dark night they loomed furrily above the still figure. It was that of a lean, dark man in his early thirties, dressed in clean, much-washed corduroy pants and checkered wool lumberjack shirt. He was unconscious, but breathing slowly, deeply and easily.

"I'll take it up by the head, here," said the senior. "You take the other end. Got it? Lift! Now, carry it into the boat."

The junior backed away, up through the spaceboat's open lock, grunting a little with the awkwardness of his burden.

"It feels slimy," he said.

"Nonsense!" said the senior. "That's your imagination."

Eldridge Timothy Parker drifted in that dreamy limbo between awakeness and full sleep. He found himself contemplating his own name.

Eldridge Timothy Parker. Eldridgetimothyparker. EldridgeTIMOTHYparker. ELdrIDGEtiMOthyPARKer. . . .

There was a hardness under his back, the back on which he was lying—and a coolness. His flaccid right hand turned flat, feeling. It felt like steel beneath him. Metal? He tried to sit up and bumped his forehead against a ceiling a few inches overhead. He blinked his eyes in the darkness—

*Darkness?*

He flung out his hands, searching, feeling terror leap up inside him. His knuckles bruised against walls to right and left. Frantic, his groping fingers felt out, around, and about him. He was walled in, he was surrounded, he was enclosed.

Completely.

Like in a coffin.

Buried.

He began to scream. . . .

Much later, when he awoke again, he was in a strange place that seemed to have no walls, but many instruments. He floated in the center of mechanisms that passed and re-passed about him, touching, probing, turning. He felt touches of heat and cold. Strange hums and notes of various pitches came and went. He felt voices questioning him.

Who are you?

"Eldridge Parker . . . Eldridge Timothy Parker. . . ."

What are you?

"I'm Eldridge Parker. . . ."

Tell about yourself.

"Tell what? What?"

Tell about yourself.

"What? What do you want to know? What——"

Tell about. . . .

"But I—"

*Tell.* . . .

. . . well, i suppose i was pretty much like any of the kids around our town . . . i was a pretty good shot and i won the fifth grade seventy-five yard dash . . . i played hockey, too . . . pretty cold weather up around our parts, you know, the air used to smell strange it was so cold winter mornings in january when you first stepped out of doors . . . it is good, open country, new england, and there were lots of smells . . . there were pine smells and grass smells and i remember especially the kitchen smells . . . and then, too, there was the way the oak benches in church used to smell on sunday when you knelt with your nose right next to the back of the pew ahead. . . .

. . . the fishing up our parts is good, too . . . i liked to fish but i never wasted time on weekdays . . . we were pres-byterians, you know, and my father had the farm, but he also had money invested in land around the country . . . we have never been badly off but i would have liked a motor-scooter. . . .

. . . no i did not never hate the germans at least i did not think i ever did, of course though i was over in europe i never really had it bad, combat, i mean . . . i was in a motor pool with the raw smell of gasoline, i like to work with my hands, and it was not like being in the infantry. . . .

... i have as good right to speak up to the town council as any man ... i do not believe in pushing but if they push me i am going to push right back ... nor it isn't any man's business what i voted last election no more than my bank balance ... but i have got as good as right to a say in town doings as if i was the biggest landholder among them. ...

... i did not go to college because it was not necessary ... too much education can make a fool of any man, i told my father, and i know when i have had enough ... i am a farmer and will always be a farmer and i will do my own studying as things come up without taking out a pure waste of four years to hang a piece of paper on the wall. ...

... of course i know about the atom bomb, but i am no scientist and no need to be one, no more than i need to be a veterinarian ... i elect the men that hire the men that need to know those things and the men that i elect will hear from me johnny-quick if things do not go to my liking. ...

... as to why i never married, that is none of your business ... as it happens, i was never at ease with women much, though there were a couple of times, and i still may if jeanie lind. ...

... i believe in god and the united states of america. ...

He woke up gradually. He was in a room that might have been any office, except the furniture was different. That is, there was a box with doors on it that might have been a filing cabinet, and a table that looked like a desk in spite of the single thin rod underneath the center that supported it. However, there were no chairs—only small, flat cushions, on which three large, woolly, bearlike creatures were sitting and watching him in silence.

He himself, he found, was in a chair, though.

As soon as they saw his eyes were open, they turned away from him and began to talk among themselves. Eldridge Parker shook his head and blinked his eyes, and would have blinked his ears if that had been possible. For the sounds the creatures were making were like nothing he had ever heard before; and yet he understood everything they were saying. It was an odd sensation, like a double image earwise, for he heard the strange mouth-noises just as they came out and then something in his head twisted them around and made them into perfectly understandable English.

Nor was that all. For, as he sat listening to the creatures

talk, he began to get the same double image in another way. That is, he still saw the bearlike creature behind the desk as the weird sort of animal he was, while out of the sound of his voice, or from something else, there gradually built up in Eldridge's mind a picture of a thin, rather harassed-looking gray-haired man in something resembling a uniform, but at the same time not quite a uniform. It was the sort of effect an army general might get if he wore his stars and a Sam Browne belt over a civilian double-breasted suit. Similarly, the other creature sitting facing the one behind the desk, at the desk's side, began to look like a young and black-haired man with something of the laboratory about him, and the creature farther back, seated almost against the wall, appeared neither as soldier nor scientist, but a heavy older man with a sort of book-won wisdom in him.

"You see, Commander," the young one with the black-haired image was saying, "perfectly restored. At least on the physical and mental levels."

"Good, Doctor, good," the outlandish syllables from the one behind the desk translated themselves in Eldridge's head. "And you say it—he, I should say—will be able to understand?"

"Certainly, sir," said the doctor-psychologist—what-ever-he-was. "Identification is absolute——"

"But I mean comprehend . . . encompass. . . ." The creature behind the desk moved one paw slightly. "Follow what we tell him. . . ."

The doctor turned his ursinoid head toward the third member of the group. This one spoke slowly, in a deeper voice.

"The culture allows. Certainly."

The one behind the desk bowed slightly to the oldest one.

"Certainly, Academician, certainly."

They then fell silent, all looking back at Eldridge, who returned their gaze with equivalent interest. There was something unnatural about the whole proceeding. Both sides were regarding the other with the completely blunt and unshielded curiosity given to freaks.

The silence stretched out. It became tinged with a certain embarrassment. Gradually a mutual recognition arose that no one really wanted to be the first to address an alien being directly.

"It . . . he is comfortable?" asked the commander, turning once more to the doctor.

"I should say so," replied the doctor, slowly. "As far as we know...."

Turning back to Eldridge, the commander said, "Eldridge-timothyparker, I suppose you wonder where you are?"

Caution and habit put a clamp on Eldridge's tongue. He hesitated about answering so long that the commander turned in distress to the doctor, who reassured him with a slight movement of the head.

"Well, speak up," said the commander. "We'll be able to understand you, just as you're able to understand us. Nothing's going to hurt you, and anything you say won't have the slightest effect on your ... er ... situation."

He paused again, looking at Eldridge for a comment. Eldridge still held his silence, but one of his hands unconsciously made a short, fumbling motion at his breast pocket.

"My pipe—" said Eldridge.

The three looked at each other. They looked back at Eldridge.

"We have it," said the doctor. "After a while we may give it back to you. For now ... we cannot allow ... it would not suit us."

"Smoke bother you?" said Eldridge, with a touch of his native canniness.

"It does not bother us. It is ... merely ... distasteful," said the commander. "Let's get on. I'm going to tell you where you are, first. You're on a world roughly similar to your own, but many ..." he hesitated, looking at the academician.

"Light-years," supplemented the deep voice.

"... light-years in terms of what a year means to you," went on the commander, with growing briskness. "Many light-years distant from your home. We didn't bring you here because of any personal ... dislike ... or enmity for you, but for ..."

"Observation," supplied the doctor. The commander turned and bowed slightly to him, and was bowed back at in return.

"... observation," went on the commander. "Now, do you understand what I've told you so far?"

"I'm listening," said Eldridge.

"Very well," said the commander. "I will go on. There is something about your people that we are very anxious to discover. We have been, and intend to continue, studying you to find it out. So far—I will admit quite frankly and freely—we

41

GORDON R. DICKSON

have not found it, and the consensus among our best minds is that you, yourself, do not know what it is. Accordingly, we have hopes of . . . causing . . . you to discover it for yourself. And for us."

"Hey. . . ." breathed Eldridge.

"Oh, you will be well treated, I assure you," said the commander, hurriedly. "You have been well treated. You have been . . . but you did not know . . . I mean you did not feel——"

"Can you remember any discomfort since we picked you up?" asked the doctor, leaning forward.

"Depends what you mean. . . ."

"And you will feel none." The doctor turned to the commander. "Perhaps I'm getting ahead of myself?"

"Perhaps," said the commander. He bowed and turned back to Eldridge. "To explain—we hope you will discover our answer for it. We're only going to put you in a position to work on it. Therefore, we've decided to tell you everything. First—the problem. Academician?"

The oldest one bowed. His deep voice made the room ring oddly.

"If you will look this way," he said. Eldridge turned his head. The other raised one paw and the wall beside him dissolved into a maze of lines and points. "Do you know what this is?"

"No," said Eldridge.

"It is," rumbled the one called the academician, "a map of the known universe. You lack the training to read it in four dimensions, as it should be read. No matter. You will take my word for it . . . it is a map. A map covering hundreds of thousands of your light-years and millions of your years."

He looked at Eldridge, who said nothing.

"To go on, then. What we know of your race is based upon two sources of information. History. And legend. The history is sketchy. It rests on archaeological discoveries for the most part. The legend is even sketchier and—fantastic."

He paused again. Still Eldridge guarded his tongue.

"Briefly, there is a race that has three times broken out to overrun this mapped area of our galaxy and dominate other civilized cultures—until some inherent lack of weakness in the individual caused the component parts of this advance to die out. The periods of these outbreaks have always been disastrous for the dominated cultures and uniformly without

42

benefit to the race I am talking about. In the case of each outbreak, though the home planet was destroyed and all known remnants of the advancing race hunted out, unknown seed communities remained to furnish the material for a new advance some thousands of years later. That race," said the academician, and coughed, or at least made some kind of noise in his throat, "is your own."

Eldridge watched the other carefully and without moving.

"We see your race, therefore," went on the academician, and Eldridge received the mental impression of an elderly man putting the tips of his fingers together judiciously, "as one with great or overwhelming natural talents, but unfortunately also with one great natural flaw. This flaw seems to be a desire—almost a need—to acquire and possess things. To reach out, encompass, and absorb. It is not," shrugged the academician, "a unique trait. Other races have it—but not to such an extent that it makes them a threat to their coexisting cultures. Yet, this in itself is not the real problem. If it was a simple matter of rapacity, a combination of other races should be able to contain your people. There is a natural inevitable balance of that sort continually at work in the galaxy. No," said the academician, and paused, looking at the commander.

"Go on. Go on," said the commander. The academician bowed.

"No, it is not that simple. As a guide to what remains, we have only the legend, made anew and reinforced after each outward sweep of you people. We know that there must be something more than we have found—and we have studied you carefully, both your home world and now you, personally. There *must* be something more in you, some genius, some capability above the normal, to account for the fantastic nature of your race's previous successes. But the legend says only—*Danger, Human! High Explosive. Do not touch*—and we find nothing in you to justify the warning."

He sighed. Or at least Eldridge received a sudden, unexpected intimation of deep weariness.

"Because of a number of factors—too numerous to go into and most of them not understandable to you—it is our race which must deal with this problem for the rest of the galaxy. What can we do? We dare not leave you be until you grow strong and come out once more. And the legend expressly warns us against touching you in any way. So we have chosen to pick one—but I intrude upon your field, Doctor."

The two of them exchanged bows. The doctor took up the talk, speaking briskly and entirely to Eldridge.

"A joint meeting of those of us best suited to consider the situation recommended that we pick up one specimen for intensive observation. For reasons of availability, you were the one chosen. Following being brought under drugs to this planet, you were thoroughly examined, by the best of medical techniques, both mentally and physically. I will not go into detail, since we have no wish to depress you unduly. I merely want to impress on you the fact that we found nothing. Nothing. No unusual power or ability of any sort, such as history shows you to have had and legend hints at. I mention this because of the further course of action we have decided to take. Commander?"

The being behind the desk got to his hind feet. The other two rose.

"You will come with us," said the commander.

Herded by them, Eldridge went out through the room's door into brilliant sunlight and across a small stretch of something like concrete to a stubby, egg-shaped craft with ridiculous little wings.

"Inside," said the commander. They got in. The commander squatted before a bank of instruments, manipulated a simple sticklike control, and after a moment the ship took to the air. They flew for perhaps half an hour, with Eldridge wishing he was in a position to see out one of the high windows, then landed at a field apparently hacked out of a small forest of mountains.

Crossing the field on foot, Eldridge got a glimpse of some truly huge ships, as well as a number of smaller ones such as the one in which he had arrived. Numbers of the furry aliens moved about, none with any great air of hurry, but all with purposefulness. There was a sudden single, thunderous sound that was gone almost before the ear could register it, and Eldridge, who had ducked instinctively, looked up again to see one of the huge ships falling—there is no other word for it—skyward with such unbelievable rapidity it was out of sight in seconds.

The four of them came at last to a shallow, open trench in the stuff that made the field surface. It was less than a foot wide and they stepped across it with ease. But once they had crossed it, Eldridge noticed a difference. In the five hundred yard square enclosed by the trench—for it turned at right angles off to his right and to his left—there was an air of tightly established desertedness, as of some highly restricted area, and the rectangular concrete-looking building that occupied the square's very center glittered unoccupied in the clear light.

They marched to the door of this building and it opened without any of them touching it. Inside was perhaps twenty feet of floor, stretching inward as a rim inside the walls. Then a sort of moat—Eldridge could not see its depth—filled with a dark fluid with a faint, sharp odor. This was perhaps another twenty feet wide and enclosed a small, flat island perhaps fifteen feet by fifteen feet, almost wholly taken up by a cage whose walls and ceiling appeared to be made of metal bars as thick as a man's thumb and spaced about six inches apart. Two more of the aliens, wearing a sort of harness and holding a short, black tube apiece, stood on the ledge of the outer rim. A temporary bridge had been laid across the moat, protruding through the open door of the cage.

They all went across the bridge and into the cage. There, standing around rather like a board of directors viewing an addition to the company plant, they faced Eldridge, and the commander spoke.

"This will be your home from now on," he said. He indicated the cot, the human-type chair and the other items furnishing the cage. "It's as comfortable as we can make it."

"Why?" burst out Eldridge, suddenly. "Why're you locking me up here? Why——"

"In our attempt to solve the problem that still exists," interrupted the doctor, smoothly, "we can do nothing more than keep you under observation and hope that time will work with us. Also, we hope to influence you to search for the solution yourself."

"And if I find it—what?" cried Eldridge.

"Then," said the commander, "we will deal with you in the kindest manner that the solution permits. It may be even possible to return you to your own world. At the very least, once you are no longer needed, we can see to it that you are quickly and painlessly destroyed."

Eldridge felt his insides twist within him.

"Kill me?" he choked. "You think that's going to make me help you? The hope of getting killed?"

They looked at him almost compassionately.

"You may find," said the doctor, "that death may be something you will want very much, if only for the purpose of putting a close to a life you've become weary of. Look,"—he gestured around him—"you are locked up beyond any chance of ever escaping. This cage will be illuminated night and day, and you will be locked in it. When we leave, the bridge will be withdrawn, and the only thing crossing that moat—which is filled with acid—will be a mechanical arm which will extend across and through a small opening to bring you food twice a day. Beyond the moat, there will be two armed guards on duty at all times, but even they cannot open the door to this building. That is opened by remote control from outside, only after the operator has checked on his vision screen to make sure all is as it should be inside here."

He gestured through the bars, across the moat, and through a window in the outer wall.

"Look out there," he said.

Eldridge looked. Out beyond, and surrounding the building, the shallow trench no longer lay still and empty under the sun. It now spouted a vertical wall of flickering, weaving distortion, like a barrier of heat waves.

"That is our final defense, the ultimate in destructiveness that our science provides us—it would literally burn you to nothingness if you touched it. It will be turned off only for seconds, and with elaborate precautions, to let guards in, or out."

Eldridge looked back in, to see them all watching him.

"We do this," said the doctor, "not only because we may discover you to be more dangerous than you seem, but to impress you with your helplessness so that you may be more ready to help *us*. Here you are, and here you will stay."

"And you think," demanded Eldridge hoarsely, "that this's all going to make me want to help you?"

"Yes," said the doctor, "because there's one thing more that enters into the situation. You were literally taken apart physically, after your capture, and as literally put back together again. We are advanced in the organic field, and certain things are true of all life forms. I supervised the work on you myself. You will find that you are, for all practical purposes immortal and irretrievably sane. This will be your home forever, and you will find that neither death nor insanity will provide you a way of escape unless we allow them to you."

They turned and filed out of the cage. From some remote control, the door was swung shut. He heard it click and lock. The bridge was withdrawn from the moat. A screen lit up and a woolly face surveyed the building's interior.

The guards took up their patrol around the rim in opposite directions, keeping their eyes on Eldridge and their weapons ready in their hands. Outside, the flickering wall blinked out for a second and then returned.

The silence of a warm, summer, mountain afternoon descended upon the building. The footsteps of the guards made shuffling noises on their path around the rim. The bars enclosed him.

Eldridge stood still, holding the bars in both hands and looking out.

He could not believe it.

He could not believe it as the days piled up into weeks, and the weeks into months. But as the seasons shifted and the year came around to a new year, the realities of his situation began to soak into him like water into a length of dock piling. For outside, Time could be seen at its visible and regular motion, but in his prison there was no Time.

Always the lights burned overhead, always the guards paced about him. Always the barrier burned beyond the building, the meals came swinging in on the end of a long metal arm extended over the moat and through a small hatchway which opened automatically as the arm approached; regularly, twice weekly, the doctor came and checked him over, briefly, impersonally—and went out again with the changing of the guard.

He felt the unbearableness of his situation, like a hand winding tighter and tighter day by day the spring of tension within him. He took to pacing feverishly up and down the cage. He went back and forth, back and forth, until the room swam. He lay awake nights, staring at the endless glow of illumination from the ceiling. He rose to pace again.

The doctor came and examined him. He talked to Eldridge, but Eldridge would not answer. Finally there came a day when everything split wide open and he began to howl and bang on the bars. The guards were frightened and called the doctor. The doctor came, and with two others entered the cage and strapped him down. They did something odd that hurt at the back of his neck and he passed out.

When he opened his eyes again, the first thing he saw was the doctor's woolly face, looking down at him—he had learned to recognize that countenance in the same way a sheepherder eventually comes to recognize an individual sheep in his flock. Eldridge felt very weak, but calm.

"You tried hard," said the doctor, "but you see, you didn't make it. There's no way out *that* way for you."

Eldridge smiled.

"Stop that!" said the doctor sharply. "You aren't fooling us. We know you're perfectly rational."

Eldridge continued to smile.

"What do you think you're doing?" demanded the doctor. Eldridge looked happily up at him.

"I'm going home," he said.

"I'm sorry," said the doctor. "You don't convince me." He turned and left. Eldridge turned over on his side and dropped off into the first good sleep he'd had in months.

In spite of himself, however, the doctor was worried. He had the guards doubled, but nothing happened. The days slipped into weeks and still nothing happened. Eldridge was apparently fully recovered. He still spent a great deal of time walking up and down his cage and grasping the bars as if to pull them out of the way before him—but the frenzy of his earlier pacing was gone. He had also moved his cot over next to the small, two-foot square hatch that opened to admit the mechanical arm bearing his meals, and would lie there, with his face pressed against it, waiting for the food to be delivered. The doctor felt uneasy, and spoke to the commander privately about it.

"Well," said the commander, "just what is it you suspect?"

"I don't know," confessed the doctor. "It's just that I see him more frequently than any of us. Perhaps I've become sensitized—but he bothers me."

"Bothers you?"

"Frightens me, perhaps. I wonder if we've taken the right way with him."

"We took the only way." The commander made the little gesture and sound that was his race's equivalent of a sigh. "We must have data. What do you do when you run across a possibly dangerous virus, Doctor? You isolate it—for study, until you know. It is not possible, and too risky to try to study his race at close hand, so we study him. That's all we're doing. You lose objectivity, Doctor. Would you like to take a short vacation?"

"No," said the doctor, slowly. "No. But he frightens me."

Still, time went on and nothing happened. Eldridge paced his cage and lay on his cot, face pressed to the bars of the hatch, staring at the outside world. Another year passed, and another. The double guards were withdrawn. The doctor came reluctantly to the conclusion that the human had at last accepted the fact of his confinement, and felt growing within him that normal sort of sympathy that feeds on familiarity. He tried to talk to Eldridge on his regularly scheduled visits, but Eldridge showed little interest in conversation. He lay on the cot watching the doctor as the doctor examined him, with something in his eyes as if he looked on from some distant place in which all decisions were already made and finished.

"You're as healthy as ever," said the doctor, concluding his examination. He regarded Eldridge. "I wish you would, though—" He broke off. "We aren't a cruel people, you know. We don't like the necessity . . . that makes us do this."

He paused. Eldridge considered him without stirring.

"If you'd accept that fact," said the doctor, "I'm sure you'd make it easier on yourself. Possibly our figures of speech have given you a false impression. We said you are immortal. Well, of course, that's not true. Only practically speaking are you immortal. You are now capable of living a very, very, very long time. That's all."

He paused again. After a moment of waiting, he went on.

"Just the same way, this business isn't really intended to go on for eternity. By its very nature of course it can't. Even races have a finite lifetime. But even that would be too long. No, it's just a matter of a long time as you might live it. Eventually, everything must come to a conclusion—that's inevitable."

Eldridge still did not speak. The doctor sighed.

"Is there anything you'd like?" he said. "We'd like to make this as little unpleasant as possible. Anything we can give you?"

Eldridge opened his mouth.

"Give me a boat," he said. "I want a fishing rod. I want a bottle of applejack."

The doctor shook his head sadly. He turned and signaled the guards. The cage door opened. He went out.

"Get me some pumpkin pie," cried Eldridge after him, sitting up on the cot and grasping the bars as the door closed. "Give me some green grass in here."

The doctor crossed the bridge. The bridge was lifted up and the monitor screen lit up. A woolly face looked out and saw that all was well. Slowly the outer door swung open.

"Get me some pine trees!" yelled Eldridge at the doctor's retreating back. "Get me some plowed fields! Get me some earth, some dirt, some plain, earth dirt! *Get me that!*"

The door shut behind the doctor, and Eldridge burst into laughter, clinging to the bars, hanging there with glowing eyes.

"I would like to be relieved of this job," said the doctor to the commander, appearing formally in the latter's office.

"I'm sorry," said the commander. "I'm very sorry. But it was our tactical team that initiated this action, and no one has the experience with the prisoner you have. I'm sorry."

The doctor bowed his head; and went out.

Certain mild but emotion-deadening drugs were also known to the woolly, bearlike race. The doctor went out and began to indulge in them. Meanwhile, Eldridge lay on his cot, occasionally smiling to himself. His position was such that he could see out the window and over the weaving curtain of the barrier that ringed his building, to the landing field. After a while one of the large ships landed and when he saw the three members of its crew disembark from it and move, ant-like, off across the field toward the buildings at its far end, he smiled again.

He settled back and closed his eyes. He seemed to doze for a couple of hours and then there was the sound of the door opening to admit the extra single guard bearing the food for his three o'clock midafternoon feeding. He sat up, pushed the cot down a little, and sat on the end of it, waiting for the meal.

The bridge was not extended—that happened only when someone was to enter his cage. The monitor screen lit up and a woolly face watched as the tray of food was loaded on the mechanical arm. It swung out across the acid-filled moat, stretched itself toward the cage, and under the vigilance of the face in the monitor the two-foot square hatch opened just before it to let it extend into the cage.

Smiling, Eldridge took the tray. The arm withdrew; as it cleared the cage the hatch swung shut and locked. Outside the cage, guards, food carrier, and face in the monitor relaxed. The food carrier turned toward the door, the face in the monitor looked down at some invisible control board before it, and the outer door swung open.

In that moment, Eldridge moved.

In one swift second he was on his feet and his hands had closed around the bars of the hatch. There was a single screech of metal, as—incredibly—he tore it loose and threw it aside. Then he was diving through the hatch opening.

He rolled head over heels like a gymnast and came up with his feet standing on the inner edge of the moat. The acrid scent of the acid faintly burnt at his nostrils. He sprang forward in a standing jump, arms outstretched—and his clutching fingers closed on the end of the food arm, now halfway in the process of its leisurely mechanical retraction across the moat.

The metal creaked and bent, dipping downward toward the acid, but Eldridge was already swinging onward under the powerful impetus of his arms from which the sleeves had fallen back to reveal bulging ropes of smooth, powerful muscle. He flew forward through the air, feet first, and his boots took the nearest guard in the face, so that they crashed to the ground together.

For a second they rolled, entangled, then the guard flopped and Eldridge came up on one knee, holding the black tube of the guard's weapon. It spat a single tongue of flame and the other guard dropped. Eldridge thrust to his feet, turning to the still-open door.

The door was closing. But the panicked food carrier, unarmed, had turned to run. A bolt from Eldridge's weapon took him in the back. He fell forward and the door jammed on his body. Leaping after him, Eldridge squeezed through the remaining opening.

Then he was out under the free sky. The sounds of alarm screechers were splitting the air. He began to run. . . .

The doctor was already drugged—but not so badly that he could not make it to the field when the news came. Driven by a strange perversity of spirit, he went first to the prison to inspect the broken hatch and the bent food arm. He traced

Eldridge's outward path and it led him to the landing field where he found the commander and the academician by a bare, darkened area of concrete. They acknowledged his presence by little bows.

"He took a ship here?" said the doctor.

"He took a ship here," said the commander.

There was a little silence between them.

"Well," said the academician, "we have been answered."

"Have we?" the commander looked at them almost appealingly. "There's no chance—that it was just chance? No chance that the hatch just happened to fail—and he acted without thinking, and was lucky?"

The doctor shook his head. He felt a little dizzy and unnatural from the drug, but the ordinary processes of his thinking were unimpaired.

"The hinges of the hatch," he said, "were rotten—eaten away by acid."

"Acid?" the commander stared at him. "Where would he get acid?"

"From his own digestive processes—regurgitated and spat directly into the hinges. He secreted hydrochloric acid among other things. Not too powerful—but over a period of time. . . ."

"Still—" said the commander, desperately, "I think it must have been more luck than otherwise."

"Can you believe that?" asked the academician. "Consider the timing of it all, the choosing of a moment when the food arm was in the proper position, the door open at the proper angle, the guard in a vulnerable situation. Consider his unhesitating and sure use of a weapon—which could only be the fruits of hours of observation—his choice of a moment when a fully supplied ship, its drive unit not yet cooled down, was waiting for him on the field. No," he shook his woolly head, "we have been answered. We put him in an escapeproof prison and he escaped."

"But none of this was impossible!" cried the commander.

The doctor laughed, a fuzzy, drug-blurred laugh. He opened his mouth but the academician was before him.

"It's not what he did," said the academician, "but the fact that he did it. No member of another culture that we know would have even entertained the possibility in their minds. Don't you see—he disregarded, he *denied* the fact that escape was impossible. *That* is what makes his kind so fearful, so dangerous. The fact that something is impossible presents no barrier to their seeking minds. That, alone, places them above us on a plane we can never reach."

"But it's a false premise!" protested the commander. "They cannot contravene natural laws. They are still bound by the physical order of the universe."

The doctor laughed again. His laugh had a wild quality. The commander looked at him.

"You're drugged," he said.

"Yes," choked the doctor. "And I'll be more drugged. I toast the end of our race, our culture, and our order."

"Hysteria!" said the commander.

"Hysteria?" echoed the doctor. "No—*guilt!* Didn't we do it, we three? The legend told us not to touch them, not to set a spark to the explosive mixture of their kind. And we went ahead and did it, you, and you, and I. And now we've sent forth an enemy—safely into the safe hiding place of space, in a ship that can take him across the galaxy, supplied with food to keep him for years, rebuilt into a body that will not die, with star charts and all the keys to understand our culture and locate his home again, using the ability to learn we have encouraged in him."

"I say," said the commander, doggedly, "he is not that dangerous—yet. So far he has done nothing one of us could not do, had we entertained the notion. He's shown nothing, nothing supernormal."

"Hasn't he?" said the doctor thickly. "What about the defensive screen—our most dangerous, most terrible weapon—that could burn him to nothingness if he touched it?"

The commander stared at him.

"But—" said the commander. "The screen was shut off, of course, to let the food carrier out, at the same time the door was opened. I assumed——"

"I checked," said the doctor, his eyes burning on the commander. "They turned it on again before he could get out."

"But he *did* get out! You don't mean—" the commander's voice faltered and dropped. The three stood caught in a sudden silence like stone. Slowly, as if drawn by strings controlled by an invisible hand, they turned as one to stare up into the empty sky and space beyond.

"You mean—" the commander's voice tried again, and died.

"Exactly!" whispered the doctor.

Halfway across the galaxy, a child of a sensitive race cried out in its sleep and clutched at its mother.

"I had a bad dream," it whimpered.

"Hush," said its mother. "Hush." But she lay still, staring at the ceiling. She, too, had dreamed.

Somewhere, Eldridge was smiling at the stars.

# REHABILITATED

I went into a bar.

"Gimme a drink," I said to the bartender.

"Brother, don't take that drink," said a voice at my elbow. I turned and there was a skinny little guy in his fifties. Thin, yellow hair and a smile on his face. "Brother, don't take that drink," he said.

I shook him off.

"Where'd you come from?" I said. "You weren't there when I sat down here one second ago." He just grinned at me.

"Gimme a drink," I said to the bartender.

"Not for you," said the bartender. "You had enough before you came in here." A fat bartender polishing shot glasses with his little finger inside a dishtowel. "Get your friend to take you home."

"He's no friend of mine," I said.

"Brother," said the little man, "come with me."

"I want a drink," I said. An idea struck me. I turned to the little man. "Let's you and I go someplace else and have a drink," I said.

We went out of the bar together, and suddenly we were somewhere else.

After I started to get over it, it wasn't too bad. The first week was bad, but after that it got better. When I found how the little man had trapped me, I tried to get away from the mission or whatever it was he'd taken me to. But after the booze died out I was real weak and sick for a long time. And after that stage was over I got to feeling that maybe I would quit after all. And I started having long talks with the little man. His name was Peer Ambrose.

"How old are you, Jack?" he asked me.

"Twenty-six," I said.

He looked at me with tight little brown eyes in his leather face, grinning.

"Can you run an elevator, Jack?"

"I can run any damn thing!" I said, getting mad.

"Can you, Jack?" he said, not turning a hair.

"Whattayou mean, can I run an elevator?" I shouted at him. "Any flying fool can run an elevator. I can run any damn thing, and you ask me can I run an elevator. Sure I can run an elevator!"

"I have one I'd like you to run for me," he said.

"Well, all right," I said. I didn't mean to yell at him. He didn't seem to be a bad little man; but he was always grinning at me.

So I went to work running the elevator. It wasn't bad. It gave me something to do around the mission or what ever it was. But it wasn't enough to do, and I got bored. I never could understand why they didn't have one of the automatics, anyway—any elevator with an operator was a museum piece.

But we were only about half a mile from the spaceport, and when there wasn't anything doing I'd take the elevator up to the transparent weather bubble that opened on the roof garden and watch the commuters and the sky with its clouds and the big ships taking off all sharp and black like a black penpoint at the end of a long white cone of exhaust. I didn't do much—just sat and watched them. When the signal rang in the elevator, I'd press the studs and we'd float down the tube to whatever floor wanted an elevator, and that'd be that.

After a few weeks, old Peer rang for me one day on the office level and told me to leave the elevator and come on in to his office. When I went in with him there was another man there, a young man with black hair and wearing a business cut on his jacket.

"Jack," said Peer, "this is counselor Toby Gregg. Toby, this is Jack Heimelmann. Jack's been with us for over a month now."

"Is that a fact?" said Toby. "Well, I'm glad to meet you, Jack." He put out his hand, but I didn't take it.

"What's this?" I asked, looking at Peer. "What're you cooking up for me now?"

"Jack," said Peer, putting his hand on my arm and looking up into my face, "you need help. You know that. And Gregg here has training that'll help him give it to you."

"I don't know about that," I said.

"Jack," said Peer, "you know I wouldn't recommend anything that was bad for you. Now, I'm going to ask you to talk to Gregg. Just talk to him."

Well, I gave in. Peer said he'd get somebody else for the elevator and I was to come and talk to Gregg three times a week, and meantime I was to be given some books to read.

The first time I went to see Gregg in his office on office level, he offered me a drink.

"A drink!" I said. And right away the old thirst came charging up. And then, while I stood there, it faded again, all by itself.

"I guess not," I said. Then I stared at him. "What's the idea of offering me a drink?" I asked. "What're you trying to do?"

"I'm just proving something to you, Jack," he said. We were sitting in a couple of slope-back easy chairs with a little low table between us that fitted up against one wall of the office. He reached over and pressed a stud on the table and a little panel in the wall above the table opened and a bottle and some glasses slid out on a tray. "Go ahead, you can have the drink if you want. I'm just showing you that it isn't your drinking that we have to fix, but what's behind it. When we get through with you, you'll be able to take a drink without going out on a bender."

"I will?" I said. I looked at the tray. "I still guess I won't have anything."

"Cigarette?" he said, offering me one.

I took that.

"Tell me, Jack," he said, when I had the cigarette going between my lips, "how long have you been smoking, now?"

"Why," I told him, "let's see. I was smoking in general prep school when I was twelve. That'd be . . . let's see . . ."

"Fourteen years," he said. "That's a long time. You started early. You must have had a pretty rough bunch of kids around that general prep."

"Bunch of damn sissies," I told him. "Catch *them* smoking! I bet there isn't a dozen of them that smoke today."

"Most people don't, you know," said Gregg.

"My dad started at ten," I said.

"That was back a few years," he smiled. "Habits change with the years, Jack. Most of those kids you were in school with were probably looking forward to jobs where smoking wouldn't be practical."

"Yeah. Yeah, I bet they were," I said. "They sure figured to be big shots."

"All of them?" he asked.

"Most of them," I said. This talk was getting on my nerves. I didn't like to talk about general prep school. I had five years of it after I got out of secondary and I was seventeen before I cut loose. And that was plenty.

"Didn't you have a few friends?" he asked.

"Hell, yes!" I said. "D'you think I was an introvert?"

"No, Jack," he said, soothingly. "I can tell by looking at you you're not an introvert. But these friends of yours. Do you ever see any of them any more?"

I jumped up out of the chair.

"Listen, what is this?" I shouted at him. "What're you getting at? What're you trying to find out? I don't see any sense to this kind of questioning. I don't have to sit and listen to these kind of stupid questions. I'm leaving."

And I turned and headed toward the office door.

"All right, Jack," he said behind me, not irritated at all. "Come back any time you feel like it."

At the door, I turned once more to look at him. But he had his back to me. He was putting the tray with the bottles and glasses on it back into the wall.

I told Peer I had changed my mind about the counseling and went back to work on the elevator. The old man didn't seem annoyed at all. And I worked on the elevator for several weeks, riding people up and down and going up by myself to watch the sky and the people flying around and the ships. But after a while it began to wear on me.

I don't know what actually made me decide to go back to Gregg. I suppose it was because there just wasn't anything else. There was nothing much doing with the elevator, and there wasn't much sense in leaving the place and going back to the old drinking again. I really didn't want to start that all over again, but I knew if I got out by myself I would. Finally I figured I'd go back to Gregg and tell him I'd listen to just enough questions to cure me of my drinking, but nothing else.

When I went back to see him for the first time, though, he told me that wouldn't work.

"You see, Jack," he told me, "to get rid of the drinking, we have to get rid of whatever it is that's making you want to drink. And whatever that is, it's what's causing all your other troubles. So, it's up to you whether you want a complete job done or not."

I thought for a minute. Somehow talking with him made it seem easy.

"Oh, hell!" I said, finally. "Let's dig it out. I can't be any worse off, anyway."

So we went to it. And it was one rough time. Even Gregg said it was rougher than he figured. At first I was always blowing up and stamping out. But I finally got to the point where I could tell him anything. And it came out that I'd started getting a chip on my shoulder back as a kid because I thought the other kids were better than I was. Actually, Gregg said, it was my adverse environment that was hampering me. My mother was a state ward because of her unstable mental condition, and the only woman we had around the house was the housekeeper Government Service paid for. My dad was a portable-operating-room driver for a country hospital, and he was away from home on calls most of the time. He wanted me to be a driver like him when I got out of school, but by that time they had the automatic routers in, so I didn't.

But Gregg figured out that, even though I never really liked the idea, my dad wanting me to do a manual job had given me an inferiority complex. Like my driving a portable operating room, when all the other kids in school were looking forward to being Earthside deskmen, or professionals, or getting schooled for new-world trades; the sort of work that means learning half a dozen different lines that'll be needed on a new planet. Gregg figured it started hitting me as soon as I got into prep school and that was why I got into all kinds of trouble with the instructors and ran with a knify bunch and took up smoking and drinking. And he said that my inferiority complex had made me believe that I hated work; while actually, I was just taking out my dislike for my classmates on it. He said it was quite to be expected under those conditions that I would just come out of prep school and draw my social maintenance year after year without really trying to find anything to do. And then, as time went on, the drink was bound to start to get me.

Anyway we went back over all my life and he started pointing out to me where I had been wrong in thinking I wasn't as good as the other kids; and after a while I began to see it myself. And from that time on I began actually to change.

It's not easy to explain just what it was like. I had had a basically good schooling, as Gregg pointed out, and with the learning techniques used in our modern schools, the knowledge was all there, still. I had just not been using it. Now, as we talked together, he began to remind me of little odds and ends of things. My vocabulary increased and my reading speed picked up. He had me study intensively; and though at some times it was real hard, little by little I began to talk and act like someone of professional, or at least desk level.

"What you need now," Gregg said to me one day, "is to decide on some specific plan of action."

"I beg your pardon?" I said, puzzled.

"A job, or some work you can devote yourself to," said Gregg. "You've been refusing to face the fact for years, but in our modern society everyone is busy at their chosen work. Now, what would you like to do?"

I stared at him.

"Have you ever thought of emigrating, for instance?" he went on. "You're large and young and strong and—active-natured. The new-world life might suit you."

I thought about it.

"The new worlds aren't like Earth," Gregg went on. "We're overstocked here on second-raters, bogged down in a surplus of inferior talent. All the bright young men and women in each generation graduate and get off planet as quickly as they can. On a newer world, you'd be freer, Jack. Your social unit would be smaller, and your personal opportunity to develop greater. It'd mean a lot of hard work, of course."

"I wouldn't mind that," I said.

While he talked, I had been thinking. I remembered the

teachers teaching about the new worlds in prep school. Hitherto untouched planets, they'd told us, which in every case present a great challenge and offer a great reward to the pioneer. Twenty-four percent of our young people emigrating every year. That meant, of course, the ones who had completed their schooling and passed the physical. The more I thought of it, the better it sounded for me.

"I'd like to leave Earth," I said. "There's nothing for me here."

"Well, good," said Gregg. "If your mind's made up, then you've come a long way from the man I first met. You know you'll have to go back to school and get your certificate?"

"Sure. I know."

"Fine," said Gregg. He punched some buttons. "We'll start you tomorrow. Well, I guess that's enough for today."

He got up and went with me to the door and out into the main corridor of office level. Coming down the hall was Peer, and he had a little girl with brown hair with him. They stopped to talk with us and I got introduced to the girl. That was the first time I met Leena Tore.

I liked Leena a lot.

I had bumped into a lot of women in the past years; but either they had been no-goods, hitting the alcohol as hard as I was, or else they were stuck up and you couldn't get along with them. I'd seen them once or twice, but we wouldn't get along and that would be the limit. They all talked too much and looked down on anybody who wasn't professional level at least.

Leena wasn't like that. She didn't talk too much; and to tell the truth, she wasn't bright at all. In fact, she was stupid. But we got along very well together. She was an orphan, raised under State supervision in a private home. They found a job for her when she got old enough, but she didn't like it and finally went on social maintenance, and didn't do anything but sit around and watch shows all day. Finally Peer heard of her and brought her down to the place.

Gregg was working with her, too. But he hadn't been going on her long enough to make any real difference, and, privately, I didn't think he ever would. She was really too stupid. But she was an easy sort of person to get along with and after a while I began to think of marrying her.

Meanwhile, I was going back to school. It was hard as

hell—I'd forgotten how hard it was. But then I hadn't really worked at it before, and I'd been away from the preliminary stuff a long time.

But I'd been through it all once before, as Gregg reminded me—I'd forgotten—which helped; and they really do have good techniques and associative equipment in the schools nowadays. So after a while, I began to know my stuff and it perked me up. And when I got stuck Gregg would talk to me, and then things would come easy.

I got myself some new clothes and I began to mix with my classmates. Most of them were young kids, but by keeping my mouth shut I got along with them pretty well. And, you know, I began to feel this stuff they talk about, the sense of personal and racial destiny. I'd look around at these tall, good-looking kids talking big about the stars and the future. And then I'd look at myself in the mirror and say, "Boy, you're part of all this." And I began to see what Gregg had said my inferiority complex had cut me off from before.

They said Leena was making progress. She had been going to school too, but she was several classes behind me and she still had some time to go when I graduated. So we talked it over, all four of us, Leena and me, and Peer and Gregg, and we decided I'd go ahead and get cleared and ship out for some world. And then when Leena came along later she could just specify the same destination when she went through emigration.

Leena didn't look too pleased at having to wait. She pouted a bit, then finally gave in. But I was eager to go. These past months had gotten me thoroughly into the mood of emigration, and I was a happy man the day I went down to the big section outside the spaceport where clearing and routing went on for those who went spaceward from our city. Gregg had had a long talk with me, and I felt real good.

There wasn't to be too much to it. I presented my certificate of graduation and my credentials. The deskman glanced them over and asked me if I had any preference about examiners.

"Celt Winter," I said. This was the man Peer and Gregg had told me to ask for. They said he was a friend of Gregg's who had heard about me from Gregg and was very interested in me. It seems he didn't have much time off, ordinarily, so he never had any chance to drop around the place; and if I asked for him as my examiner, that would give us a chance to meet before I left.

The deskman ran his finger down his file and pressed a few studs. A message jumped out on the screen set in his desk.

"Celt Winter has just stepped out for a minute," he said. "Do you want to wait, or shall I give you someone else?"

I sort of hesitated. I hated to disappoint this Winter, but I was too wound up just to sit and twiddle my thumbs until he got back. I saw the deskman looking at me, waiting for my answer, and I got kind of nervous.

"Oh, anyone'll do," I said. "Just give me anybody that's free."

"Sven Coleman, then," said the deskman. "Desk four sixty-two." He gave me a little plastic tab and directed me through a door to his right.

I went through the door and came out into a big hall covered with desks at which examiners sat. Most of them had people sitting with them. I went ahead down a lane between the desks until I reached the four-sixty row, and two places off to my right I came to a desk where a tall young deskman with black hair and a long, straight nose waved me to a seat.

I handed him my credentials: my graduation certificate, my government registration card, and my physical okay sheet, for I'd taken that exam a couple of days before. He read through them.

"Well, Mr. Heimelmann," he said, smiling at me, and laying the credentials down. "You realize this is just a sort of formality. We interviewers are set up here just for the purpose of making sure that those of our people who go out to the new worlds won't want to turn back when they get there. In fact, this is just a last-minute chance for you to change your mind."

"There's no danger of that," I said.

He smiled and nodded.

"That's fine," he said. "Now perhaps you'd like to tell me, Mr. Heimelmann, what you particularly want to do when you get to your pioneer world and any preferences you might have as to location."

Gregg had told me that they'd ask me that, and I had my answer ready.

"I'd like to get out on the edge of things," I said. "I like singleton jobs. As for location, any place that's got plenty of outdoors is fine."

He laughed.

"Well, we can certainly suit those preferences," he said. "Most of our prospective emigrants are looking forward to team work in a close colony."

I laughed, too. I found myself liking this man.

"Probably afraid to get their feet wet," I said.

His smile went a little puzzled. Then he laughed again.

"I see what you mean," he said. "Too much community emphasis is a bad thing, even though the motives are good."

"Sure," I said. "If you like a crowd, you might as well stay here on Earth."

He looked puzzled again, and then serious. He picked up my credentials and went through them once more.

"You're in your late twenties, aren't you, Mr. Heimelmann?" he said.

"That's right," I answered.

"But I see that according to your graduation certificate you just finished your trade learnings."

"Oh," I said. "Well, you see, I fooled around for a few years there. I couldn't seem to make up my mind about what I wanted to do."

"I see," he said. He put down my credentials and sat for a moment, tapping the top of the desk with his forefinger and looking as if he was thinking. "Excuse me a moment, Mr. Heimelmann."

He got up and left. After a few minutes he was back.

"Will you come with me, please?" he asked.

I wondered a bit, but I got up and followed him. I didn't see any of the other interviewers doing this with the people they had at their desks. But you can't tell what the procedure is in these kind of places by just looking. Sven Coleman took me over to one side of the big room and through a door into an office where a sort of nervous older-looking man got up from a desk to greet us.

"Mr. Heimelmann," said Coleman. "This is Mr. Jos Alter. He'd like to talk to you for a moment."

"Hello," I said, shaking hands.

"How do you do, Mr. Heimelmann," answered Alter. "Sit down beside my desk here, will you? That'll be all, Sven."

"Yes, sir," said Coleman and went out. I followed Alter to the desk and sat down. He had two tired lines between his eyes and a little mustache.

"Mr. Heimelmann," he said. "I've got a little test here I

64

want you to take. I'm going to give you a tape and I'd like
you to take it over to the machine there and put it in. As the
questions pop up on the screen, you press either the true stud
or the false to register your choice. Will you do that? I've got
to step out for a minute, but I'll be right back."

And he handed me the tape. It all seemed sort of strange
to me, but as Sven himself said, this business was just a
formality. I did what Alter wanted me to.

The questions were easy at first. If I have ten credits and I
give two-thirds of them away, how many do I have left? If
the main traffic strips are closed to children below the age of
responsibility and I have a five-year-old nephew with me, can
I send him home alone? But after a while they began to get
harder, and I was still working when Alter came back. He
took the tape and we went back to his desk, where he ran it
through a scorer and set it aside. Then he just looked at me.

"Mr. Heimelmann," he said, finally. "Where've you spent
the last six months or a year?"

"Why, at the place," I said. "I mean, the Freemen Independent Foundation Center."

"I see," he said. "And will you tell me briefly how you
happened to go there in the first place and what you've been
doing while you were there?"

I hesitated. There was something strange about all this. But
I had to give him some answer, and there was no point in
telling him anything but the truth when he could just press a
stud on his desk and call Peer to ask him.

"Well," I said, squirming some inside, for it isn't easy to
admit you've been an alcoholic, "I was drinking one day in a
bar. . . ."

And I went through the whole story for him, down to the
present. After I'd finished, he sat for a long while without
saying anything. I didn't say anything, either. I was feeling
pretty low down after admitting what I'd been. Finally he
spoke.

"Blast those people!" he said, viciously. "Blast and damn
them!"

I stared at him.

"Who?" I said. "Who? I don't understand."

He turned and looked me full in the face.

"Mr. Heimelmann," he said, "your friends at the Foundation—" he hesitated. "Nobody hates to tell you this more

than I do, but the fact of the matter is we can't approve you for emigration."

"Can't?" I echoed. His words seemed to roar in my ears. The room tilted and I seemed to have a sudden feeling as if I was falling, falling from a great, high place. And all the time I knew I was just sitting beside his desk. I grabbed at the desk to steady myself. I had a terrible feeling then as if everybody was marching away and leaving me—all the tall young people I'd gone to classes and graduated with. But I *had* graduated. My credentials were in order.

"Listen," I said; and I had to struggle to get the words out. "I'm qualified."

"I'm sorry," he said. And he did look sorry—sorry enough to cry. "You're not, Mr. Heimelmann. You're totally unfit, and your friends at the Foundation knew it. This isn't the first time they've tried to slip somebody by us, counting on the fact that modern education can get facts into anybody."

I just looked at him. I tried to say something, but my throat was too tight and the words wouldn't come out.

"Mr. Heimelmann . . . Jack . . ." he said. "I'll try and explain it to you, though it's not my job and I really don't know how. You see, in many ways, Jack, you're much better off than your ancestors. You're in perfect physical health. You're taller and stronger. You have faster reflexes and better coordination. You're much better balanced mentally, so much so, in fact, that it would be almost impossible for you to go insane, or even to develop a severe psychosis, but—"

I tasted blood in my mouth, but there was no pain. The room was beginning to haze up around me, and I felt something like a time bomb beginning to swell and tick in the back of my brain. His voice roared at me like out of a hurricane.

"—you have an IQ of ninety-two, Jack. Once upon a time this wasn't too bad, but in our increasingly technical civilization—" he spread his hands helplessly.

The hurricane was getting worse. I could hardly hear him now and I could hardly see the room. I felt the time bomb trembling, ready to explode.

"What these people at the Foundation did to you," he was saying, "was to use certain psi techniques to excite your own latent psi talents—a procedure which isn't yet illegal, but shortly will be. This way, they were able to sensitize you to amounts and types of knowledge you wouldn't otherwise be able to absorb—in much the same way we train animals, using these psi techniques, to perform highly complicated actions. Like an animal——"

The world split wide open. When I could see again, I found little old, leather-faced Peer had joined us in the room. Alter was slumped in his chair, his eyes closed. Peer crossed over to him, looked him over, then glanced at me with a low whistle.

"Easy Jack," he said. "Easy now. . . ." And I suddenly realized I was trembling like a leaf. But with his words, the tension began to go. Peer was shaking his head at me.

"We got a shield on Alter just in time," he said. "He's just going to wake up thinking you left and he dozed off for a while. But you don't realize what kind of a mental punch you've got, Jack. You would have killed him if I hadn't protected him."

For the first time, that came home to me. My hurricane could have killed Alter. I understood that, now. My knees weakened.

"No, it's all right. He's just out temporarily," said Peer. "Unfreeze yourself, Jack, and we'll teleport out of here. . . . What's the matter?"

"I want to know—" the words came hard from my throat. "I want to know, right now. What'd you do to me?"

Peer sighed.

"Can't it wait?—no, I guess not," he said, looking at me. "If you must know, you were an experiment. The first of your particular kind. But there'll be lots like you from now on; we'll see to that. Earth is starving, Jack; starving for the very minds and talents and skills it ships out each year. It's behind the times now and falling further every year, because the first-class young people all emigrate and the culls are left behind."

"Thanks!" I said, between my teeth and with my fists clenched. "Thanks a lot."

"Why not face facts?" said Peer cheerfully. "You're a high-grade moron, Jack—no, don't try that on me, what you did on Alter," he added, as I took a step forward. "You're not that tough, yet, Jack, though someday we hope you may be. As I was saying, you're a high-grade moron. Me, I've got an aneurysm that can't stand any kind of excitement, let alone spaceflight. Gregg, for your information, has a strong manic-depressive pattern—and so on, at the Foundation."

"I don't know what you mean," I said, sullenly.

"Of course you don't. But you will, Jack, you will," said Peer. "A government of second-raters were afraid to trigger your kind of talent in a high-grade moron, so they passed restrictive laws. We've just proved that triggering your abilities can not only be safe but practical. More evidence for a change that's coming here on Earth."

"You lied to me!" I shouted, suddenly. "All the time you were lying to me! All of you!"

"Well, now, we had to," Peer said. "It required a blockbuster of an emotional shock to break through all the years of conditioning that told you someone like yourself couldn't compete. You had to be so frustrated on a normal level that you'd go to your abnormal powers in desperation. Your desire to get off Earth to a place where life would be different was real enough. Gregg just built it up to where you couldn't face being turned down. And then we arranged the turndown."

I was crying.

"You shouldn't have done it!" I said. "You shouldn't have! For the first time, I thought I had some friends. For the first time——"

"Who says we're not your friends?" snapped Peer. "You think we went to all that trouble to break the law and bust you loose without figuring that you could be as close to us as anyone in the world could be? You—well, there's no use trying to explain it to you. You've got to be shown. Lock on, gang!"

And suddenly—they did lock on. For a second, I almost fell over, I was so scared. I felt Peer's mind slip into mine, then Toby Greggs's—and, without warning, there too was Leena. And she was not the same Leena I knew at all, but somebody almost as bright as Gregg. Only she was an epileptic.

All of a sudden, I knew too much. I heaved, with all the strength that was in me, trying to break loose. But the three of them held me easily.

"You just want to use me!" I shouted at them—with my mouth and my mind, both. "You just want me for what I can do for you—like a big, stupid horse." I was crying again, this time internally as well. "Just because you're all smarter than I am and you can make me do what you say!"

"Calm down, Jack," came the thought of Toby. "You've

got the picture all wrong. What kind of a team is that, the three of us riding on your back? What do you think keeps Peer nicely calmed down all the time? And what do you think keeps Leena's epileptic attacks under control and me sane? Let me show you something."

And then he did something which was for me like heaven opening up and showing a rainbow in all its glory to a blind man.

"You want a few extra IQ points to think with?" said Toby. "Take mine!"

# LISTEN

Reru did not like to see humans eat. So he was waiting in the living room while Taddy and his parents finished breakfast.

"And quite right, too," boomed Taddy's father. "He has as much right to his own ways as we have to ours. Remember that, Taddy, when you grow up. The only reason humans have been successful conquerors throughout the galaxy is because they have always respected the attitudes and opinions of the people they conquered."

"Oh, Harry!" said Taddy's mother. "He's too young to understand all that."

"I am not young," said Taddy defensively, through a mouthful of breakfast food. "I'm four years old."

"See there, Celia," said Taddy's father, laughing. "He's four years old—practically grown up. But seriously, honey, he's going to be growing up into a world in which the great majority of thinking beings are Mirians like Reru. He should start to understand the natives early."

"Well, I don't know," said Taddy's mother, worriedly. "After all, he was born in space on the way here and he's a delicate child——"

"Delicate, nonsense!" boomed Taddy's father. "He comes from the toughest race in the galaxy. Look at these Mirians, chained to their planet by a symbiosis so extensive that our biologists haven't reached the end of the chain yet. Look at Reru himself, gentle, noncombative, unenergetic, a stalwart example of the Mirian race, and therefore the ideal nursemaid for our son."

"Oh, I don't have a word of complaint to say against

Reru," answered Taddy's mother. "He's been just wonderful with Taddy. But I can't help it—when he cocks his head on one side and starts *listening* the way they all do, I get a little bit scared of him."

"Damn it, Celia!" said Taddy's father. "I've told you a thousand times that he's just hearing one of their cows calling that it wants to be milked."

Taddy squirmed in his chair. He knew all about the cows. They were six-legged Mirian animals that roamed around much as Reru and his mind roamed around. When they were full of milk they would start making a high, whistling sound, and Reru or some other Mirian would come along and attach his suckers to them and drink the milk. But the cows were no longer interesting, Reru was, and Taddy had finished his breakfast food.

"I'm all through," he broke in suddenly on his parents' conversation. "Can I go now? Can I?"

"I guess so," said Taddy's mother, and Taddy scrambled from the chair and ran off toward the living room.

"Don't go too far!" his mother's voice floated after him, followed by his father's deep bass.

"Let him go. Reru will bring him back all right. And, anyway, what on this planet of vegetarians could harm him?"

But Taddy had already forgotten his mother's words. For Reru was waiting for him, and Reru was fascinating.

He looked, at first glance, like a miniature copy of an old Chinese mandarin, with robe, bald head, and little wispy beard. It was only when you got to know him that you realized that there were tentacles beneath the robe, that he had never had hair on his head, and that the wispy beard hid and protected the suckers with which he milked the cows that were his source of food.

But Taddy liked him very much, and Taddy didn't think that there was anything the least bit strange about him.

"Where are we going today, Reru?" demanded Taddy, bouncing up and down before the little Mirian who was not quite twice as tall as he was.

Reru's voice was like the voice of a trilling bird, and it sang more than it spoke.

"Good morning, Taddy," it trilled. "Where would you like to go?"

"I want to go to the silver-and-green place," cried Taddy. "Can we go?"

Reru's dark little mandarin face did not smile because it did not have the muscles to do so. But the mouth opened and the Mirian gave a short wordless trill expressive of happiness and pleasure.

"Yes, small Taddy," Reru answered. "We can go." And, turning with a kind of stately dignity, he led the way out of the dwelling and into the soft yellow Mirian sunlight.

"Oh good, good, good!" sang Taddy, skipping along beside him.

They went away from the buildings of the humans, out across the low rolling grassland of Miria, Taddy bounding and leaping in the light gravity and Reru gliding along with effortless ease. And if that dignified glide was the result of twisting tentacles hidden beneath the robe, what of it? Where older humans might have felt squeamish at the thought of the twisting ropes of white muscle, Taddy took it entirely for granted. To him, Reru was beautiful.

They went on across the grasslands. Several times Reru stopped to *listen* and each time Taddy tried to imitate him, standing with his tousled head cocked on one side and an intent expression on his baby face. After one of these stops his brow furrowed and he seemed to be thinking. The little Mirian noticed him.

"What is it, Taddy?" he trilled.

"Daddy says that when you listen, you're listening to the cows," Taddy answered. "You hear more than that, don't you, Reru?"

"Yes, Taddy," said Reru, "I am listening to all my brothers."

"Oh," said the boy, wisely. "I thought so."

As they went on, the grassland began to dip, and after a while a patch of deeper green came into sight in the distance.

"There it is," trilled the Mirian. Taddy broke into a run.

"Let's hurry, Reru," cried the boy, pulling at the mandarin robe. "Come *on,* Reru!"

Reru increased his glide and they hurried forward until they came to the silver-and-green place.

It was like a storybook land in its beauty. Little green islands and clumps of vegetation were interspersed with flashing slivers of water, so that no matter where you stood some small reflective surface caught the yellow light of the sun and sent it winking into your eyes. It looked like a toy landscape on which some giant had broken his mirror and left the bits to sparkle and shine in the daytime brightness. Reru squatted and Taddy sat down on the edge of one of the pools.

"What does it say?" asked the boy. "Tell me what it says, Reru."

The Mirian trilled again his little trill of pleasure; then composed himself. For a long time he sat silent, *listening,* while the boy squirmed, impatient, yet not daring to say anything that might interrupt or delay what Reru was about to say. Finally, the Mirian spoke.

"I can hear my brother the cow down in the tall grass at the edge of a pool. I can hear him as he moves among the grass; and I hear what he hears, his little brother, the dweller in the ground who stores up rich food for my brother the cow. And I can hear still further to all the other little brothers of the world as they go about their appointed tasks, until the air is thick with the sound of their living and their memories are my memories and their thoughts my thoughts.

"So the green-and-silver place is filled with a mighty thought, and this is what that thought says:

" 'The green-and-silver place is a coming together of waters that have traveled a long way. Our brothers in the earth have told us that there are three waters that come together here, and none flow in the light of day. Our brothers of the waters have told us that these waters run far, for they have traveled the waters.

" 'One comes from the south, but the other two from the north. And the ones from the north travel side by side for a long way, with the dark and silent earth between and around them, until they come out in a colder land to the far north of here. And, in the far north, the two come together and their source is a single river that comes from a high mountain where the winds blow over bare rock. And in that place there is a brother who lives on the stones of the hillside and watches the stars at night. He has listened along the water and heard us down here in the warm grasslands; and he dreams of the green-and-silver place as he lies at night on the bare rock, watching the stars.

" 'But the water that comes from the south comes from deep beneath the mountains of the south, from a silent lake in the heart of the rock. The lake is filled by the water that trickles down the veins of the mountains, and in it lives another brother who is blind and has never seen the yellow sun. But he lies in the dark on a rock shelf above the silent lake and listens to the grumbling of the world as it talks to itself deep in the heart of the planet. And he, too, has heard us here in the warm grasslands, under the light of the yellow sun, and he dreams of the green-and-silver place as he lies on his rock ledge listening to the grumbling of the world.' "

Reru ceased talking and opened his eyes.

"That is only one story, Taddy," he said, "of the green-and-silver place."

"More," begged the boy. "Tell me more, Reru."

And he looked up into the alien face with eyes glowing in the wonder and excitement of what he had just heard. And Reru told him more.

The morning was nearly gone when they returned to Taddy's home, and Taddy's father and mother were already seated at the table eating lunch.

"Late again, Taddy," said his mother.

"No, I'm not," Taddy retorted, sliding into his place. "You're early."

"You *are* a little early at that, Celia," said Taddy's father. "How come?"

"Oh, I promised to go over to visit Julia this afternoon," answered Taddy's mother. "Taddy! Did you wash your hands?"

"Uh-huh," said Taddy with a vigorous nod, his mouth already full. "Look!" He displayed them at arms' length.

"Where did you go today, anyway?" asked his mother.

"To the green-and-silver place," answered Taddy.

"Green-and-silver place?" She looked across at her husband. "Where's that, Harry?"

"Darned if I know," answered Taddy's father. "Where is it, son?"

Taddy pointed in a southwesterly direction.

"Out there," he said. "There's lots of little pieces of water and lots of little bushes and things."

"Why," said Harry, "he must mean the swamp."

"The swamp!" echoed Taddy's mother. "He spent the whole morning out at the swamp! Harry, you have to do something. It isn't healthy for a boy to go mooning around like these Mirians."

"Now, Celia," grumbled Taddy's father. "The Mirians put their planet before everything else. It's almost a form of worship with them. But that can't possibly affect Taddy. Humans are just too big and strong to be seduced into that dead-end sort of philosophy. Anyway, that swamp's going to be drained shortly and they're going to put a building in its place."

He leaned across the table toward Taddy.

"You'd like that better, now, wouldn't you, Son?" he said. "A big new building to run around in instead of that water and muck!"

The boy's face had gone completely white and his mouth was open.

"You can get Reru to take you over and watch it go up," his father went on.

"No!" said the boy, suddenly and violently.

"Why, Taddy!" said his mother. "Is that any way to talk to your father? You apologize right now!"

"I won't," said Taddy.

"Taddy!" his father's big voice rumbled dangerously.

"I don't care!" cried Taddy. Suddenly the words were tumbling out of him all at once. "I hate you! I hate your old buildings. When I grow up I'm going to tear down that old building and put all the water and things back." He was crying now, and his words came interspersed with sobs. "I don't like you here. Nobody else likes you, either. Why don't you go 'way? Why don't you all go 'way?"

Taddy's father sat dumbfounded. But Taddy's mother got quickly up from her chair and around to Taddy's. She took him by the arm and pulled him away from the table.

"It's his nerves," she said. "I knew all this running around was bad for him." And she led him off in the direction of his room, his wails diminishing with distance and the closing of a door.

After a little while she came back.

"You see?" she said triumphantly to her husband. "Now he'll have to stay in bed all afternoon and I can't go over to Julia's because I'll have to stay here and watch him."

But Taddy's father had recovered his composure.

"Nonsense, Celia," he said. "It's just a case of nerves, like you said. Every boy has them one time or another. We can let the young pioneer kick up a few fusses without worrying too much about it. It won't hurt his character any. Now, you go on over to Julia's as you planned. He'll stay put."

"Well," said Taddy's mother slowly, wanting to be convinced, "if you say so. . . . I don't suppose it would do any harm to run over for a few minutes. . . ."

Up in his room, Taddy's sobs diminished until they no longer racked his small body. He got up and went to the window and looked out at the rolling grasslands.

"I will, too," he said to himself, "I will too tear down all their old buildings when I grow up."

And, immediately as he said it, a strange thing seemed to happen. A wave of peace flooded over him and he stopped crying. It was as if all the brothers that Reru had been talking about were here in the room and just outside his window, comforting him. He felt them all around him; and at the same time he sensed that they were all waiting for him to say something, waiting and listening. For just a few seconds he could feel all of Miria listening to him, to Taddy.

And he knew what they wanted, for he stretched both his arms out the window to them, a love filling his heart like no love he had ever felt before, as he spoke the two words they were waiting to hear.

"I promise," said Taddy.

# ROOFS OF SILVER

"Because you're a fool, brother," said Moran.

The words hung on the hot air between them. A small breeze blew through the rectangular window aperture in the thick mud wall to the rear. Through the window could be seen a bit of a garden, a few blue mountain flowers, and the courtyard wall of mud. The breeze disturbed the air but did not cool the room. In an opposite wall the hide curtain did not quite cover the doorway. The curtain's much-handled edge was scalloped and worn thin. Hot sunlight from the square came through the gap. Beasts like Earth donkeys, with unnatural-looking splayed hooves drowsed around the fountain in the center of the square.

"Why don't you call me a donkey?" said Jabe, looking at them.

"Fair enough," said Moran. He sat, gowned and fat among his grain sacks, his slate balanced on his knees, his creased fingers of both hands white with chalk. "Because it's just what you aren't. Any more than those variforms out there are, no matter what they're called."

Jabe moved uneasily. His spurs clinked.

"You think I'm overadapted?" he said.

"No. You're just a fool," said Moran. "As I said and keep saying. You've been here ten years. You started out a liberal and you've become conservative. When you started to work with these settlers, the returns weren't in yet."

"It's not a hundred per cent," said Jabe.

"How can it be?" said Moran. "But what's a statistical chance of error of three per cent?"

"I can't believe it," said Jabe. "I might have believed it, back on Earth, when these people were just population figures to me. Now, I've lived with them ten years. I can't believe it."

"I've lived with them, too."

"Eight years," said Jabe.

"Long enough. I didn't marry into them, though. That's why my eyes are still clear."

"No," said Jabe. He beat his hands together softly with a curious rhythmic and measured motion until he became suddenly aware of Moran's eyes upon them, and checked their motion, guiltily.

"No," he said again, with an effort. "It can't be true. It must be sociological."

"Indigenous."

"I can't believe that," said Jabe.

"You aren't arguing with me, man," said Moran. "You're arguing with a ten-year survey. I showed you the report. It's not a matter of living conditions or local superstitions. It's a steady, progressive deterioration from generation to generation. Already the shift is on from conscience to taboo."

"I haven't seen it."

"You've got a single point of view. And a technologically high level of community at that mine."

"No," said Jabe, shifting his weight from one foot to the other, and looking down at Moran. "Report or no report, I'm not condemning a world full of human beings."

Moran sat heavily among the grain sacks.

"Who's condemning?" he said. "It's just quarantine for the present, and you and I and the rest of the agents have to go back."

"You could hold up the report."

"No," said Moran. "You know better than that."

"It could be stolen. The agent bringing it to you could have been knifed."

"No. No," said Moran. "The report goes in." He looked with a twist of anger on his face at Jabe. "Don't you think I feel for them? I've been here almost as long as you have. It's just quarantine for a time—fifty years, maybe."

"And after the fifty years runs out?"

"We'll figure out something in that much time."

"No," said Jabe. "No more than they did on Astarte, or on Hope. They'll sterilize."

"Rather than let them breed back down into the animal."

"There's no danger of that here, I tell you," said Jabe.

"Report says there is," said Moran. "I'm sending it in. It has to be done."

"Earth has to protect Earth, you mean."

Moran sighed heavily.

"All right," he said. "I'm through talking about it. You get yourself ready to leave, along with the other agents—though if you take my advice, the kindest thing you can do for that wife of yours is to leave right now, just vanish."

"I don't think I'll go," said Jabe. "No." His spurs clinked again. "I'm not leaving."

"I haven't any more time to waste with you," said Moran. He twisted around and pulled one of the grain sacks out of position. Behind it was revealed a black board with several buttons and dials upon it. He pressed a button and turned a dial. He spoke to the board.

"Survey ship? I've got an agent here who——"

Jabe leaned down and forward, and struck. Moran choked off in midsentence and stiffened up. His fat arm came back and up, groping for the knife hilt standing out between his shoulder blades. Then he fell forward, half covering the black board.

"Moran?" said the board in a small, buzzing voice. "Moran? Come in, Moran. . . ."

Two hours later, out on the desert with Alden Mann who had come into the city with him to buy medicines for the mine, Jabe stopped automatically to rest the horses, and Alden drew up level with him.

"Something on your mind, Jabe Halvorsen?" said Alden.

"Nothing," said Jabe. "No, nothing." He looked into Alden's frank, younger face, made himself smile, and went back to staring out past Alden at the sherry-colored, wavering distance of the hot sandy plain. Behind him, to the right of their road was the edge of the cultivated area with palmlike trees about thirty feet high.

"Let me know, if," said Alden, cheerfully, got out his pipe and began to fill it, throwing one leg over his saddlehorn. The spur below the floppy leather pantleg flashed the sun for a moment in Jabe's eyes.

"If, I will," answered Jabe automatically. Alden, he thought, was the closest thing to an actual friend that he had.

Moran he had known for a long time, but they had not really been close. They had been relatives in a foreign land.

Jabe lit his own pipe. He did not feel guilt, only a hollow sick feeling over the killing of Moran. Over the necessity of his killing Moran. He thought there would be no immediate danger from it. The knife was a city knife he had bought there an hour before for the purpose. He had worn gloves. He had taken Moran's purse, the report, and nothing else. The survey ship would not be able to identify him as the murderer and send men to arrest him in much less than three months. He should be able to do something in three months. If he did, after that nothing mattered.

It was good that he had suspected the report's coming. He puffed on his pipe, staring at the sandy distance. He knew where they had gone wrong. But Moran was proof of the fact that argument would be useless. They wanted something concrete.

"I was wild out here, once," said Jabe, to Alden.

"Yeah," Alden glanced at him, with some sympathy. "Nobody holds it against you any more."

"I still don't belong."

"For me, you do. And for Sheila." Alden blew smoke at him. "When your son's born he'll have a place on the staff of the mine."

"Yes," said Jabe. His thoughts veered. "You people never had much to do with the wild ones."

"Oh, we shoot a few every year."

"Did you ever keep any for a while? Just to get a notion of what makes them tick?"

"No," said Alden. "We're miners with work to do. If one gets caught, he's hung; and we're back on the job in an hour."

"You didn't hang me."

"That was different," said Alden. "You came in with that trader's packtrain, and when it was time to leave Sheila spoke for you."

"You didn't maybe take me for a trader crewman, myself?"

"Oh no," said Alden. "We knew. You can tell, a wild one."

"I'm surprised," said Jabe, a little sadly, "you'd want to risk it."

"If Sheila spoke for you—" Alden shrugged. He stared at Jabe. "What got you thinking of wild ones?"

"Nothing," said Jabe. "The sand, I guess."

It was not true, of course. What had started him was the knowledge of his advantage over Moran and the rest. All the other agents on this world had played one role, one character. By chance of luck, or fate, it had fallen on him to play two. He had not meant to be taken up by the community around the silver mine back in the mountains. It had merely happened. Love had happened—to himself as well as Sheila. And the survey ship, concerned only with its routine hundred-year check on this planetful of emigrants from old Earth, had okayed his change of status.

The result, he thought now, as the smoke of the pipe came hot from low in the bowl of it, almost burned out, was that he had two points of view where Moran and the rest had one. Two eyes instead of one, binocular vision instead of the one-dimensional view a single seeing organ could achieve. There was a recessive strain cropping up on this world, all right, but it was carried and spread by the wild ones—the degenerate individuals that had neither clan nor community to uphold them.

And the check to it, he was sure, was right in his own adopting community. The tight-held social unit of the mine people, who had preserved their purity of strain by keeping the degenerates killed off and at a distance. There was no doubt in his mind that if he had been actually a wild one Sheila would never have been attracted to him, or he to her. It was because, though she did not know it, he was unalloyed with the spreading degeneracy of this world—as she herself was pure, untainted silver like that the mine refinery turned out of the common, mingled ore of the mountains—that she had demanded him of the trader.

He knocked his pipe out on his boot. And there was the answer, he thought. A natural tendency to breed for the best that was a counterforce to what Moran and the others had discovered. In the long run, the superior, pure breed would kill off the degenerates. All he had to do was prove it to the survey ship.

Only for that he needed a specimen of each type. One of the mine people would not be hard to come by. But he would need one of the wild ones as well. After that, it was up to the testing facilities of the survey ship to monitor and make findings. But the findings could only substantiate what he already knew.

And that was the important thing. For himself, he had burnt his bridges with the knife he had driven into Moran. But Sheila and his unborn son would be safe.

"Let's get on," he said to Alden. Alden knocked out his own pipe and the two horses went forward once more. The gait of their wide hooves—not splayed so badly as were the hooves of the donkeys but spread for the sand as camel hooves are spread—was smooth. Jabe wondered how it could be done—attracting one of the wild ones. He and Alden would be passing through wild territory in the early part of the mountains. But bait was needed.

After a while a thought came to him. He reached down and unhooked one of the large silver buckles from his boot. Alden, riding a little ahead, did not notice. As they rode on, Jabe set himself to rubbing the buckle to a high shine on the pant's leg hidden from Alden by the horse's bulk.

When they saw the first low crests of the mountains rising ahead of them, Jabe stuck the buckle into the headband of his wide-brimmed hat—on the side away from Alden.

When darkness came, they camped. They were only a few hours from the mine, but they were deep in the mountains. In a little shallow opening in the rocks, all but clear of scrub variform pine and native bush, they lit a fire and ate. Alden rolled himself early in his blankets, but Jabe sat up, feeding the fire and frowning into its licking flames.

He had not even reached for the chunk of dead limb an hour or so later. He had only thought about it—his hand had not yet moved—but some preliminary tensing of the body must have given him away, because the voice, dry as the desert wind that had followed them all through the day, whispered suddenly in his ear.

"Don't move, mister."

He did not move. His rifle was lying across his spread knees, its trigger guard scant inches from his right index finger, but the whisper had come from the dark immediately behind him, and a thrown knife takes very little time to cover the distance a whisper can carry, even in the stillness of a mountain night. He glanced past the flames of the fire to where the dim shape of the blanket-wrapped body of Alden lay like a long, dark log against the further rim of darkness. But whether Alden slept or waked, whether he had heard the whisper or not, the young miner gave no sign of being aware of what was happening.

"Reach out with your right arm. Slow," said the whisperer. "Fill me a cup of that coffee and hand it back. And don't you turn, mister."

Jabe moved slowly as he had been told. The last word had been pronounced *turun*. The accentual difference from the speech of Alden announced a wild one, one of the groupless wandering savages roaming about the deserted lands. The speaker behind Jabe—was it a man, or a woman?—used his words like a child, with sing-song cadences.

Slowly and steadily, Jabe passed back the full cup without turning. He felt it taken from him and heard the soft noise of drinking.

"Fill again, mister." The cup was sitting again, empty, at his side "Fill yourself, too."

Jabe obeyed.

"What do you want?" he asked, when he had his own hot, full cup between his hands. He stared into the flames, waiting for the answer.

"Some things. That silver do-thing in your hat. Some talk. You riders from that mine town?"

"Yes," said Jabe. He had been easing his hand, a millimeter at a time toward the rifle on his knees. He found himself whispering his answer. If Alden still slumbered, so much the better. The rifle on his knees was like any that the mine people carried, but there was an anesthetic cartridge in its chamber now instead of an ordinary shell.

"It's them goats you're after?"

"Goats?" said Jabe. The community of the mine kept goats for hide and meat. He had been set to guarding some himself in the beginning, before his marriage ceremony with Sheila. Usually the old people watched them. "Some strays?"

"They aren't not strays," came back the answer. "One's eat and the other two butchered ready to eat. They's mine now."

"You stole them."

"Was you never hungry, mister?"

"Yes," said Jabe. "I was wild once, myself."

He was waiting for the response to that. It was one of the things he had hoped would help. In addition to the bullet that was not a bullet in his gun, there were other things that belonged to him as an agent. There was a match box in his pocket that was not a match box, but an emotional response recorder. A moment's cooperation, a moment's relaxation from the wild one behind him was all that he needed. A chance to bring the rifle to bear. And meanwhile, the recorder was running. He had started it the minute Alden had rolled up and turned away in his blankets.

"Then you know," said the whisperer. "You know it, then." There was a moment of pause. "It's rich you is, down there at that mine. I seen the packtrains come and go. I seen the goats. And I seen you all down there, all rich with silver."

"The silver," said Jabe, "you like the silver?"

"Mighty rich, you is. All that silver."

"We have to mine for it," said Jabe. "We have to make it." He could not feel the recorder in his pocket, but he knew it was there, taking down the colors of the wild one's responses. "It isn't just there to be picked up."

"Yeah," there was something almost like a whispery chuckle behind him. "I found her so, watching. I couldn't walk down in through your gates, not me. But I took t'myself a high place and watched—all day—the fire going in the tall building and the bright silver things about the town. And the women with silver on them, so that they shine here and there in the sun, coming and going down there 'tween the houses. And the houses, all the big ones and the little ones with roofs of silver."

"Roofs—?" said Jabe, and then to his mind's eye came a picture of the corrugated metal sheathing, dating indestructibly back over a hundred years to the first coming of the settlers to this world, and the first establishment of the mine. "But they're——"

"What, mister?"

"Part of the buildings," said Jabe, "that's all. . . ."

A whispery laugh sounded in his ear.

"Don't fear, mister. I tell you something. If it were me comin' in with horses and men to take all you got, I wouldn't let nobody touch them roofs, but leave them there for the sun to shine on. I never seen nothing so fine, so fine anywhere, as them roofs of silver all to-shine in the sun." The whisper changed a little in tone, suddenly. "You feel that way too, don't you, mister?"

"Yes," said Jabe, out of a suddenly dry throat. "Oh, yes. The roofs—the roofs, all silver."

"I tell you what," said the whisperer. "I take this from

your hat"—Jabe felt the buckle lightly plucked from his hat-
band—"and I got some other little silver bits from your
saddles. But I want you to know, I'm going to make me little
houses and roof them houses with the silver, just like yours,
and come day put them out for the sun to bright-shine on. So
you know your silver, it in the sun."

"Good," said Jabe, whispering. His throat was still dry.

"And now mister . . . don't move," said the voice from
behind him, "I got to——"

The whispered words ceased suddenly. Caught in a sudden
cold ecstasy of fear, Jabe sat frozen, the breath barely trick-
ling in and out of his throat. *For Sheila,* he prayed internally,
*for all of them at the mine—not now. Don't let me be killed
now. . . .* The long seconds blew away into silence. Then, a
far shout broke the plaster cast of his tension.

"Alden! Jabe! Coming up!"

In one motion, Jabe snatched up his rifle and whirled to
face the darkness beyond the firelight behind him. But it
hung there before him emptily. And even as he relaxed and
turned away from it, there rode up from the other side of the
fire three of the mine men on nervous horses, their rifle bar-
rels gleaming in the light of the fire.

"We were after a goat lifter, and the hounds started baying
off this way. We rode over from our camp," said Jeff Connel,
the assay engineer, as he led the way in. His long dark face
gleamed under gray hair as he looked down into Jabe's face.
"What's the matter with Alden, sleeping like that?"

"Alden!" Jabe turned and stepped over the fire to shake his
friend out of his blankets. Alden rolled over at the first touch,
his head lolling backward.

His throat had been neatly cut.

Their return to the mine with Alden's body took place in
silence. Jabe rode in their midst, aware of their attitude,
whether right or wrong. When two men went out from the
mine together on a journey, one was responsible for the
other, no matter what the circumstances. He could accept
that; it was part of their customs. But what touched him with
coldness now was the fact that he seemed to feel suspicion in
them. Suspicion of the fact that it had been him who lived,
while Alden was murdered.

That suspicion might block his chance of getting a clean
recording from one of them to place in comparison with the

recording he had made of the wild one. And the recording was all he had, now. Back by the fire he had been full of hope. If he could have captured the wild one and compared his recording with Alden's when he awoke Alden to tell him of the capture. . . . But there had never been any hope of waking Alden.

Yet, there was a sort of chill hope still in him. He did have the recording he had made. And he had himself to make a recording of for control purposes. It was not impossible; it was still quite possible that he could get a parallel recording yet from one or another of the mine people. It was a field sort of expedient, but the survey ship could not ignore it. If they were faced with three recordings of responses to parallel situations, and there was an identity between the two belonging to Jabe and one of the mine people, and a variance between those two and the wild one, they would have to check further.

With luck, they would send down assistance to capture at least one miner and one savage and take them, drugged, to the ship for full tests. And then. . . .

The sad caravan carrying Alden's body had wound its way through the mine streets picking up a cortege of women and children, for the available men were out on the hunt as the three who had come on Jabe and Alden had been. At the mine manager's house they stopped, brought in the body of Alden and told their story. Lenkhart, the mine manager, stood with his gray eyes in a bearded face, watching Jabe as they talked. But he said nothing in blame—if nothing in comfort. He beat his hands together with a curious rhythmic and measured motion, and dismissed them to their homes.

Sheila was kinder.

"Jabe!" she said, and held him, back at last in the privacy and safety of their own home. "It might have been you killed!"

"I know," he said. He sat down wearily. "But it was Alden."

"Oh, that animal!" said Sheila with sudden violence. "That *animal*! They ought to burn him at the pass and leave him there as a warning to the rest!"

He felt a certain sense of shock.

"Sheila," he said. She looked at him. She was a slim, tall girl with heavy, black hair. Under that hair her eyes seemed darker in this moment than he had ever seen them before, and almost feverish. "He didn't burn Alden. Alden probably never even woke up."

"But he's an animal—a wild animal!" she said again. "If he is a man, that is. It might be one of those horrible women. Was it a woman, Jabe?"

He caught a new note of hatred in the question, the thought that it might have been a woman. He had never seen her like this; he had not known she could be so dangerous where things close to her were concerned. He thought of the child she was carrying, and a little fear came for a moment into the back of his mind.

"I don't think so. No," he said. He felt the lie like a heavy weight on him. For it had been impossible to tell the sex of the whisperer. Weariness swept over him like a smothering wave. "Let's go to bed."

In the obscurity and privacy of their bed, later, she held him tightly.

"They'll get him tomorrow," she whispered. And she was fiercely loving. Later, much later, when he was sure that she slept heavily, he rose quietly in the dark and went into the living room-dining room of their three-room cottage, and extracting the recorded strip from the imitation match box, processed it. In the little light of an oil lamp, he held it up to examine it behind closed shades. And his breath caught for a second.

An angry fate seemed to pursue him. The strip was a long band of colors, a code for emotional profile that he could read as well as the men up on the survey ship. And the profile he read off now was that of a lone savage all right, but by some freak of luck one with crippled but burning talents—talents far surpassing even Jabe's own. In the range of artistic perception, the profile of the whisperer shone powerfully with a rich and varied spectrum of ability and desire wherever the silver roofs had been mentioned.

Dropping the proof of a bitter exception to all he knew about the wild ones, Jabe beat his hands together with the measured rhythm that signalled frustration among the people of the mine.

In the morning, the men that could be spared formed for the posse in the open space below the mine buildings and above the houses. There were some forty of them, including Jabe; all superbly mounted, all armed with rifles, side-arms and knives. Every two-man unit had a saddle radio. The hounds, leashed, bayed and milled in their pack.

Standing on the platform from which mine meetings were held, the mine manager laid out the orders of the hunt. A senior engineer for many years before he had become manager, Lenkhart was stooped and ascetic-looking with his long gray beard.

"Now," he said to them, "man or woman, he can't have gone far since last night if he's on foot. And a man on horseback doesn't need to steal goats. You'll stay in contact with radios at all times. At the sign of any marauder or his trail, fire two spaced shots in the air. If you hear the shots fired by someone else, wait for radio orders from the senior engineer of your group before moving in. Any questions?"

There were none. To Jabe, watching, there was a heartwarming quality in the cool, civilized way they went about it. He was paired, himself, with Sheila's father for the hunt. He reined over next to the older man and they all moved out together. The hounds, loosed at last from their leashes, yelped and belled, streaming past them.

They moved as a group for the first two hours, back to the camp where Alden had been killed. From there they fanned out, picked up the trail of the whisperer, running northwest and quartering away from the mining town. A little later, they lost the trail again and they split up into pairs, each pair with a hound or two, and began to work the possible area.

Sheila's father had said little or nothing during the early part of the ride. And Jabe had been busy thinking of his own matters. There must, he had told himself desperately again and again after the moment of discovering the freakish quality of the whisperer's profile, be some way yet of saving the situation. Now, as they turned into a maze of small canyons, hope on the wings of an idea suddenly returned to him.

He had been assuming that the whisperer's profile was useless as a means to point up the relative purity of one of the mine people. But this need not be so. The recorder took down only what it was exposed to. If he could make a recording of the whisperer where roofs of silver and all the area of the whisperer's artistic perception was carefully avoided the wild one would show in the color code as only the lonely savage he was. All the primitiveness, the bluntedness of the whisperer would be on show—his degeneracy in all other fields. A recording of any of the other mine people, and a recording of Jabe, matched with this second attempt, would show Jabe and the mine person's profile falling into one separate class, and the whisperer's into another. Better yet—the whisperer would be executed when he was caught. There would then be no chance of the survey ship sending down to make other recordings of the whisperer as a check. All that was necessary was to find the chance to make the second recording, under conditions that would be favorable. And if the whisperer was captured and held for a day or so while a trial was being set up, the chance would be there for the finding. . . .

"Jabe," said Sheila's father. "Pull up."

Jabe reined his horse to a halt and turned to face his father-in-law. Tod Harnung had called a halt in a little amphitheater of scrub pine and granite rock. As Jabe watched, the older man threw one leg over his saddle and began to fill his pipe. Like all who had achieved the status of engineer he wore a beard, and his beard had only a few streaks of gray in it. His straight nose, his dark eyes like Sheila's, above the beard, were not unkind as they looked at Jabe now.

"Smoke if you like," he said.

"Thank you, sir," said Jabe. Gratefully, he got out his own pipe and tobacco, which he had not dared reach for before. The "sir" no longer stuck in his throat as it had in his first days among these people. He understood these signs of authority in a small, compact society which had persisted virtually unchanged since the planet's first settlement, a hundred and sixteen years before. It was such things, he was convinced, that had kept the pure silver of their strain unalloyed by the base metals of the disintegrating wild ones and the softening people of the desert and lower lands. By harshness and rigidity they had kept themselves shining bright.

Even, he thought, lighting his pipe—and it was a suddenly startling thought—in comparison to the very Earth strain in the survey ship now presuming to sit in judgment upon them. For the first time Jabe found himself comparing his own so-called "most-civilized" Earth strain with these hard-held descendants of pioneers. In such as Moran, in agents and sociologists, even in himself, wasn't there a softness, a selfish blindness bolstered by the false aid of many machines and devices?

He thought of himself as he had been ten years ago. Even five years ago. He was still largely of Earth then, still hesitant, fumbling and unsure. He could never then have reacted so swiftly, so surely, and so decisively to Moran's announcement about the report. Above all, he could not have killed Moran, even if he had seen the overwhelming necessity of it. This world, and in particular, the people of the mine here, had pared him down to a hard core of usefulness.

"—Sir?" he said, for Sheila's father had just spoken to him again. "I didn't catch just what you said, Mr. Harnung."

"I said—you don't by any chance know this killer, do you?"

Jabe looked sharply up from the pipe he was just about to light. He sat in his saddle, the pipe in one hand, the match in the other.

"Know him?" said Jabe.

"Do you?"

"Why—no!" said Jabe. "No sir. Of course not. I don't. Why should I?"

Tod Harnung took his own pipe out of his bearded mouth.

"Sheila's my only child," he said. "I've got a grandson to think of."

"I don't understand," said Jabe, bewildered.

The dark eyes looked at him above the beard.

"My grandson," said Harnung, harshly, "will one day be an engineer like I am. There's going to be no stain on his reputation, nothing to make him be passed over when a vacancy occurs in one of the senior positions." There was a moment's silence.

"I see," said Jabe. "You mean, me."

"There'll be no fault about his mother's line. I'm responsible for that," said Harnung. "I've always hoped there would be no fault about his father to be remembered against him, either."

Jabe felt himself stirred by a profound emotion.

"I swear," he said, "I never saw or heard that wild one before in my life! Alden was my friend—you know that!"

"I always thought so," said Harnung.

"You know," said Jabe, reining his horse close to the older man, "you know how much Sheila means to me, what you all mean to me. You know what it's meant for me to be accepted here as Sheila's husband among people"—Jabe's voice cracked a little in spite of himself—"people with a firm, solid way of life. People who know what they are and what everybody else is. All my life I wanted to find people who were sure of themselves, sure of the way the universe works and their own place in it. I always hated the business of not being completely sure, of only being mostly right, of having to guess and never having anyone in authority to turn to. And do you think," cried Jabe, "I'd throw that away, all that, for some moronic savage?"

He stopped, shaking a little, and wiped his mouth with the back of his hand. For a moment, he thought he had said too much. But then Harnung's eyes, which had been steady on him, relaxed.

"No," said Harnung, "I don't believe you would." He nodded at Jabe's pipe. "Go ahead and light up there. I had to make sure, Jabe. I have my responsibility as Sheila's father."

"Yes sir. I understand." Fingers still trembling a little, Jabe got his pipe lit. He drew the smoke gratefully deep into his lungs.

"Very well, then," said Harnung. "As soon as you've finished your pipe, we'll get on."

"Sir!" said Jabe. An idea had just come to him. He took his pipe out of his mouth, and turned quickly to the other man. "I just thought of something."

Harnung peered at him.

"Yes?"

"I just remembered something that killer said. . . ." Jabe put his hand on the pommel of Harnung's saddle to hold the two horses together as they began to grow restive with the halt. "He said he'd been watching the town from some high place close at hand. Now we've circled almost a full turn back toward the town. Right ahead of us is a spot where we can cut over to the rock faces north of town. I'll bet that's where he's holed up."

Harnung frowned.

"He'd have had to cut back through us earlier to be there now," the older man said. "How could he have cut through us—and past the hounds?"

"Some of these desert runners could do it," Jabe said. "Believe me, sir, I know from when I was one of them. It's worth a try. And if I'm the one to lead us to where we capture him. . . ."

Harnung scratched his beard with the stem of his pipe.

"I don't know," he said. "I'll have to radio and ask permission for you and I to try it. And if we get it, we'll be leaving a hole in the search pattern when we drop out. If it turned out later he got away through that hole. . . ."

"I give you my word, sir——"

"All right," said Harnung, abruptly. "I'll do it." He picked up his radio set from the saddle before him and rang the senior engineer of the search. He listened to the answering voice for a minute.

"All right," he said at last, and put the radio back. "Come on, Jabe."

They reined their horses around and went off in a new direction. The impatient bitch hound that had been waiting with them leaped hungrily ahead once more, the red tongue lolling out of her mouth.

They angled their approach so as to come up on the blind side of the heights of rock north of the mine town. It was past noon when they reached the first of these and they began slowly to work around the perimeter of the rocks. This part of the mountain was all narrow canyons and sudden upthrusts of granite. The sun moved slowly, as slowly as they, across the high and cloudless sky above, as they prospected without success.

It was not until nearly midafternoon that the hound, running still ahead of them up a narrow cut in the rock, checked, stiffened, and whimpered, lifting her nose in the air. She turned sharply and trotted up a slope to the right, where she paused again, sniffing the breeze.

The two men looked off in the direction she pointed.

"The Sheep's Head!" said Jabe. "Sir, he's up on the Sheep's Head. He has to be. And there's only one way down from there."

"He couldn't see much from there unless he wanted to climb away out . . . well, let's look," said Harnung. They put their horses to a trot and went up the slope to emerge from the canyon and cut to their right up around an overhanging lump of bare rock that was the base of the granite pinnacle known from its shape as the Sheep's Head.

The hound was eager. A sharp command from Harnung held her to no more than the customary five yards in front of the horses' heads, but she shivered and danced with the urge to run. Breasting a steeper slope as they approached the top of the pinnacle, the two riders were forced to slow to a walk.

The bald dome of the Sheep's Head was just a short distance vertically above them.

They were perhaps a hundred feet from a view of the summit, when the hound suddenly belled, loud and clear. Looking up together, they saw a flicker of movement disappearing over the shoulder of the Sheep's Head. Harnung and Jabe angled their horses off in that direction, but when Jabe would have forced his animal to a trot Harnung laid his hand on the reins.

"We'll catch him now," he said. "A walk's good enough."

"Yes sir," said Jabe.

They walked their horses on up to the crest of the rise, the hound dancing ahead of them. As they came level with the top they found themselves at the head of a long gully cutting away down from the side of the Sheep's Head, out toward a smaller pinnacle of rock. A few short yards to the right of them, they saw all the litter of a cold camp, the half-demolished carcasses of the missing goats, and some little, toylike objects the tops of which caught the glitter of the sun. Jabe reined his horse over to them, and reached down. They were all attached to a smoothed piece of wood, and they came up as a group as he leaned from his saddle to scoop them in. Sitting in the saddle, he stared at them. Proof of the artistic perception he had read in the whisperer's profile glowed before him. They were tiny models of buildings with pieces of silver fitted onto them for roofs. And it was not just that they were well made—it was more than that. Some genius of the maker had caught the very feel and purpose of the mine and the life of their people, in their making.

"Jabe!" snapped Harnung. "Come along!"

Jabe turned his horse to join the older man, slipping the piece of wood with the house models into his saddle bag. They headed together at a steady trot up the slope and down into the mouth of the gully.

Harnung was talking into the radio, the black bush of his bearded lips moving close to its mouthpiece.

"The rest'll move in behind us," he said to Jabe, replacing the radio on his saddle. "But we'll be the ones to take him. Let's go."

They trotted down the gully, which deepened now and narrowed. Its walls rose high around them. The winding semi-level upon which they traveled was clear except for the occasional rock or boulder. The almost vertical rock of the walls was free of vegetation except for the occasional clump of brush. After a little distance, they came to another gully cutting off at near right angles; and the hound informed them with whines and yelps that the fugitive had taken this new way.

They followed.

Coming around a corner suddenly, they faced him at last. There had been no place else for him to go. This gully was blind. He stood with his back against the farther rock of the gully's end, a long knife balanced in one hand in throwing position—a thin, gangling figure in scraggly beard and dirt-darkened hide clothing. At the sight of them, he flipped his hand with the knife back behind his head ready to throw, and Harnung shot him through the shoulder to bring him down.

They brought their prisoner back to the town as the last rays of the sunset were fading from the peaks where he had secretly looked down on the life of the mine. They locked him in a toolshed behind the ore-crushing mill and split up among their various homes. Word had gone in ahead of how the wild one had been taken. Sheila was waiting in their living room for Jabe. She opened her arms to him.

"Jabe!" she said. "You did it! It was *you* that led them to him!" She hugged him, but something he was holding got in her way. "What's that?"

"Nothing." He reached out and dropped the piece of wood with the little silver-roofed houses on it down on the table beside her. "He used my silver buckle to make the roofs on them—the buckle he took from me when Alden was killed." He put his arms around her, and kissed her.

"Eat now," she said, leading him to the table. "You haven't had anything decent since breakfast." He let her steer him to his chair. She had set the table as if for a celebration, with a fresh tablecloth and some blue mountain flowers in a vase.

She sat with him. She had waited to eat until he should get back. She wanted to know all about the hunt. He listened to her questions and, a little uneasily, thought he caught an echo of the doubt that had been in the mind of her father, a doubt about his loyalty to the mine people. She did not doubt now, but earlier she must have, he thought, and now she was trying to make up for it. She came back again and again to the matter of the marauder's execution.

". . . I suppose it'll be hanging, though burning's too good for someone like——"

"Sheila!" he put his coffee cup down again in the saucer so hard some of it spilled. "Can't you at least wait until I'm done eating?"

She stared at him.

"What's the matter?" she wanted to know.

"Nothing. Nothing. . . ." He picked up the cup carefully again, but it trembled slightly in his hand in spite of all he could do. "We have to be just, that's all. It's a matter of justice with this man."

"But he killed Alden!" Her eyes were quite large, and he moved uncomfortably under their look.

"Of course. Of course . . ." he said. "A murderer has to be punished. But you have to remember the man's limitations. He isn't like you or me—or Alden was. He hasn't any sense of right or wrong as we know it. He operates by necessity, by taboo, or superstition. That's why"—he looked appealingly at her—"we mustn't lose our own perspective and get down to his own animal level. We have to execute him—it's necessary. But we shouldn't hate him for being something he can't control."

"But Alden was your friend!" she said. "Doesn't that mean anything to you, Jabe? What's all this about the creature mean, beside the fact Alden was your friend?"

"I know he was my friend!" Even as he lost his temper with her, he knew it was the wrong thing to do, the wrong way to handle the situation. "Do you think I don't know—he was the only friend I had in this place! But I happen to know what it's like to be like that man we've got locked up in the toolshed."

"You were never like that!" she cried.

"I was."

"You were a freighter on a pack train. You had a job. You weren't a crawling thief or murderer like that——"

"But you remembered that I might have been. Didn't you?" He half rose from the table, shouting. He wanted to throw the accusation squarely in her face. "Last night you remembered that——"

"No!" she cried, suddenly, jumping to her feet. "*You* had to make me do that! And not last night. Just now! You had to mention yourself in the same breath with that animal, that crawling beast in the shape of a man!"

"He is not," said Jabe, trying to make an effort to speak slowly and calmly, "an animal yet. He is only on the way to being one. We who can still think like human beings——"

"Human!" she cried. "He's a filthy, wild animal and he doesn't deserve to be hung. Why do you say he isn't? Why is it everything that's perfectly plain and straight and right to everybody else gets all tangled up when you start hashing it over? Alden was your friend and this wild one killed him. It doesn't seem bad enough that creature already stole goats that took the food out of people's mouths—maybe even the mouth of your own son, next winter——"

"Why, there's not going to be any shortage of food—" he began, but she had gone right on talking.

"——not even that. But he killed your friend. And you say he ought to be dealt with, but you want me to feel bad about it at the same time. Nothing I do ever is right, according to you! I'm always wrong, always wrong, according to you! If you feel like that all the time why did you marry me in the first place?"

"You know why I married you——"

"No I don't!" she cried. "I never did!" And she turned and ran from him, suddenly. The bedroom door slammed behind him, and he heard the bolt to it snap shut.

Silence held the house. He got up and went across to the cupboard on the opposite wall. He opened it and took out a small thick bottle of the whisky made at the mine still. For a moment he held it, and then he put it back. Reason returned to him. He felt for the recorder in his pocket. It was there, and he turned toward the door.

Quietly, he let himself out of the house.

The toolshed where the whisperer was held was unguarded and locked only by a heavy bar across the door on the outside. In the darkness, he merely lifted the bar from the door and stepped inside. For a moment he could see nothing; and then as his eyes adjusted to the deeper gloom, the lights on the outer wall of the ore-crushing mill, striking through the gaps between the heavy planks of the toolshed wall, showed him the wild one, tightly bound.

"Hello," he said, feeling the word strange on his lips. A gaunt whisper replied to him.

"I mighty thirsty, mister."

He heard the words with a feeling of shock. He went back outside the shed to a pipe down the hill, filled the tin cup hanging from it and brought it back. The prisoner drank, gulping.

"I thank you, mister."

"That's all right," he said. Reaching in his pocket, he started the recorder. He searched for the expression on the prisoner's face in the darkness, but all he could make out was a vague blur of features and any expression was hidden. It did not matter, he thought.

Skillfully, he began to question the prisoner. . . .

He woke with a sudden jerk and came fully awake. For a second he felt nothing, and then the cruel, dry hands of a hangover clamped unyieldingly upon his head and belly. He could not remember for a moment what had happened. He lay still, on his back, staring at the ceiling above his bed and trying to remember what had happened. Bright sunlight was coming around the edges of the curtain on the window, and Sheila was not in the bed with him.

He must be late for work—but Sheila would never have permitted that. He tried once more to put the previous evening together in his mind, and slowly, it came back.

He had got a good recording from the wild one. He had not even had to look at it to know that it was what he wanted. The prisoner was like any creature in a trap, and there was nothing in him of the dangerous perception Jabe had found earlier. He had got a good recording, and after it was over he had cautioned the prisoner against telling anyone else about the interview. But it did not really matter whether the prisoner spoke or not. They would think, whoever heard it, that Jabe had simply stumbled in on the man while drunk—to taunt or bully him.

For Jabe had made sure that he was drunk, later. But first he had made a parallel recording of himself and one of the supervisors on night shift at the ore-crusher mill, and broadcast the results of all three to the survey ship from a transmitter hidden behind his own house. Then he had gone over to the bachelors' barracks to make sure of his alibi for the evening. There was always a group drinking at the barracks and it was the natural place for a husband who had just had a fight with his wife.

When he stumbled home at last, he had found the bedroom door unbolted.

Now, lying in the bed, he wondered again at the lateness

of the morning hour. A thought came to him. Perhaps he had been allowed the day off by the mine manager because of his usefulness in capturing the prisoner. He listened, but could not hear Sheila in the next room. He rolled over and saw a note from her on the bedside table.

"—Back soon, darling. Breakfast on the stove to warm."

Things were evidently well once more between them. He thought of the three profiles safely messaged off to the survey ship the night before and a great sense of relief and happiness rose in him. He rolled out of bed and headed for the shower.

By the time he was showered, dressed, and shaved, the hangover had all but disappeared. He drew the curtain on the bedroom window and looked out on a mid-morning bright with the clear mountain sunshine. Up the little slope behind the house, near the storage shed where his transmitter was hidden, a clump of the same blue flowers Sheila had filled into the vase the evening before were growing wild. Their heads stirred in the small breeze passing by, and they struck him suddenly as a token of good luck.

He turned away from the window, walked across the bedroom, and pushing open the door to the main room of the house, stepped into it. The room was clean, tidied-up, and empty of Sheila's presence, but he had not taken more than a step into it before he was aware of his invisible visitors.

The first glimpse showed only a sort of waveriness of the air in two corners of the room—and that was all anyone but he, or one of the other agents, would have seen. He, however, now that he had become aware of them, felt a small device implanted in the bone of his skull begin to operate. The waveriness fogged, then cleared, and he saw watching him two men from the survey ship, both armed and in uniform. They were, it seemed to him, remarkably young-looking, and he did not know their names. But there was nothing so surprising in that, for the personnel of the ship had turned over a number of times since he had first been landed on this world.

"Well, this is quick," he said. The lips of one of them moved and a voice sounded inside Jabe's ear.

"I'm afraid you're under arrest," the voice said. "You'll have to come up with us."

"Under arrest?"

"For the killing of"—the one speaking hesitated for a tiny moment—"your brother."

"Brother. . . ." Jabe stopped suddenly. About him every-thing else seemed to have halted, too. Not merely the room and the people in it, but the world in its turning beneath them seemed to have stopped with the word he had just heard. "Brother? . . . Oh, yes. Moran." The world and all things started to move again. He felt strangely foolish to have hesitated over the word. "Moran Halversen. We were never very close. . . ." His mind cleared suddenly. "How did you find out so soon it was me?" he asked.

Outside, at some little distance off, there was a sudden out-burst of cheering. It seemed to come from the open space where they had gathered yesterday for the hunt. It drowned out the answer of the man from the ship.

"What?" Jabe had to ask.

"I say," said the other, "your profile was one of the three you sent up to the ship, some hours ago. It showed aberran-cies of pattern. It was too much of a coincidence, taken with the recent death of—Moran Halversen. We checked, and there was a good deal of indication it was you."

"I see," said Jabe. He nodded. "I—expected it," he said, "but not so soon."

"Shall we go, then?" said the man from the ship.

"Could we wait a few minutes? A minute or two?" said Jabe. He turned to look out the window. "My wife . . . she ought to be back in just a few minutes."

The man from the ship glanced at his watch, and then over at his partner. Jabe could feel rather than hear them inside his ear speaking to each other on another channel.

"We can wait a few minutes, I guess," said the one who had done all the talking. "But just a few."

"She'll be right back, I'm sure," said Jabe. He moved to the window, looking out on the narrow, sloping cobble-stoned street before the row of houses. "You'll make sure she doesn't see me go?"

"Sure," said the man from the ship. "We can take care of that all right. She'll just forget you were here when she got here."

"Thank you," said Jabe. "Thanks. . . ." He turned away from the window. People were beginning to hurry down the street from the direction of the open space, but he did not see Sheila. He moved back into the room, and caught sight of the board with the little model houses, still on the table.

"I'll take this," he said, picking it up. He turned to the one who had been doing the speaking. "So the three recordings got through all right?"

The other two looked at each other.

"Yes—" said one. There was a sudden, rapid step outside the house. The door burst open and Sheila almost ran in. Her face was flushed and happy.

"Jabe!" she cried. "We're going to have a dance! Isn't that wonderful? Manager Lenkhart just announced it! Did you get your breakfast yet? How do you like the holiday?" She spun about gleefully. "And—guess?"

"What?" he said, filling his eyes with the sight of her.

"Why, they're going to burn him after all! Up at the pass. Isn't that marvelous? And we'll all have an outdoor dinner up there, and burn him just as it starts to get dark, then everybody comes back here for the dance. Isn't that wonderful, Jabe? We haven't had a dance for so long!"

He stood staring at her.

"Burn?" he said stupidly. "Burn? But why——"

"Oh, *Jabe!*" she pirouetted about to face him. "Because we haven't caught one like this for such a long time, of course." She held out her arms to him. "Everybody thought because production in the mine wasn't up last month Manager Lenkhart wouldn't let us have anything but an ordinary hanging. But the staff engineers pleaded with him and said how badly everybody needed a holiday—so we got the whole thing." She reached for him, but he stepped back, instinctively. "Burning, and picnic, and dance! Jabe—" she said, stopping, and looking at him in some puzzlement. "What's wrong? Aren't you happy. . . ."

The word died suddenly on her lips. Suddenly she stopped moving. She stood arrested, like a wax figure in a museum—only her chest moved slightly with her breathing. Jabe made a move toward her, but one of the armed men stopped him.

"No," said the voice in his head. "She's in stasis now, until we leave. Better not touch her."

Jabe turned numbly toward them.

"No . . ." he said. "I sent recordings that proved these people were different. You know about them. What she says isn't what it sounds like. I tell you, those recordings——"

"I'm sorry," said the voice. Both men were looking at him with something like pity on their faces. "You're over-adapted, Jabe. You must have suspected it yourself. You couldn't seriously believe that thousands of men working over a ten-year period could come to a wrong conclusion. Or that that report Moran was going to send in would be the only way we'd have of knowing about things here——"

"I tell you, no!" said Jabe, breaking in. "I *know* these people here. They're different. Maybe I am a little . . . overadapted. But these people operate according to standards of justice and conscience. It's not just taboo and ritual, not just——"

"Come along, Jabe," said the voice and the two men moved in on him. "You'll have a chance to talk later."

"No," he said, backing away from them. People were beginning to stream past outside the front window. Jabe evaded the two men and went to the door, opening it. At the top of the street, leading from the square, two of the bachelors appeared carrying rifles. The prisoner walked silently between them.

"Jabe——" began the voice in his head.

"I tell you, no!" said Jabe, desperately. "Sheila's expecting. She makes things sound different than they are."

"Oh, Jabe!" said one of two women, hurrying past. "Did you hear about the jam? You'll have to tell Sheila!"

"Jam?" said Jabe, stupidly.

"That marauder. They asked him what he wanted and he wanted bread and jam for a last meal. Imagine. Two pounds he ate! Not my jam, thank goodness——"

"Come on, Etty!" said the other woman. "All the good places'll be gone. . . ." They hurried off.

The two bachelors with the rifles and the prisoner were only a few steps behind the women.

"Wait——" said Jabe, desperately.

The bachelors stopped at this command from a senior and married man. The prisoner also stopped. He had not been cleaned up, in his ragged suit of badly tanned hide, except for a clean white bandage on his arm. The whites of his eyes were as clear as a child's and his beard was the soft silk of adolescence. All three of them looked inquiringly at Jabe.

"Wait," said Jabe again, unnecessarily. He appealed to the nearest bachelor. "Why's Manager Lenkhart doing this?"

The bachelor frowned, looked at the other bachelor, then back at Jabe. He guffawed in uneasy fashion.

"What was his reason?" said Jabe.

The bachelor shrugged elaborately. He looked at the ground, spat, and kicked a pebble aside.

"We've got to get going," said the other bachelor. He looked over at the prisoner, who had moved aside to reach up and feel the low edge of the metal roof on Jabe's cottage; the roof made of corrugated aluminum.

"Silver," he said, glancing a moment at Jabe. "It's mighty rich—and fine."

The bachelors guffawed again. They took the prisoner's elbows and marched him off, down the slope of the road.

"You see there? You see?" said Jabe, staring after them, but speaking to the invisible warders just behind him. "He thought the sheet metal was silver, that the roofs were made of silver. There's your true degenerate. But the men with him——"

"Let's go, Jabe," said the voice gently in his head. He felt the warders take hold of him on either side. Invisibly, they led him out into the street, on the same way down which the other prisoner had already gone. He felt the uselessness of it all suddenly cresting over him like a wave, the sudden realization that there was no hope and there had never been any hope, no matter how he had tried to delude himself. He had known it from the beginning, but something in him would not let him admit the truth about these people—about his own wife, and his own child soon to be born—to himself.

From the beginning he had known that there was no saving them. Yet he had tried, anyway—had killed his own brother in an attempt he knew was quite hopeless, to save a people who were already regressing to the animal. Why? Why had he done it? He could not say.

All he knew was that there had never been any choice about it—for him. He had done what he had to do.

"Come along now," said the gentle voice in his head. Dumbly, and plodding like a donkey, he let them lead him as they would. To where, it no longer mattered.

# BY NEW HEARTH FIRES

The last dog on Earth was dying. It was a small, but important, crisis. None other of his kind was known to still exist on any of the other worlds. It was quite probable that there were no others and that with him the race would end. Nothing seemed to be wrong with this dog named Alpha. He was still young and in no way hurt or diseased. But still he was dying.

The curator at this time of the museum world that was Earth was quite concerned about the situation. He had done everything he could with the large, brown and white canine, utilized every device and therapy available at the hospital center in the Adirondack Mountains. But the dog, unlike all the other sick animals brought in from the various parks and exhibit areas of the Earth, responded to none of his efforts. It was not the curator's fault, of course. But still he felt the matter as a sort of failure—that the race of dogs, important as it had been to the past history of man, should terminate during his term of office.

He coded a request to the Galactic Center for the person most likely to be of help to him in this situation, and a few weeks later a well-known historical psychologist Dr. Anius, arrived on Earth, accompanied by his son, a bright twelve-year-old named Geni. The curator was on hand to meet them as they stepped off the transportation platform at the edge of the hospital area.

"Dr. Laee?" said Anius, descending from the platform and offering his hand. He was a tall, brown-haired man in his first hundred years, and his handgrip was firm. "I brought my boy along to give him this chance to look over the home world.

He won't be in the way. Geni, this is the curator here, Dr. Laee."

Laee shook hands also with the boy, a slim lad well over two meters in height and showing signs of being another lean, tall individual like his father. Laee, originally from the far side of the galaxy, was from a rather shorter ancestral strain than these Center people, but age had put him past the point of noticing that difference.

"Come along into the hospital," he said.

They strolled up the narrow, resilient walk through the hospital area. The grassy grounds were occupied by a number of different animals, arranged by species, that were currently at the hospital and undergoing treatment. The boy stared in fascination at a whooping crane which was turning around and around in an attempt to get a better look at one of its wings, which had been set for a break and bound in stasis.

"I had no idea there were so many I wouldn't know," he said to the curator.

"The original Earth was very rich in varieties," replied the curator. "One way or another, we have specimens of nearly all, though in many cases we had to breed back for extinct forms."

"How do you keep them separate?" asked Geni, his gray eyes ranging over the apparently open grounds.

"Tingle barriers separate the groups into small areas," answered Laee. "Remind me to give you a key, when you want to examine the animals more closely."

They reached the entrance to the curator's quarters after seeing a buffalo who had just had his horn amputated, a Kodiak bear with an infected ear, and a large gorilla with a skin rash allergy who sat back in the shadows of his little groves of bushes and watched their passing with sad, intelligent eyes.

"I assume," said the tall Dr. Anius, as they passed into the main lounge of the curator's area, "you could also rebreed the domestic dog from one of your other canine forms if we're completely unsuccessful in saving this specimen?"

"Oh, of course," said Laee. "But naturally, I like to know what his affliction is, so we can stop it if it ever pops up again. And then," he paused, turning his eyes on Anius, "it would be nice to maintain the original line."

They went on into a farther room that was half library, half patio. The bright afternoon spring sun came in through the invisible ceiling and struck warmly upon the patches of grass and flowers. On the white flagstone a furry body lay outstretched, eyes closed and clean limbs stretched out and still, with only the slow rise and fall of the narrow chest to indicate life.

"Is that him?" asked the boy.

"That's him," said the curator. They all three came up and stood over the dog who lifted his eyelids to look at them, then closed the lids again, without stirring.

"Is he helpless?" asked Anius.

"No . . . not helpless," said the curator. "He's weak, mainly from not eating anything to speak of these last few weeks. But he's got energy enough to move around when he wants to. Alpha," he said, sharply. "Alpha."

The dog opened his eyes again, and half lifted his head. He moved his tail, briefly, and then, as if it were too much of an effort, lay back again. His eyes, however, remained open, watching them. The boy, Geni, stared at those eyes in an odd sort of fascination. They were as brown and liquid as a human's but they had something different—he thought of it as a clearness or transparency—that he had never noticed before in eyes of any kind.

"If you two don't mind stepping out," said his father, "I'd like to examine him with no one else around to distract him."

The boy and the curator went out together.

"As long as we have to wait," said the curator, "how'd you like to look around the planet a bit?"

"I'd enjoy that," said Geni. "If it's not too much trouble——"

"No trouble at all," said the curator. He led the way to a small platform, sitting by the fireplace in the main lounge, and they both got on. "This job's something of a sinecure, generally."

He set the controls that took them directly to a spot a little ways out from the world where they could see the North American Continent as a whole, and, pointing out various features of historic interest, moved on around the globe.

". . . There are capsules of detail on this information back in my library," Laee said, between paragraphs of his talk. "You can pick them out later, if you want. This world, of course, is too crammed with history for anyone to do justice to it on a quick sweep like this, but it's my belief that immediacy is a great virtue. You may get more of the feel of it from this sort of presentation."

"I'm overwhelmed," said the boy. "I am."

"Ah, then, you're a responsive," said Laee. "So few are. Many of the visitors here make a valiant effort—I see them at it—but for all their trouble they achieve no emotional response. And I think they go away thinking that it's all a rather unnecessary expense."

They descended at random and landed on Salisbury plain, in England, within the toothed circle of a reconstructed Stonehenge. The midafternoon July sun struck warmly between the upright blocks as it had for thousands of years, but the heavy shadows were cold.

The boy shivered suddenly, looking about him.

"They were different, weren't they?" he said.

"Anthropologists deny it," said Laee, "that we have changed. But I know what you feel. I feel it myself, sometimes—and particularly on this world."

"Should we go?" asked Geni.

They went on, to see the Louvre and the Forum, and the Taj Mahal and the Angkor Thom and Angkor Vat—and so by way of the Christ of the Andes back to the hospital.

Anius was sitting in the main lounge when they came in, the dog Alpha not far from him, lying stretched out on the rosy tile of the floor with the brown fur of his back turned to the fireplace, as if in disdain at its illusion of a blaze.

"Been seeing the Earth, have you?" he said, smiling up at them as they approached.

"We hit some of the high spots," replied the curator, as he and the boy sat down. "Have you discovered anything about the dog?"

Anius shook his head slowly and looked over at Alpha.

"He's dying because he has no will to live," he answered. "But you know that already. These creatures are strange." He stared at the dog, who returned the gaze without stirring. "Their psychology is baffling."

"But I thought," said the curator, who had turned to the table beside him and was coding for a meal to be served the three of them, "animal psychology was at least as well understood as the human."

"Oh yes, most of them," said Anius. "The monkey and ape family, now"—he smiled suddenly across his lean face—"how we know that bunch! And the wild strains, and the herd animals. But the dog—and to a lesser extent, the cat, and the horse. All of those that had some peculiar partnership in man's history. These, we do not understand." A cart came gliding into the room with the meal upon it and stopped between them. Anius reached out for a tumbler of clear liquid. "Perhaps that's why—they were too close."

"You mean it would be like understanding ourselves?" said Laee. "But we do, don't we?"

"In everything that's pin-downable, we do," said Anius. "But there's more than that, or each one of us wouldn't be an individual, in his own right."

"Father," said the boy, "what were they like—the ones who built Stonehenge?"

Anius laughed and set his glass down.

"You see there?" he said to the curator. "I can't answer that." He turned to his son. "The original Stonehenge, you mean? I can tell you what they looked and talked like and even something of what they thought. But what they felt——"

"That's what I mean," said the boy, eagerly.

His father spread his hands helplessly.

"The science of emotions is no science," he said. "It's an art. Which was why Art developed automatically to express it. Look at what ancient man has done—and you're as close to him as I can come with all I know."

"Yes," said the curator, musingly over a biscuit held in one hand. "I understand that, I think."

"But——" began the boy.

"It's not natural for men to be martyrs and heroes and tyrants," his father continued, as if he had not heard. "But they had them. We can attempt to explain the bad in men of those times by saying these were warped personalities. But how do you explain the good—the better than normal—" he interrupted himself, looking at the curator.

"A code of ethics——" said the curator.

"Does not completely explain it," said Anius. "There was a very good paper written several hundred years back by somebody whose name slips my mind at this moment," he frowned for a second over the effort of remembering, then gave it up, "which attempted to prove that an ethical existence is the most practical one for any intelligent species as a species, from the time that they first begin to show intelligence. But there were flaws in his argument . . . there were flaws. . . ."

He fell silent, and the boy and the curator were both just opening their mouths to speak, thinking he was through, when he looked up and addressed Laee, directly.

"I believe you told me Alpha, here, started his decline from the time he was left alone in the world, so to speak."

"Well, yes," said the curator. "But his symptoms are unique in that. I mean . . . we used to have quite a number of these dogs."

"In a separate area?"

"Yes. We had something like a farm, or a country place, covering several square miles. There was a building, circa 1880s, old reckoning, a barn, some farm animals."

"And some robots in human form, I suppose," said Anius.

"That's right. But they weren't put there for the dogs' benefit," said the curator. "They were just part of the exhibit—as the dogs themselves were, originally."

"And then they started to die off? I mean, the dogs, of course," said Anius.

"The group began to dwindle. Smaller litters were born, the puppies did all right during their growing period, but began to give up, like Alpha, here, and die shortly after maturity. Alpha was one of a litter of two. His sister was born dead, and he and his mother were the last two of the species. When she died——"

"He began to go this way?"

The curator nodded.

"I see," said Anius, thoughtfully, nodding at the glass in his hand. "I see. . . ."

"Father," said Geni, the fresh, tight skin of his brow stretching in a frown, "about these men who *did* build Stonehenge. . . ."

In the following days Dr. Anius gave himself over wholly to the observation and care of the dog. To the curator watching, it all seemed a little marvelous, and he himself felt a touch of humbleness at the thought of having harnessed so much intelligence and erudition, as it were, to such a small and common problem. For a few days Alpha actually seemed to revive under this attention. He occasionally followed Anius around, and even consented to eat several times. But shortly after that it could be seen that he was sinking back into his apathy again.

"Perhaps," Laee suggested, offering the ready-made excuse like a polite host, "it was impossible to begin with. You've been very generous with your time."

"When there's life, there's hope, as that hoary saying goes," objected Anius. They were sitting in the same library-patio, with Alpha stretched out at their feet and apparently dozing. "And the challenge is . . . well, a challenge." He smiled at the curator. "It wouldn't take much imagination to pretend that there's some old magic still at work on this world of yours. You've noticed Geni?"

"He's very interested in the local past," said Laee.

"He's head over heels interested in the local past," said Anius. "But I suppose it's natural at his age."

"That reminds me," said Laee, almost a trifle shyly, "he's dropping by in a few minutes. He wants to ask you something."

Anius raised his head and looked closely at the curator.

"It must be something he suspects I won't approve of," he said dryly, "if he has to send advance warning through you, this way."

"I don't know what he has in mind," said Laee, quickly. And changed the subject.

Some ten minutes later, Geni came into the patio and sat down. His father stared at him. The boy was dressed in an odd, archaic costume consisting of boots, slacks, and jacket.

"I see," said Anius. "You want to play-act some historical role or other? That's your plan."

"Well, yes," said Geni. He shifted a little uncomfortably on his chair. He had been very sure of himself, but now the words would not come for his argument. He had been out, roaming the face of the Earth by himself, and he had seen the fresh, clean soil black with the dampness of spring and smelled the many odors of the open wind. Something in all this had moved him, but he found that now, facing his father, he had no term for it. "I'd like to try living . . . a little like they used to. And I'd like to take the dog along. It might work for him."

"Fantasy!" said his father. "You realize, you can't go back?"

"Oh, I know that," said Geni quickly. "It'd be play-acting, as you say. But there's something there I'd like to touch."

"The past is the past," said his father. "There's a certain emotional danger in entertaining the notion that it might be otherwise. Everyone who works in the field of history has to realize that. It's like studying something attractive through a glass which can't be broken. You risk frustration."

"It would be good for the dog," said the boy. "He's not improving, is he? If I took him out and exposed him to nothing but the kind of environment his kind flourished in, then maybe. . . ." He let the sentence hang, watching his father.

"I'm not sure I approve of that, either," said Anius, slowly. "It's rather on the order of tinkering at random with a mechanical device whose principle of operation you do not understand. By accident you may cure its malfunction, but there's an equal or greater chance you may damage it further."

"Alpha's dying," said the boy, "And you aren't saving him. Nobody's saving him. I could try my experiment without him, but I'd rather have him, and it wouldn't hurt to try."

"What do you think?" asked Anius, turning to the curator.

"I've been bitten by Geni's bug many years now." Laee rubbed his short-fingered hands together and smiled wryly. "And I've never got over it. Call me devil's advocate, if you wish. But it might help the dog, at that."

"Has anything like it ever been tried before?" asked Anius.

Laee shook his head.

"Not as far as the records show," he said. "Give the two of them a week or so, why don't you? At the end of that time we should be able to tell about Alpha, one way or another. Of course, I realize it would leave you at loose ends—but now that you're here on Earth, perhaps there's material here in our files or otherwise you may have wanted to examine, a week's worth of it, anyway."

"Much more than that. I'd planned to stay over anyway—" Anius waved his hand, dismissing that element of the problem. "It's just that I feel a certain professional responsibility toward the dog, now . . . well, go ahead, if you want to," he wound up, turning to Geni.

The boy's face lit up.

Early the next morning they left the clinic, Geni, and Alpha. The dog, like all the other animals there, had been restrained by the invisible tingle barriers from straying into areas where he was not wanted to go, and, in spite of the fact that now he, like Geni, wore a key that cut out a barrier as soon as he touched it, he had to be urged to strike out across the grounds, and cringed slightly as he followed the boy at the end of a leash.

"You won't stray off the grounds?" Anius said to Geni, as they left.

"Not if you don't want us to, Father," said the boy, looking up at the man with an expression of slight puzzlement. "It really doesn't matter where we go, as long as we stay out of the clinic itself."

"Fine," said Anius. "Because I'd like to check on the dog from time to time by local scan."

"All right, Father."

They turned and went, walking away through the areas of the sick and injured animals, Alpha's head glancing to right and left at the wild creatures with a wariness, but Geni moving with the unconscious unconcern of a being who knew his science.

Anius and Laee watched them go. The dog, Alpha, trotting at the end of his leash, shied from the Kodiak with the infected ear and sniffed curiously, a second later, at the gorilla with the allergy rash. They moved on, dwindling, and passing at length from sight among a small grove of pines.

"And now," said Anius, turning to the curator, "I'll start my poking through your files."

The files, indeed, turned out to be even far more interesting to an historical psychologist than Anius had expected. They consisted of nothing more—and nothing less—than a great mass of statistics and information about all periods of human history on Earth. Taken item by item, they were as dry as old newsprint, but investigating them was like looking up an item in an encyclopedia, where each page turned over sowed fishhooks for the attention, in the shape of odd and hitherto unknown avenues of knowledge. Anius felt caught, as he had not been caught in decades, by a lust that drew him down these obscure paths and into the wilderness of civilizations long dead and put to rest. The mirage of something not fully understood fled always just a little ways ahead of him, and the more he overtook it in his absorption of facts from the past, the more it drew away from him, and drew him on; until in the end he pursued it headlong, without attempting analysis or self-understanding, like a man in love.

In this occupation he suddenly lost himself, and several

days went by as if the time they represented had unexpectedly evaporated. He was startled to find Laee at his elbow one afternoon.

"Eh?" he said, looking up from the screen before him. "What's that?"

"You said you wanted to check on Alpha's condition from time to time," Laee was standing close, with his round face bent a little curiously over him. "You haven't made any attempt, and I just now happened to pick up Geni and the dog on a routine check of the grounds."

"Oh . . . oh, yes," said Anius, getting to his feet. "Where's your scan board?"

"Through here."

Laee led him into a little side room. They looked over a small ornamental railing into a little area of imaged outdoors, solid enough appearing in its three dimensions to be an actuality. Anius saw his son, still in the archaic jacket and boots, seated cross-legged before an actual wood fire, burning on the grass of an open space surrounded by pine and birch. On the other side of the fire, Alpha lay on his belly, nose between his paws. His eyes were open, but they were not on Geni. They were gazing instead into the almost invisible flames of the fire.

Seeing them there, Anius felt a sudden entirely irrational and new twinge of panic, as if he were watching his son out of reach and drowning in some strange waters.

"Geni!" he called.

"Just a minute," said Laee. The boy had not looked up. The curator adjusted a control and nodded at Anius.

"Geni!" he said again, loudly.

The boy looked up. The dog's ears flicked and stirred, but he did not move. Geni looked over to one side as if he could actually see them, but the gaze of his image went past the two men in the room, the way the gaze of a blind man does.

"Father?" he said.

"It's all right," said Anius more calmly. "I just didn't realize the sound element wasn't on." He took a breath and went on more calmly. "Alpha looks good. How've you been doing?"

"I don't know. I think he's better," said the boy. "We've been moving around the grounds a lot. He's pretty interested in the other animals. He perked up the first day—and he's been eating pretty well until just today."

"Something happen today?" asked the curator.

"No," said Geni, shifting his gaze at the other voice, but still looking past them. "But when I stopped and built the fire here for our midday meal, he didn't seem hungry. And he doesn't seem to want to follow me away from the fire."

"If he shows any obvious signs of physical illness, let me know," said Laee.

"I will," answered Geni. "Father?"

"Yes, Geni?" said Anius.

"Are you keeping occupied all right?"

Anius smiled.

"Yes," he said. "I'm quite busy on some files here. Geni—how far from the clinic are you?"

"About ten kilometers, I imagine," said Geni. "Why?"

"I just wondered. Keep in touch with us, son."

"I will."

"Good-by."

"Good-by, Father."

"Good-by," said Laee.

"Good-by."

Laee touched a control and the scene vanished, leaving a small area of bare, bright yellow floor enclosed by the little railing.

"I've a little more scanning to do," said Laee, looking up at his tall guest. "I won't keep you from your own work."

"Oh, yes . . . yes," said Anius, starting a little. He lifted his hand in a friendly gesture and went out the door of the scan room. But he did not go back to the files. Deep in thought, he wandered through the living quarters of the clinic and out onto the grounds. The afternoon was reddening into its later hours just before sunset and the long shadows lay across his path. Again he felt the whisper of something like a panic, but it sank and mellowed into a sadness, a feeling of regret no deeper than the transience of the passing day. He found himself standing by the area where the gorilla sat and he looked across the distance of a few short meters into its wrinkle-hooded eyes. And the gorilla looked back with a wondering unhappiness that had no language to explain itself, its great and hairy arms crossed on its knees.

"What do you know?" Anius asked it. "What do *you* know?"

And the gorilla blinked and turned its head shyly and painfully away.

113

Anius sighed and turned back toward the clinic, and the files.

"I hesitate to mention this," said Laee, over lunch two days later, "but have you run across something in the files that disturbs you? It's not my intention to pry, but as curator here——"

"Of course," said Anius. He put down the glass he was holding and shook his head. "There's nothing, except——" he hesitated. "There is nothing, that's just it."

"I'm afraid——" began Laee.

"I know, I'm not being clear," Anius waved a hand in apology. "It's not the files. It's this whole world of yours . . . I'm half prepared to believe it's haunted. It puts questions into my mind."

"For example?" said Laee, encouragingly.

"Do you suppose," said Anius, very slowly, "that something could be lost without its loss being known?"

"Lost from the files?"

"No," said Anius. "Lost to us, by us, as a people, without our knowing it. Do you suppose it would be possible for us to have taken a turning, somewhere along the way—a turning that was maybe right, and maybe wrong—but a turning that put us past the hope of going back to find our original path?"

Laee spread his hands and smiled, with a little shrug.

"No!" said Anius, forcefully. "I mean it as a serious question." Laee frowned at him.

"In that case——" he said, and paused. "No, I still don't understand you."

"There was an old legend on this world, once," said Anius, "about the elephants' graveyards."

"I know it," Laee nodded.

"Because the remains of dead elephants were not found, because of the value of ivory if great boneyards existed, a theory of a dramatic end for elephants was invented. Only the truth was that the scavengers, small and large, in the jungle disposed of all remains. The true end was not remarkable, not impressive, but natural and a little dull. Gradually, the dead elephant disappeared. As if"—Anius hesitated—"he had never been."

"Come now," said Laee smiling, "the human race is a long way from the end of its existence—if, indeed, it's going to end at all."

"I think," said Anius, with a slight shiver, "all things end."

A sudden mellow note, like the sound of a gong, echoed through the clinic. Both men looked up, startled, and Laee, frowning in surprise, reached over and pressed a stud on the table by his chair. A bright little shimmer sprang into existence in front of the imitation fire on the hearth of the lounge and resolved itself into the face of Geni, looking up at them.

"What is it, Son?" asked Anius, for the boy's face was strained.

"I'm sorry, Father," said Geni. "But I've lost Alpha. I thought I could find him by myself and not bother you. But I can't."

"Tell us what happened," said Laee, leaning forward.

"He ran off yesterday, during the night, I guess," said Geni. "He was gone in the morning. I hunted for him yesterday, and found some tracks this morning crossing a couple of tingle barriers. No other animal could do that—Alpha's the only one carrying a key—" the boy broke off. "I think . . . I think the gorilla got him. You know . . . the one just a little way from the clinic. I'm at the gorilla's area, now. But I don't have anything protective with me. I don't dare go in."

"We'll be right there," said the curator, getting to his feet.

"Wait where you are, Geni," said Anius, also rising.

"All right, Father. I'm sorry," said the boy. He broke the connection.

Laee got a paralyzer from his stores and the two men set out on foot toward the area where the gorilla was enclosed. It was just a couple of minutes' walk from the clinic, and as they rounded a little clump of lilac bushes they saw Geni standing unhappily at the edge of the area, and the gorilla itself squatting in front of the little grove of bushes that had been designed to give it the privacy the powerful but shy anthropoid desired.

Geni turned to look at them as the two men approached together, Laee carrying the paralyzer with a practiced and competent grip.

"I'm sure he's back in there," Geni said, as they came up. "I can't quite see him now, but I saw him before."

"Let me call him," said Laee. He stepped up to the edge of the tingle barrier and raised his voice. "Alpha!" He waited a second, and then called again. *"Alpha!"*

There was no immediate response from the shadows of the bushes, but the gorilla, his attention suddenly directed to

115

Laee, all at once recognized the paralyzer in the curator's hand and threw up one thick clumsy arm before his face, shrinking back and away.

Immediately, there was movement in the bushes and the dog came out. Pushing in front of the huddled gorilla, he stood squarely, facing the men.

"There he is," said Laee, raising the paralyzer. The gorilla whimpered. Alpha snarled suddenly, and Anius caught at the curator's arm.

"No!" he said. "Don't."

Laee turned and stared at him. The boy cried out.

"But he's got Alpha!"

"Come along," said Anius, putting a hand on both of them. "Leave them."

Slowly, the curator lowered the paralyzer. He was frowning at Anius. Then his frown cleared and he slowly nodded.

"But," cried the boy again, "he's got Alpha. He's got our dog."

Anius put his long arm around his son's shoulders and turned him about. And the three of them walked away, toward the silver dome of the clinic, which from where they were seemed to shimmer in the noon sun like a bright bubble, Earth-tethered there for only a little time and against its will.

"No, Son," he said, gently. "Not our dog. He's not our dog any more."

# IDIOT SOLVANT

The afternoon sun, shooting the gap of the missing slat in the Venetian blind on the window of Art Willoughby's small rented room, splashed fair in Art's eyes, blinding him.

"Blast!" muttered Art. "Got to do something about that sun."

He flipped one long, lean hand up as an eyeshield and leaned forward once more over the university news sheet, unaware that he had reacted with his usual gesture and litany to the sun in his eyes. His mouth watered. He spread out his sharp elbows on the experiment-scarred surface of his desk and reread the ad.

Volunteer for medical research testing. $1.60 hr., rm., board. Dr. Henry Rapp, Room 432, A Bldg., University Hospital.

"Board—" echoed Art aloud, once more unaware he had spoken. He licked his lips hungrily. *Food,* he thought. Plus wages. And hospital food was supposed to be good. If they would just let him have all he wanted. . . .

Of course, it would be worth it for the $1.60 an hour alone.

"I'll be sensible," thought Art. "I'll put it in the bank and just draw out what I need. Let's see—one week's work, say—seven times twenty-four times sixteen. Two-six-eight-eighth to the tenth. Two hundred sixty-eight dollars and eighty cents. . . ."

That much would support him for—mentally, he totted up

his daily expenses. Ordinary expenses, that was. Room, a dollar-fifty. One and a half pound loaf of day-old bread at half price—thirteen cents. Half a pound of peanut butter, at ninety-eight cents for the three-pound economy size jar—seventeen cents roughly. One all-purpose vitamin capsule—ten cents. Half a head of cabbage, or whatever was in season and cheap—approximately twelve cents. Total, for shelter with all utilities paid and a change of sheets on the bed once a week, plus thirty-two hundred calories a day—two dollars and two cents.

Two dollars and two cents. Art sighed. Sixty dollars and sixty cents a month for mere existence. It was heart-breaking. When sixty dollars would buy a fine double magnum of imported champagne at half a dozen of the better restaurants in town, or a 1954 used set of the Encyclopaedia Britannica, or the parts from a mail order house so that he could build himself a little ocean-hopper shortwave receiver so that he could tune in on foreign language broadcasts and practice understanding German, French, and Italian.

Art sighed. He had long ago come to the conclusion that since the two billion other people in the world could not very well all be out of step at the same time, it was probably he who was the odd one. Nowadays he no longer tried to fight the situation, but let himself reel uncertainly through life, sustained by the vague, persistent conviction that somewhere, somehow, in some strange fashion destiny would eventually be bound to call on him to have a profound effect on his fellow men.

It was a good twenty-minute walk to the university. Art scrambled lankily to his feet, snatched an ancient leather jacket off the hook holding his bagpipes, put his slide rule up on top of the poetry anthologies in the bookcase so he would know where to find it again—that being the most unlikely place, Q.E.D.—turned off his miniature electric furnace in which he had been casting up a gold pawn for his chess set, left some bread and peanut butter for his pet raccoon, now asleep in the wastebasket, and hurried off, closing the door.

"There's one more," said Margie Hansen, Dr. Hank Rapp's lab assistant. She hesitated. "I think you'd better see him." Hank looked up from his desk, surprised. He was a short, cheerful, tough-faced man in his late thirties.

"Why?" he said. "Some difficulties? Don't sign him up if you don't want to."

"No. No . . . I just think maybe you'd better talk to him. He passed the physical all right. It's just . . . well, you have a look at him."

"I don't get it," said Hank. "But send him in."

She opened the door behind her and leaned out through it.

"Mr. Willoughby, will you come in now?" She stood aside and Art entered. "This is Dr. Rapp, Mr. Willoughby. Doctor, this is Art Willoughby." She went out rather hastily, closing the door behind her.

"Sit down," said Hank, automatically. Art sat down, and Hank blinked a little at his visitor. The young man sitting opposite him resembled nothing so much as an unbearded Abe Lincoln. A *thin* unbearded Abe Lincoln, if it was possible to imagine our sixteenth President as being some thirty pounds lighter than he actually had been.

"*Are* you a student at the university here?" asked Hank, staring at the decrepit leather jacket.

"Well, yes," said Art, hoping the other would not ask him what college he was in. He had been in six of them, from Theater Arts to Engineering. His record in each was quite honorable. There was nothing to be ashamed of—it was just always a little bit difficult to explain.

"Well—" said Hank. He saw now why Margie had hesitated. But if the man was in good enough physical shape, there was no reason to refuse him. Hank made up his mind. "Has the purpose of this test been explained to you?"

"You're testing a new sort of stay-awake pill, aren't you?" said Art. "Your nurse told me all about it."

"Lab assistant," corrected Hank automatically. "There's no reason you can think of yourself, is there, why you shouldn't be one of the volunteers?"

"Well, no. I . . . I don't usually sleep very much," said Art, painfully.

"That's no barrier." Hank smiled. "We'll just keep you awake until you get tired. How much do you sleep?" he asked, to put the younger man at his ease at least a little.

"Oh . . . six or seven hours."

"That's a little less than average. Nothing to get in our way . . . why, what's wrong?" said Hank, sitting up suddenly, for Art was literally struggling with his conscience, and his Abe Lincoln face was twisted unhappily.

"A . . . a week," blurted Art.

"A week! Are you—" Hank broke off, took a good look at his visitor and decided he was not kidding. Or at least, believed himself that he was not kidding. "You mean, less than an hour a night?"

"Well, I usually wait to the end of the week—Sunday morning's a good time. Everybody else is sleeping then, anyway. I get it over all at once—" Art leaned forward and put both his long hands on Hank's desk, pleadingly. "But can't you test me, anyway, Doctor? I need this job. Really, I'm desperate. If you could use me as a control, or something——"

"Don't worry," said Hank, grimly. "You've got the job. In fact if what you say is true, you've got more of a job than the rest of the volunteers. This is something we're all going to want to see!"

"Well," said Hank, ten days later. "Willoughby surely wasn't kidding."

Hank was talking to Dr. Arlic Bohn, of the Department of Psychology. Arlic matched Hank's short height, but outdid him otherwise to the tune of some fifty pounds and fifteen years. They were sitting in Hank's office, smoking cigarettes over the remains of their bag lunches.

"You don't think so?" said Arlic, lifting blond eyebrows toward his half-bare, round skull.

"Arlie! Ten days!"

"And no hallucinations?"

"None."

"Thinks his nurses are out to poison him? Doesn't trust the floor janitor?"

"No. No. No!"

Arlie blew out a fat wad of smoke.

"I don't believe it," he announced.

"I beg your pardon!"

"Oh—not you, Hank. No insults intended. But this boy of yours is running some kind of a con. Sneaking some sort of stimulant when you aren't looking."

"Why would he do that? We'd be glad to give him all the stimulants he wants. He won't take them. And even if he was sneaking something—ten days. Arlie! Ten days and he looks as if he just got up after a good eight hours in his own bed."

Hank smashed his half-smoked cigarette out in the ash tray. "He's not cheating. He's a freak."

"You can't be that much of a freak."

"Oh, can't you?" said Hank. "Let me tell you some more about him. Usual body temperature—about one degree above normal average."

"Not unheard of. You know that."

"Blood pressure a hundred and five systolic, sixty-five diastolic. Pulse, fifty-five a minute. Height, six feet four, weight when he came in here a hundred and forty-two. We've been feeding him upwards of six thousand calories a day since he came in and I swear he still looks hungry. No history of childhood diseases. All his wisdom teeth. No cavities in any teeth. Shall I go on?"

"How is he mentally?"

"I checked up with the university testing bureau. They rate him in the genuis range. He's started in six separate colleges and dropped out of each one. No trouble with grades. He gets top marks for a while, then suddenly stops going to class, accumulates a flock of incompletes, and transfers into something else. Arlie," said Hank, breaking off suddenly, lowering his voice and staring hard at the other, "I think we've got a new sort of man here. A mutation."

"Hank," said Arlie, crossing his legs comfortably, "when you get to be my age, you won't be so quick to think that Gabriel's going to sound the last trump in your own particular back yard. This boy's got a few physical peculiarities, he's admittedly bright, and he's conning you. You know our recent theory about sleep and sanity."

"Of course I——"

"Suppose," said Arlie, "I lay it out for you once again. The human being deprived of sleep for any length of time beyond what he's accustomed to, begins to show signs of mental abnormality. He hallucinates. He exhibits paranoid behavior. He becomes confused, flies into reasonless rages, and overreacts emotionally to trifles."

"Arthur Willoughby doesn't."

"That's my point." Arlie held up a small, square slab of a hand. "Let me go on. How do we explain these reactions? We theorize that possibly sleep has a function beyond that of resting and repairing the body. In sleep we humans, at least, dream pretty constantly. In our dreams we act out our unhappinesses, our frustrations, our terrors. Therefore sleep, we guess, may be the emotional safety valve by which we maintain our sanity against the intellectual pressures of our lives."

"Granted," said Hank, impatiently. "But Art——"

"Now, let's take something else. The problem-solving mechanism——"

"Damn it, Arlie——"

"If you didn't want my opinion, why did you ring me in on this . . . what was that you just said, Hank?"

"Nothing. Nothing."

"I'll pretend I didn't hear it. As I was saying—the problem-solving mechanism. It has been assumed for centuries that man attacked his intellectual problems consciously, and consciously solved them. Recent attention to this assumption has caused us to consider an alternate viewpoint, of which I may say I"—Arlie folded his hands comfortably over his bulging shirtfront—"was perhaps the earliest and strongest proponent. It may well be—I and some others now think— that Man is inherently incapable of consciously solving any new intellectual problem."

"The point is, Art Willoughby—what?" Hank broke off suddenly and stared across the crumpled paper bags and wax paper on his desk, at Arlie's chubby countenance. "What?"

"Incapable. Consciously." Arlie rolled the words around in his mouth. "By which I mean," he went on, with a slight grin, "Man has no *conscious* mechanism for the solution of new intellectual problems." He cocked his head at Hank, and paused.

"All right. All right!" fumed Hank. "Tell me."

"There seems to be a definite possibility," said Arlie, capturing a crumb from the piece of wax paper that had enwrapped his ham sandwich, and chewing on it thoughtfully, "that there may be more truth than poetry to the words *inspiration, illuminating flash,* and *stroke of genius.* It may well turn out that the new-problem solving mechanism is not under conscious control at all. Hm-m-m, yes. Did I tell you Marta wants me to try out one of these new all-liquid reducing diets? When a wife starts that——"

"Never mind Marta!" shouted Hank. "What about nobody being consciously capable of solving a problem?"

Arlie frowned.

"What I'm trying to say," he said, "is that when we try to solve a problem consciously, we are actually only utilizing an attention-focusing mechanism. Look, let me define a so-called 'new problem' for you——"

"One that you haven't bumped into before."

"No," said Arlie. "No. Now you're falling into a trap." He waggled a thick finger at Hank; a procedure intensely irritating to Hank, who suffered a sort of adrenalin explosion the moment he suspected anybody of lecturing down to him. "Does every hitherto undiscovered intersection you approach in your car constitute a new problem in automobile navigation? Of course not. A truly new problem is not merely some variation or combination of factors from problems you have encountered before. It's a problem that for you, at least, previously, did not even exist. It is, in fact, *a problem created by the solution of a problem of equal value in the past.*"

"All right. Say it is," scowled Hank. "Then what?"

"Then," said Arlie, "a true problem must always pose the special condition that no conscious tools of education or experience yet exist for its solution. Ergo, it cannot be handled on the conscious level. The logic of conscious thought is like the limb structure of the elephant, which, though ideally adapted to allow seven tons of animal a six-and-a-half foot stride, absolutely forbids it the necessary spring to jump across a seven-foot trench that bars its escape from the zoo. For the true problem, you've got to get from hyar to thar without any stepping stone to help you across the gap that separates you from the solution. So, you're up against it, Hank. You're in a position where you can't fly but you got to. What do you do?"

"You tell me," glowered Hank.

"The answer's simple," said Arlie, blandly. "You fly."

"But you just said I couldn't!" Hank snapped.

"What I said," said Arlie, "was two things. One, you can't fly; two, you got to fly. What you're doing is clinging to one, which forces you to toss out two. What I'm pointing out is that you should cling to two, which tosses out one. Now, your conscious, experienced, logical mind *knows* you can't fly. The whole idea's silly. It won't even consider the problem. But your unconscious—aha!"

"What about my unconscious?"

"Why, your unconscious isn't tied down by any ropes of logical process like that. When it wants a solution, it just goes looking for it."

"Just like that."

"Well," Artie frowned, "not just like that. First it has to fire up a sort of little donkey-engine of its own which we might call the intuitive mechanism. And that's where the trickiness comes in. Because the intuitive mechanism seems to be all power and no discipline. Its great usefulness comes from the fact that it operates under absolutely no restrictions—and of course this includes the restriction of control by the conscious mind. It's a sort of idiot savant . . . no, idiot solvant would be a better term." He sighed.

"So?" said Hank, after eyeing the fat man for a moment. "What's the use of it all? If we can't control it, what good is it?"

"What good is it?" Arlie straightened up. "Look at art. Look at science! Look at civilization. You aren't going to deny the existence of inspirations, are you? They exist—and one day we're going to find some better method of sparking them than the purely inductive process of operating the conscious, attention-focusing mechanism in hopes that something will catch."

"You think that's possible?"

"I know it's possible."

"I see," said Hank. There was a moment or so of silence in the office. "Well," said Hank, "about this little problem of my own, which I hate to bring you back to, but you did say the other day you had some ideas about this Art Willoughby. Of course, you were probably only speaking inspirationally, or perhaps I should say, without restriction by the conscious mind——"

"I was just getting to that," interrupted Arlie. "This Art Willoughby obviously suffers from what educators like to call poor work habits. Hm-m-m, yes. Underdevelopment of the conscious, problem-focusing mechanism. He tries to get by on a purely intuitive basis. When this fails him, he is helpless. He gives up—witness his transfers from college to college. On the other hand, when it works good, it works very, very good. He has probably come up with some way of keeping himself abnormally stimulated, either externally or internally. The only trouble will be that he probably isn't even conscious of it, and he certainly has no control over it. He'll fall asleep any moment now. And when he wakes up you'll want him to duplicate his feat of wakefulness but he won't be able to do it."

Hank snorted disbelievingly.

"All right," said Arlie. "All right. Wait and see."

"I will," said Hank. He stood up. "Want to come along and see him? He said he was starting to get foggy this morning. I'm going to try him with the monster."

"What," wondered Arlie, ingenuously, rising, "if it puts him to sleep?"

Hank threw him a glance of pure fury.

"Monster!" commanded Hank. He, Arlie, and Margie Hansen were gathered in Art's hospital room, which was a pleasant, bedless place already overflowing with books and maps. Art, by hospital rules deprived of such things as tools and pets, had discovered an interest in the wars of Hannibal of Carthage. At the present moment he was trying to pick the truth out of the rather confused reports following Hannibal's escape from the Romans, after Antiochus had been defeated at Magnesia and surrendered his great general to Rome.

Right now, however, he was forced to lay his books aside and take the small white capsule which Margie, at Hank's order, extended to him. Art took it; then hesitated.

"Do you think it'll make me very jittery?" he asked.

"It should just wake you up," said Hank.

"I told you how I am with things like coffee. That's why I never drink coffee, or take any stimulants. Half a cup and my eyes feel like they're going to pop out of my head."

"There wouldn't," said Hank a trifle sourly, "be much point in our paying you to test out the monster if you refused to take it, now would there?"

"Oh . . . oh, no," said Art, suddenly embarrassed. "Water?"

Margie gave him a full glass and threw an unkind glance at her superior.

"If it starts to bother you, Art, you tell us right away," she said.

Art gulped the capsule down. He stood there waiting as if he expected an explosion from the region of his stomach. Nothing happened, and after a second or two he relaxed.

"How long does it take?" he asked.

"About fifteen minutes," said Hank.

They waited. At the end of ten minutes, Art began to

brighten up and said he was feeling much more alert. At fifteen minutes, he was sparkling-eyed and cheerful, almost, in fact, bouncy.

"Awfully sorry, Doctor," he said to Hank. "Awfully sorry I hesitated over taking the monster that way. It was just that coffee and things——"

"That's all right," said Hank, preparing to leave. "Margie'll take you down for tests now."

"Marvelous pill. I recommend it highly," said Art, going out the door with Margie. They could hear him headed off down the corridor outside toward the laboratory on the floor below, still talking.

"Well?" said Hank.

"Time will tell," said Arlie.

"Speaking of time," continued Hank. "I've got the plug-in coffee pot back at the office. Have you got time for a quick cup?"

". . . Don't deny it," Hank was saying over half-empty cups in the office a short while later. "I heard you; I read you loud and clear. If a man makes his mind up to it, he can fly, you said."

"Not at all. And besides, I was only speaking academically," retorted Arlie, heatedly. "Just because I'm prepared to entertain fantastic notions academically doesn't mean I'm going to let you try to shove them down my throat on a practical basis. Of course nobody can fly."

"According to your ideas, someone like Willoughby could if he punched the right buttons in him."

"Nonsense. Certainly he can't fly."

There was the wild patter of feminine feet down the hallway outside the office, the door was flung open, and Margie tottered in. She clung to the desk and gasped, too out of wind to talk.

"What's wrong?" cried Hank.

"Art . . ." Margie managed, "flew out—lab window."

Hank jumped to his feet, and pulled his chair out for her. She fell into it gratefully.

"Nonsense!" said Arlie. "Illusion. Or"—he scowled at Margie—"collusion of some sort."

"Got your breath back, yet? What happened?" Hank was demanding. Margie nodded and drew a deep breath.

"I was testing him," she said, still breathlessly. "He was talking a blue streak and I could hardly get him to stand still. Something about Titus Quintus Flamininius, the three-body problem, Sauce Countess Waleska, the family Syrphidae of the order Diptera—all mixed up. Oh, he was babbling! And all of a sudden he dived out an open window."

"Dived?" barked Arlie. "I thought you said he *flew?*"

"Well, the laboratory's on the third floor!" wailed Margie almost on the verge of tears.

Further questioning elicited the information that when Margie ran to the window, expecting to see a shattered ruin on the grass three stories below, she perceived Art swinging by one arm from the limb of an oak outside the window. In response to sharp queries from Arlie, she asserted vehemently that the closest grabable limb of the oak was, however, at least eight feet from the window out which Art had jumped, fallen, or dived.

"And then what?" said Hank.

Then, according to Margie, Art had uttered a couple of Tarzanlike yodels, and swung himself to the ground. When last seen he had been running off across the campus through the cool spring sunlight, under the budding trees, in his slacks and shirt unbuttoned at the throat. He had been heading in a roughly northeasterly direction—*i.e.*, toward town—and occasionally bounding into the air as if from a sheer access of energy.

"Come on!" barked Hank, when he had heard this. He led the way at a run toward the hospital parking lot three stories below and his waiting car.

On the other side of the campus, at a taxi stand, the three of them picked up Art's trail. A cab driver waiting there remembered someone like Art taking another cab belonging to the same company. When Hank identified the passenger as a patient under his, Hank's, care, and further identified himself as a physician from the university hospital, the cab driver they were talking to agreed to call in for the destination of Art's cab.

The destination was a downtown bank. Hank, Arlie, and Margie piled back into Hank's car and went there.

When they arrived, they learned that Art had already come and gone, leaving some confusion behind him. A vice-president of the bank, it appeared, had made a loan to Art of two hundred and sixty-eight dollars and eighty cents; and was now, it seemed, not quite sure as to why he had done so.

"He just talked me into it, I guess," the vice-president was saying unhappily as Hank and the others came dashing up. It further developed that Art had had no collateral. The vice-president had been given the impression that the money was to be used to develop some confusing but highly useful discovery or discoveries concerning Hannibal, encyclopedias, the sweat fly and physics—with something about champagne and a way of preparing trout for the gourmet appetite.

A further check with the cab company produced the information that Art's taxi had taken him on to a liquor store. They followed. At the liquor store they discovered that Art had purchased the single jeroboam of champagne (Moet et Chandon) that the liquor store had on hand, and had mentioned that he was going on to a restaurant. What restaurant, the cab company was no longer able to tell them. Art's driver had just announced that he would not be answering his radio for the next half hour.

They began checking the better and closer restaurants. At the fourth one, which was called the Calice d'Or, they finally ran Art to the ground. They found him seated alone at a large, round table, surrounded by gold-tooled leather volumes of a brand-new encyclopedia, eating and drinking what turned out to be Truite Sauce Countess Waleska and champagne from the jeroboam, now properly iced.

"Yahoo!" yelped Art, as he saw them approaching. He waved his glass on high, sloshing champagne liberally about. "Champagne for everybody! Celebrate Dr. Rapp's pill!"

"You," said Hank, "are coming back to the hospital."

"Nonsense! Glasses! Champagne for m'friends!"

"Oh, Art!" cried Margie.

"He's fried to the gills," said Arlie.

"Not at all," protested Art. "Illuminated. Blinding flash. Understand everything. D'you know all knowledge has a common point of impingement?"

"Call a taxi, Margie," commanded Hank.

"Encyclopedia. Champagne bubble. Same thing."

"Could I help you, sir?" inquired a waiter, approaching Hank.

"We want to get our friend here home——"

"All roads lead knowledge. Unnerstand ignorance, unnerstand everything——"

"I understand, sir. Yes sir, he paid the check in advance——"

"Would *you* like to speak three thousand, four hundred and seventy-one languages?" Art was asking Arlie.

"Of course," Arlie was saying, soothingly.

"My assistant has gone to get a taxi, now. I'm Dr. Rapp of the university hospital, and——"

"When I was child," announced Art, "thought as child, played child; now man—put away childish things."

"Here's the young lady, sir."

"But who will take care of pet raccoon?"

"I flagged a taxi down. It's waiting out front."

"Hoist him up," commanded Hank.

He and Arlie both got a firm hold on a Willoughby arm and maneuvered Art to his feet.

"This way," said Hank, steering Art toward the door.

"The universe," said Art. He leaned confidentially toward Hank, almost toppling the three of them over. "Only two inches across."

"That so?" grunted Hank.

"Hang on to Arlie, Art, and you won't fall over. There——" said Margie. Art blinked and focused upon her with some difficulty.

"Oh . . . there you are——" he said. "Love you. Naturally. Only real woman in universe. Other four point seven to the nine hundred seventeenth women in universe pale imitations. Marry me week Tuesday, three P.M. courthouse, wear blue." Margie gasped.

"Open the door for us, will you?"

"Certainly sir," said the waiter, opening the front door to the Calice d'Or. A pink and gray taxi was drawn up at the curb.

"Sell stock in Wehauk Cannery immediately," Art was saying to the waiter. "Mismanagement. Collapse." The waiter blinked and stared. "News out in ten days."

"But how did you know I had—" the waiter was beginning as they shoved Art into the back seat of the cab. Margie got in after him.

"Ah, there you are," came Art's voice from the cab. "First son Charles Jonas—blond hair, blue eyes. Second son, William——"

"I'll send somebody to pick up that encyclopedia and anything else he left," said Hank to the waiter and got into the taxi himself. The taxi pulled away from the curb.

"Well," said the waiter, after a long pause in which he stared after the receding cab, to the doorman who had just joined him on the sidewalk, "how do you like that? Ever seen anything like that before?"

"No, and I never saw anyone with over a gallon of champagne in him still walking around, either," said the doorman.

". . . And the worst of it is," said Hank to Arlie, as they sat in Hank's office, two days later, "Margie *is* going to marry him."

"What's wrong with that?" asked Arlie.

"What's wrong with it? Look at that!" Hank waved his hand at an object in the center of his desk.

"I've seen it," said Arlie.

They both examined the object. It appeared to be an ordinary moveable telephone with a cord and wall plug. The plug, however, was plugged into a small cardboard box the size of a cheese carton, filled with a tangled mess of wire and parts cannibalized from a cheap portable radio. The box was plugged into nothing.

"What was that number again . . . oh yes," said Arlie. He picked up the phone and dialed a long series of numbers. He held the phone up so that they could both hear. There was a faint buzzing ring from the earphone and then a small, tinny voice filled the office.

". . . The time is eight forty-seven. The temperature is eighteen degrees above zero, the wind westerly at eight miles an hour. The forecast for the Anchorage area is continued cloudy and some snow with a high of twenty-two degrees, a low tonight of nine above. Elsewhere in Alaska——"

Arlie sighed, and replaced the phone in its cradle.

"We bring him back here," said Hank, "stewed to the gills. In forty minutes before he passed out, he builds this trick wastebasket of his that holds five times as much as it ought to. He sleeps seven hours and wakes up as good as ever. What should I do? Shoot him, or something? I must have some responsibility to the human race—if not to Margie."

"He seems sensible now?"

"Yes, but what do I do?"

"Hypnosis."

"You keep saying that. I don't see——"

"We must," said Arlie, "inhibit the connection of his conscious mind with the intuitive mechanism. The wall between the two—the normal wall—seems to have been freakishly thin in his case. Prolonged sleeplessness, combined with the abnormal stimulation of your monster, has caused him to break through—to say to the idiot-solvant, *'Solve!'* And the idiot solvant in the back of his head has provided him with a solution."

"I still think it would be better for me to shoot him."

"You are a physician——"

"You would remind me of that. All right, so I can't shoot him. I don't even want to shoot him. But, Arlie, what's going to happen to everybody? Here I've raised up a sort of miracle worker who can probably move the North American continent down to the South Pacific if he wants to—only it just happens he's also a feather-headed butterfly who never lit on one notion for more than five minutes at a time in his life. Sure, I've got a physician's responsibility toward him. But what about my responsibility to the rest of the people in the world?"

"There is no responsibility being violated here," said Arlie patiently. "Simply put him back the way you found him."

"No miracles?"

"None. At least, except accidental ones."

"It might be kinder to shoot him."

"Nonsense," said Arlie sharply. "It's for the good of everybody." Hank sighed, and rose.

"All right," he said. "Let's go."

They went down the hall to Art's room. They found him seated thoughtfully in his armchair, staring at nothing, his books and maps ignored around him.

"Good morning, Art," said Arlie.

"Oh? Hello," said Art, waking up. "Is it time for tests?"

"In a way," said Arlie. He produced a small box surmounted by a cardboard disk on which were inked alternate spirals of white and black. He plugged the box in to a handy electric socket by means of the cord attached to it, and set it on a small table in front of Art. The disk began to revolve. "I want you to watch that," said Arlie.

Art stared at it.

"What do you see?" asked Arlie.

"It looks like going down a tunnel," said Art.

"Indeed it does," said Arlie. "Just imagine yourself going down that tunnel. Down the tunnel. Faster and faster. . . ." He continued to talk quietly and persuasively for about a minute and a half, at the end of which Art was limply demonstrating a state of deep trance. Arlie brought him up a bit for questioning.

". . . And how do these realizations, these answers come to you?" Arlie was asking a few minutes later.

"In a sort of a flash," replied Art. "A blinding flash."

"That is the way they have always come to you?"

"More lately," said Art.

"Yes," said Arlie, "that's the way it always is just before people outgrow these flashes—you know that."

There was a slight pause.

"Yes," said Art.

"You have now outgrown these flashes. You have had your last flash. Flashes belong to childhood. You have had a delayed growing-up, but from now on you will think like an adult. Logically. You will think like an adult. Repeat after me."

"I will think like an adult," intoned Art.

Arlie continued to hammer away at his point for a few more minutes; then he brought Art out of his trance, with a final command that if Art felt any tendency to a recurrence of his flashes he should return to Arlie for further help in suppressing them.

"Oh, hello, Doctor," said Art to Hank, as soon as he woke up. "Say, how much longer are you going to need me as a test subject?"

Hank made a rather unhappy grimace.

"In a hurry to leave?" he said.

"I don't know," said Art, enthusiastically, rubbing his long hands together as he sat up in the chair, "but I was just thinking maybe it's time I got to work. Settled down. As long as I'm going to be a married man shortly."

"We can turn you loose today, if you want," said Hank.

When Art stepped once more into his room, closing the door behind him and taking off his leather jacket to hang it up on the hook holding his bagpipes, the place seemed so little changed that it was hard to believe ten full days had passed. Even the raccoon was back asleep in the wastebasket. It was evident the landlady had been doing her duty about keeping the small animal fed—Art had worried a little about that. The only difference, Art thought, was that the room seemed to feel smaller.

He sighed cheerfully and sat down at the desk, drawing pencil and paper to him. The afternoon sun, shooting the gap of the missing slat on the Venetian blind at the window, splashed fair in Art's eyes, blinding him.

"Blast!" he said aloud. "Got to do something about that—"

He checked himself suddenly with one hand halfway up to shield his eyes, and smiled. Opening a drawer of the desk, he took out a pair of heavy kitchen scissors. He made a single cut into the rope slot at each end of the plastic slat at the bottom of the blind, snapped the slat out of position, and snapped it back in where the upper slat was missing.

Still smiling, he picked up the pencil and doodled the name *Margie* with a heart around it in the upper left-hand corner as he thought, with gaze abstracted. The pencil moved to the center of the piece of paper and hovered there.

After a moment, it began to sketch.

What it sketched was a sort of device to keep the sun out of Art's eyes. At the same time, however, it just happened to be a dome-shaped all-weather shield capable of protecting a city ten miles in diameter the year around. The "skin" of the dome consisted of a thin layer of carbon dioxide such as one finds in the bubbles of champagne, generated and maintained by magnetic lines of force emanating from three heavily charged bodies, in rotation about each other at the apex of the dome and superficially housed in a framework the design of which was reminiscent of the wing structure found in the family Syriphidae of the order Diptera.

Art continued to smile as the design took form. But it was a thoughtful smile, a mature smile. Hank and Arlie had been quite right about him. He had always been a butterfly, flitting from notion to notion, playing.

But then, too, he had always been a bad hypnotic subject, full of resistances.

And he was about to have a wife to care for. Consequently it is hard to say whether Arlie and Hank would have been reassured if they could have seen Art at that moment. His new thinking was indeed adult, much more so than the other two could have realized. Where miracles were concerned, he had given up *playing*.

Now, he was *working*.

# THE IMMORTAL

The phone was ringing. He came up out of a sleep as dark as death, fumbled at the glowing button in the phone's base with numb fingers and punched it. The ringing ceased.

"Wander here," he mumbled.

"Major, this is Assignment. Lieutenant Van Lee. Scramble, sir."

"Right," he muttered.

"You're to show in Operations Room four-oh-nine at four hundred hours. Bring your personals."

"Right." Groggily he rolled over on his stomach and squinted at his watch in the glow from the button on the phone. In the pale light, the hands of his watch stood at twelve minutes after three—three hundred ten hours. Enough time.

"Understood, sir?"

"Understood, Lieutenant," he said.

"Very good, sir. Out." The phone went dead. For a moment the desire for sleep sucked at Jim Wander like some great black bog, then with a convulsive jerk he threw it and the covers off him in one motion and sat up on the edge of his bed in the darkness, scrubbing at his face with an awkward hand.

After a moment, he turned the light on, got up, showered and dressed. As he shaved, he watched his face in the mirror. It was still made up of the same roughly handsome, large-boned features he remembered, but the lines about the mouth and between the eyebrows under the tousled black hair, coarsely curling up from his forehead seemed deepened with the sleep. It could not be drink, he thought. He never drank even on rest-alert nowdays. Alcohol did nothing for him any more. It was just that nowdays he slept like a log—like a log water-soaked and drowning in some bottomless lake.

When he was finally dressed, he strapped on last of all his personals—his side-arm, the x-morphine kit, the little green thumbnail-square box holding the cyanide capsules. Then he left his room, went down the long sleeping corridor of the officers' quarters and out a side door into the darkness of predawn and the rain.

He could have gone around by the interior corridors to the Operations building, but it was a shortcut across the quadrangle and the rain and chill would wake him, drive the last longing for sleep from his bones. As he stepped out of the door the invisible rain, driven by a light wind, hit him in the face. Beyond were the blurred lights of the Operations building across the quadrangle.

Far off to his left thunder rolled. Tinny thunder—the kind heard at high altitudes, in the mountains. Beyond the rain and darkness were the Rockies. Above the Rockies the clouds. And beyond the clouds, space, stretching beyond the Pole Star to the Frontier.

Where he would doubtless be before the dawn rose, above this quadrangle, above these buildings, these mountains, and this Earth.

He entered the Operations building, showed his identification to the Officer of the Day, and took the lift tube up to the fourth floor. The frosted pane of the door to room four-oh-nine glowed with a brisk, interior light. He knocked on the door and went in without waiting for an answer.

Behind the desk inside sat General Mollen, and in a chair half facing the general was a civilian of Jim's own age, lean and high-foreheaded, with the fresh skin and clear eyes of someone who has spent most of his years inside walls, sheltered from the weather. Both men looked up as Jim came in and Jim felt a twinge of sudden and reasonless dislike for the civilian. Perhaps, he thought, it was because the other looked so wide awake and businesslike this unnatural hour of the morning. Of course, so did General Mollen, but that was different.

As Jim came forward, both of the other men stood up.

"Jim," said the general, deep-voiced, his square face unsmiling. "I want you to meet Walt Trey. He's from the Geriatrics Bureau."

He would be, thought Jim grimly, shaking hands with the other. Walt Trey was as tall as Jim himself, if leaner-boned. And his handshake was not weak. But still . . . here he was, thought Jim, a man as young as Jim himself, full of the juices of living and with all his attention focussed on the gray and tottering end years of life. A bodysnatcher—a snatcher of old bodies back from the brink of the grave for a few months or a few years.

"Pleased to meet you, Walt," he said, in a neutral tone.

"Good to meet you, Jim."

"Sit down," said the general. Jim pulled up a chair as they all sat down once more around the desk.

"What's up, sir?" asked Jim.

"Something special," answered Mollen. "That's why Walt here's been rung in on it. Do you happen to remember about the Sixty Ships Battle?"

"It was right after we found we had a frontier in common with the Laggi, wasn't it?" said Jim, slightly puzzled. "Back before we and they found out logistics made space wars unworkable. Sixty of our ships met forty-some of theirs beyond the Pole Star, and their ships were better. What about it?"

"Do you remember how the battle came out?" It was the civilian, Walt Trey leaning forward with strange intensity.

Jim shrugged.

"Our ships were slower then. We hadn't started to design them for guarding a spatial border, instead of fighting pitched battles. They cut us up and suckered what was left into standing still while they set off a nova explosion," he said. He looked into the civilian's eyes and spoke deliberately. "The ships on the edge of the explosion were burst up like paper cutouts. The ones in the center—well, they just disappeared."

"Disappeared," said Walt Trey. He did not seem disturbed by Jim's vivid description of the nova and death. "That's the right word. Do you remember how long ago this was?"

"Nearly two hundred years ago," said Jim. He turned and looked impatiently at General Mollen, with a glance that said plainly, *what is this?*

"Look here, Jim," said the general. "We've got something to show you." He pushed aside a few papers on the surface of the desk in front of him and touched some studs on the edge of the desk. The overhead lights dimmed. The surface of the table became transparent and gave way to a scene of stars. To the three men seated around the desk top it was as if they looked down and out into an area of space a thousand light years across. To the civilian, Jim was thinking, the stars would be only a maze. To Jim himself, the image was long familiar.

Mollen's hands did things with the studs. Two hazy spheroids of dim light, each about six hundred light years in diameter along its longest axis, sprang into view—bright enough to establish their position and volume, not so bright as to hide the stars they enclosed. The center of one of the spheroids was the sun of Earth, and the farthest extent of this spheroid in one direction inter-mixed with an edge of the other spheroid beyond the Pole Star, Polaris.

"Our area of space," said Mollen's voice, out of the dimness around the table, "and the Laggi's, Walt. They block our expansion in that direction, and we block theirs in this. The distribution of the stars in this view being what it is, it's not practical for either race to go around the other. You see the Frontier area?"

"Where the two come together, yes," said the voice of Walt.

"Now, Jim—" said Mollen. "Jim commands a wing of our frontier guard ships, and he knows that area well. But nothing but unmanned drones of ours have ever gotten deep into Laggi territory beyond the Frontier and come back out again. Agreed, Jim?"

"Agreed, sir," said Jim. "More than ten, fifteen light years deep is suicide."

"Well, perhaps," said Mollen. "But let me go on. The Sixty Ships Battle was fought a hundred and ninety-two years ago—here." A bright point of light sprang into existence in the Frontier area. "One of the ships engaged in it was a one-man vessel with semianimate automatic control system, named by its pilot *La Chasse Gallerie*—you said something, Jim?"

The exclamation had emerged from Jim's lips involuntarily. And at the same time, foolishly, a slight shiver had run down his back. It had been years since he had run across the old tale as a boy.

"It's a French-Canadian ghost legend, sir," he said. "The legend was that voyageurs who had left their homes in eastern Canada to go out on the fur trade routes and who had died out there would be able to come back home one night of the year. New Year's night. They'd come sailing in through the storms and snow in ghost canoes, to join the people back home and kiss the girls they wouldn't ever be seeing again. That's what they called the story, "*La Chasse Gallerie.*" It means the hunting of a type of butterfly that invades beehives to steal the honey."

"The pilot of this ship was a French-Canadian," said Mollen. "Raoul Penard." He coughed dryly. "He was greatly attached to his home. *La Chasse Gallerie* was one of the ships near the center of the nova explosion, one of the ones that disappeared. At that time we didn't realize that the nova explosion was merely a destructive application of the principle used in translight drive. . . . You've heard of the statistical chance that a ship caught just right by a nova explosion could be transported instead of destroyed, Jim?"

"I'd hate to count on it, sir," said Jim. "Anyway, what's the difference? Modern ships can't be anticipated or held still long enough for any kind of explosion to be effective. Neither the Laggi nor we have used the nova for eighty years."

"True enough," said Mollen. "But we aren't talking about modern ships. Look at the desk schema, Jim. Forty-three hours ago one of our deep unmanned probes returned from far into Laggi territory with pictures of a ship. Look."

Jim heard a stud click. The stars shifted and drew back. Floating against a backdrop of unknown stars he saw the cone shape of a one-man space battlecraft, of a type forgotten a hundred and fifty years before. The view moved in close and he saw a name, abraded by dust and dimmed, but readable on the hull. He read it.

*La Chasse Gallerie*—the breath caught in his throat.

"It's been floating around in Laggi territory all this time?" Jim said. "I can't believe——"

"More than that," Mollen interrupted him. "That ship's under power and moving." A stud clicked. The original scene came back. A bright line began at the extreme edge of the desk and began to creep toward the back limits of Laggi territory. It entered the territory and began to pass through.

"You see," said Mollen's voice out of the dimness, "it's coming back from wherever the nova explosion kicked it to, nearly two hundred years ago. It's headed back to our own territory. It's headed back, toward Earth."

Jim stared at the line in fascination.

"No," he heard himself saying, "it can't be. It's some sort of Laggi trick. They've got a Laggi pilot aboard——"

"Listen," said Mollen. "The probe heard talking inside the ship. And it recorded. Listen——"

Again, there was a faint snap of a stud. A voice, a human voice, singing raggedly, almost absent-mindedly to itself, entered the air of the room and rang on Jim's ears.

". . . *en roulant ma boule, roulant*—" the singing broke off and the voice dropped into a mutter of a voice in a mixture of French and English, speaking to itself, mixing the two languages indiscriminately. Jim, who had all but forgotten the little French he had picked up as a boy in Quebec, was barely able to make out that the possessor of the voice was carrying on a running commentary to the housekeeping duties he was doing about the ship. Talking to himself after the fashion of hermits and lonely men.

"Now, then," said Jim, even while he wondered why he was protesting such strong evidence at all. "Didn't you say they had the early semianimate control systems then? They used brain tissue grown in a culture, didn't they? It's just the control system, parroting what it's heard, following out an early order to bring the ship back."

"Look again," said Mollen. The view changed once more to a closeup of *La Chasse Gallerie*. Jim looked and saw wounds in the dust-scarred hull—the slashing cuts of modern light weapons, refinements of the ancient laser beam-guns.

"The ship's already had its first encounter with the Laggi on its way home. It met three ships of a Laggi patrol—and fought them off."

"Fought them off? That old hulk?" Jim stared into the dimness where Mollen's face should be. "Three modern Laggi ships?"

"That's right," said Mollen. "It killed two and escaped from the third—and by rights it ought to be dead itself, but it's still coming. A control system might record a voice and head a ship home, but it can't fight off odds of three to one. That takes a living mind."

A stud clicked. Dazzling overhead light sprang on again and the desk top was only a desk top. Blinking in the illumination, Jim saw Mollen looking across at him.

"Jim," said the general, "this is a volunteer mission. That ship is headed dead across the middle of Laggi territory and it's going to be hit again before it reaches the Frontier. Next time it'll be cut to ribbons, or captured. We can't afford to have that happen. The pilot of that ship, this Raoul Penard, has too much to tell us, even beginning with the fact of how he happens to be alive at over two hundred years of age." He watched Jim closely. "Jim, I'm asking you to take a section of four ships in to meet *La Chasse Gallerie* and bring her out."

Jim stared at him. He found himself involuntarily wetting his lips and stopped the gesture.

"How deep?" he asked.

"At least a hundred and fifty years in toward the heart of Laggi territory," said Mollen, bluntly. "If you want to turn it down, Jim, don't hesitate. The man who pulls this off has got to go into it believing he can make it back out again."

"That's me," said Jim. He laughed, the bare husk of a laugh. "That's the way I operate, General. I volunteer."

"Good," said Mollen. He sat back in his chair. "There's just one more thing, then. Raoul Penard is older than any human being has a right to be and he's pretty certainly senile, if not out and out insane. We'll want a trained observer along to get as much information out of contact with the man as we can, in case you lose him and his ship getting back. That calls for a man with a unique background and experience in geriatrics and all the knowledge of the aging process. Walt, here, is the man. He'll replace your regular gunner and ride in your two-man ship with you."

It was like a hard punch in the belly. Jim sucked in air and found he had jerked erect. Both men watched him. He waited a second, to get his voice under control. He spoke first to the general.

"Sir, I'll need a gunner. If there was ever a job where I'd need a gunner, it'd be this one."

"As a matter of fact," said Mollen, slowly, and Jim could feel that this answer had been ready and waiting for him, "Walt here is a gunner—a good one. He's a captain in the Reserves, Forty-Second Training Squadron. With a ninety-two point six efficiency rating."

"But he's still a week-end warrior—" Jim swung about on the lean geriatrics man. "Have you ever done a tour of duty? Real duty? On the Frontier?"

"I think you know I haven't, Major," said Walt, evenly. "If I'd had you'd have recognized me. We're about the same age, and there aren't that many on Frontier duty."

"Then do you know what it's like—waht it can be like out there?" raged Jim. He knew his voice was getting away from him, scaling upward in tone, but he did not care. "Do you know how the bandits can come out of nowhere? Do you know you can be hit before you know anyone's anywhere near around? Or the ship next to you can be hit and the screens have to stay open—that's regulation, in case of some miracle that there's something can be done? Do you know what it's like to sit there and watch a man you've lived with burning to death in a cabin he can't get out of? Or spilled out of a ship cut wide open, and lost back there somewhere . . . alive but lost . . . where you'll never be able to find him? Do you know what it might be like to be spilled out and lost yourself and faced with the choice of living three weeks, a month, two months in your suit in the one in a million chance of being found after all—or of taking your cyanide capsule? Do you know what that's like?"

"I know it," said Walt. His face had not changed. "The same way you do, as a series of possibilities for the most part. I know it as well as I can without having been wounded or killed."

"I don't think you do!" snapped Jim raggedly. His hands were shaking. He saw Walt looking at them.

"General," said Walt, "perhaps we should ask for another volunteer?"

"Jim's our best man," said Mollen. He had not moved, watching them both from behind the desk. "If I had a better man—or an equal man who was fresher—I'd have called him in instead. But what you're after is just about impossible, and only a man who can do the impossible can bring it off. Jim's that man. It's like athletic skills. Every so often a champion comes along, one in billions of people, who isn't just one notch up from the next contenders but ten notches up from the nearest. There's no point in sending you and five ships into Laggi territory with anyone else in command. You simply wouldn't come back. With Jim, you . . . may."

"I see," said Walt. He looked at Jim. "Regardless, I'm going."

"And you're taking him, Jim," said Mollen, "or turning down the mission."

"And if I turn it down?" Jim darted a glance at the general.

"I'll answer that," said Walt. Jim looked back at him. "If

necessary, my Bureau will requisition a ship and I'll go alone."

Jim stared back at the other for a long moment, and felt the rage drain slowly away from him, to be replaced by a great weariness.

"All right," he said. "All right, Walt—General. I'll head the mission." He breathed deeply and glanced over Walt's civilian suit. "How long'll it take you to get ready?"

"I'm ready now," said Walt. He reached down to the floor behind the desk and came up with a package of personals, side-arm, med-kit and cyanide box. "The sooner the better."

"All right. The five ships of the Section are manned and waiting for you," said Mollen. He stood up behind the desk and the two younger men got to their feet facing him. "I'll walk down to Transmission Section with you."

They went out together into the corridor and along it and down an elevator tube to a tunnel with a moving floorway. They stepped on to the gently rolling strip, which carried them forward onto a slightly faster strip, and then to a faster, and so on until they were flashing down the tunnel surrounded by air pumped at a hundred and twenty miles an hour in the same direction they traveled, so that they would not be blown off their feet. In a few minutes they came to the end, and air and strips decelerated so that they slowed and stepped at last into what looked like an ordinary office, but which was deep in the heart of a mountain. This, the memory returned to Jim, was in case the Transmission Section blew up on one of its attempts to transmit. The statistical chance was always there. Perhaps, this time . . . ?

But Mollen had cleared them with the officer of the duty guard and they were moving on through other rooms to the suiting room, where Jim and Walt climbed into the unbelievably barrel-bodied suits that were actually small spaceships in themselves and in which—if they who wore them were unlucky and still would not take their cyanide—they might drift in space, living on recycled air and nourishments until they went mad, or died of natural causes.

—Or were found and brought back. The one in a million chance. Jim, now fully inside his suit, locked it closed.

"All set?" It was Mollen's voice coming at him over the audio circuit of the suit. Through the transparent window of the headpiece he saw the older man watching him.

"All set, General." He looked over at Walt and saw him

already suited and waiting. Trying to make points by being fast, thought Jim sardonically. With the putting on of the suit, the old feeling of sureness had begun to flow back into him, and he felt released. "Let's go, body-snatcher."

"Good luck," said Mollen. He did not comment on the name Jim had thrown at the geriatrics man. Nor did Walt answer. Together they clumped across the room, waited for the tons-heavy explosion door to swing open, and clumped through.

On the floor of the vast cavern that was the takeoff area, five two-man ships sat like gray-white darts, waiting. Red "manned" lights glowed by each sealed port on the back four. Jim read their names as he stumped forward toward the open port of the lead ship, his ship, the *Fourth Mary*. The other four ships were the *Swallow*, the *Fair Maid*, the *Lela*, and the *Andfriend*. He knew their pilots and gunners well. The *Swallow* and the *Andfriend* were ships from his own command. They and the other two were good ships handled by good men. The best.

Jim led the way aboard the *Fourth Mary* and fitted himself into the forward seat facing the controls. Through his suit's receptors, he heard Walt sliding into the gunner's seat, behind and to the left of him. Already, in spite of the efficiency of the suit, he could feel the faint, enclosed stink of his own body sweat, and responding to the habit of many missions, his brain began to clear and come alive. He plugged his suit into the controls.

"Report," he said. One by one, in order, the *Swallow*, the *Fair Maid*, the *Lela*, and the *Andfriend* replied. . . .

"Transmission Section," said Jim, "this is Wander Section, ready and waiting for transmission."

"Acknowledged," replied the voice of the Transmission Section. There followed a short wait, during which as always Jim was conscious, as if through some extra sense, of the many-tons weight of the collapsed magnesium alloy of the ship's hulls bearing down on the specially reinforced concrete of the takeoff area. "Ready to transmit."

"Acknowledged," said Jim.

"On the count of four, then," said Transmission Section's calm, disembodied voice. "For Picket Nine, L Sector, Frontier Area, transmission of Wander Section, five ships. Counting now. Four. Three . . ." the unimaginable tension that always preceded transmission from one established point to another began to build a gearing-up of nerves that affected all the men on all the ships alike. "Two . . ." the voice of Transmission Section seemed to thunder at them along their overwrought nerves. "One . . ."

". . . Transmit!"

Abruptly, a wave of disorientation and nausea broke through them, and was gone. They floated in dark and empty interstellar space, with the stars of the Frontier Area surrounding them, and a new voice spoke in their ear.

"Identify yourself," it said. "Identify yourself. This is Picket Nine requesting identification."

"Wander Section. Five ships." Jim did not bother to look at his instruments to find the space-floating sphere that was Picket Nine. It was out there somewhere, with twenty ships scattered around, up to half a light year away, but all zeroed in on this reception point where he and the other four ships had emerged. Had Jim been a Laggi Wing or Picket commander, he would not have transmitted into this area with twice twenty ships—no, nor with three times that many. "Confirm transmission notice from Earth? Five ship section for deep probe bandit territory. Wander Section Leader speaking."

"Transmission notice confirmed Wander Section Leader," crackled back the voice from Picket Nine. "Mission confirmed. You will not deship. Repeat, not deship. Local Frontier area has been scouted for slipover, and data prepared for flash transmission to you. You will accept data and leave immediately. Please key to receive data."

"Major—" began the voice of Walt, behind him.

"Shut up," said Jim. He said it casually, without rancor, as if he was speaking to his regular gunner, Leif Molloy. For a moment he had forgotten that he was carrying a passenger instead of a proper gunman. And there was no time to think about it now. "Acknowledge," he said to Picket Nine. "Transmit data, please."

He pressed the data key and the light above it sprang into being and glowed for nearly a full second before going dark again. That, thought Jim, was a lot of data—at the high speed transmission at which such information was pumped into his ship's computing center. That was one of the reasons the new computing units were evolved out of solid-state physics instead of following up the development of the semi-animate brains such as the one aboard the ancient *La Chasse*

*Gallerie.* The semianimate brains—living tissue in a nutrient solution—could not accept the modern need for sudden high-speed packing of sixteen hours worth of data in the space of a second or so.

Also, such living tissue had to be specially protected against high accelerations, needed to be fed and trimmed—and it died on you at the wrong times.

All the time Jim was thinking this with one part of his mind, the other and larger part of his thinking process was driving the gloved fingers of his right hand. These moved over a bank of one hundred and twenty small black buttons, ten across and twelve down, like the stops on a piano-accordion, and with the unthinking speed and skill of the trained operator, he punched them, requesting information out of the body of data just pumped into his ship's computing center, building up from this a picture of the situation, and constructing a pattern of action to be taken as a result.

Evoked by the intricate code set up by combinations of the black buttons under his fingers, the ghost voice of the computing center whispered in his ear in a code of words and numbers hardly less intricate.

". . . transmit destination area one-eighty ell wye, Lag Sector L forty-nine c at point twelve-five, thirteen-two, sixty-four-five. Proceedings jumps ten ell wye, at inclination zforty-nine degrees frontier midpoint. Optimum jumps two, point oh three error correctible. . . ."

He worked steadily. The picture began to emerge. It would not be hard getting in. It was never hard to do that. They could reach *La Chasse Gallerie* in two transmissions or jumps across some hundred and eighty light-years of distance, and locate her in the area where she should then be, within an hour or so. Then they could—theoretically at least—surround her, lock on, and try to improve on the ten light-years of jump it seemed was the practical limit of her pilot's or her control center's computing possibilities.

With modern translight drive, the problem was not the ability to move or jump any required distance, but the ability to compute correctly, in a reasonable time, the direction and distance in which the move should be made. Such calculations took in of necessity the position and movement of the destination area—this in a galaxy where everything was in relative movement, and only a mathematical fiction, the theoretical centerpoint of the galaxy from which all distances were marked and measured, was fixed.

The greater the distance, the more involved and time-consuming the calculation. The law of diminishing returns would set in, and the process broke down of its own weight—it took a lifetime to calculate a single jump to a destination it would not take quite a lifetime to reach by smaller, more easily calculable jumps. It was this calculation time-factor that made it impractical for the human and Laggi races to go around each other's spatial territory. If we were all Raoul Penards, thought Jim grimly, with two hundred and more years of life coming, it'd be different. The thought chilled him; he did not know why. He put it out of his mind and went back to the calculations.

The picture grew and completed. He keyed his voice to the other ships floating in dark space around him.

"Wander Leader to Wander Section," he said. "Wander Leader to Wander Section. Prepare to shift into bandit territory. Key for calculations pattern for first of two jumps. Acknowledge, all ships of Wander Section."

The transmit section of his control board glowed briefly as the *Swallow*, the *Fair Maid*, the *Lela*, and the *Andfriend* pumped into their own computing centers the situation and calculations he had worked out with his own. Their voices came back, acknowledging.

"Lock to destination," said Jim. "Dispersal pattern K at destination. Repeat, pattern K, tight, hundred kilometer interval. Hundred kilometer interval." He glanced at the sweep second hand of the clock before him on his control board. "Transmit in six seconds. Counting. Five. Four. Three. Two. One. Transmit——"

Again, the disorientation, and the nausea.

Strange stars were around them.

"Check Ten," whispered Jim. It was the code for "make next jump immediately." "Three. Two. One. Transmit——"

Once again the wrench of dislocation. Nausea.

Darkness. They were alone amongst the enemy's stars. None of the other ships were in sight.

"*Swallow . . .*" came a whisper in his earphones as from somewhere unseen as a tight, short-range, light-borne beam touched the outside of the *Fourth Mary*, beaming its message to his ears. "*Fair Maid. Lela . . .*" a slightly longer pause. "*Andfriend.*"

*Andfriend* was always a laggard. Jim had braced her pilot about it a dozen times. But now was not the hour for reprimands. They were deep in Laggi territory, and the alien alert posts would have already picked up the burst of energy not only from their transmit off the Frontier, but from the second jump to over a hundred light years deep in Laggi territory. Communication between the ships of the Section must be held to a minimum while the aliens were still trying to figure out where the second jump had landed the intruders.

Shortly, since they must know by now of the approximate position of *La Chasse Gallerie* and have ships on the way to kill her, they would put two and two together and expect to find the intruders in the same area. But for the moment Wander Section, if it lay low and quiet, could feel it was safely hidden in the immensities of enemy space.

Jim blocked off outside transmission, and spoke over the intercom to Walt.

"All right, bodysnatcher," he said. "What was it you wanted to say to me back at the Frontier?"

There was a slight pause before the other's voice came back.

"Sir——"

"Never mind that," said Jim. "I don't count Reserve officers as the real thing. As far as I'm concerned you're a civilian. What was it you wanted, Wa—bodysnatcher?"

"All right, Major," said the voice of Walt. "I won't bother about military manners with what I call you, and I won't bother with what you call me." There was a slight grimness of humor in the voice of the geriatrics man. "I wanted to say—I'd like to get in close enough to *La Chasse Gallerie* so that we can keep a tight beam connection with her hull at all times and I can record everything Penard says from the time of contact on. It'll be important."

"Don't worry," said Jim. "He'll be along in a few minutes, if my calculations were right, and I'll put you right up next to him. We're going to surround him with our ships, lock him in the middle of us with magnetics, and try to boost out as a unit at something more practical than the little ten light-year at a time jumps that seem to be all he's able to compute."

"You say he'll be along?" said Walt. "Why didn't we go directly to him?"

"And make it absolutely clear to the Laggi he's what we're after?" answered Jim. "As long as they don't know for sure, they have to assume we don't even know of his existence. So we stop ahead in his line of travel—lucky he's just plugging straight ahead without trying any dodges—and wait for him. We might even make it look like an accidental meeting to the Laggi"—Jim smiled inside the privacy of his suit's headpiece without much humor—"I don't think."

"Do you think you can lock on him without too much trouble——"

"Depends," answered Jim, "on how fast he starts shooting at us when he sees us."

"Shooting at us?" there was incredulity in Walt's voice. "Why should he—oh." His voice dropped. "I see."

"That's right," said Jim, "we don't look like any human ship he could know about, and he's in territory where he's going to be expecting bandits, not friends."

"But what're you going to do to stop him shooting?"

"They dug up the recognition signals of the Sixty Ships Battle," said Jim. "Just pray he remembers them. And they've given me a voice signal that my blinker lights can translate and flash at him in the code he was working under at the time of the battle. Maybe it'll work, maybe it won't."

"It will," said Walt, calmly.

"Oh?" Jim felt harshness in his chest. "What makes you so sure?"

"It's my field, Major. It's my business to know how the aged react. And one of their common reactions is to forget recent events and remember the events of long ago. Their childhood. High points of their early life—and the Sixty Ships Battle will have been one of those."

"So you think Penard will remember?"

"I think so," said Walt. "I think he'll remember with almost hypnotic recall."

Jim grinned again, mirthlessly, privately in his suit.

"You'd better be right," he said. "It's one order of impossibility to pick him up and take him home. It's another to fight off the Laggi while we're doing it. To fight Penard at the same time would be a third order—and that's beyond mortal men."

"Yes," said Walt. "You don't like to think of man as anything but mortal, do you, Major?"

"Why, you—" Jim bit back the rest of the words that flung themselves into his throat. He sat rigid and sweating in his suit, his hand lying across the accessible flap that would let

149

him reach in and draw his side-arm without losing atmosphere from inside the suit. This crum—this *crum*—he thought, who doesn't know what it's like to see men die . . . ! The impulse to do murder passed after a moment, leaving Jim trembling and spent. There was the sour taste of stomach acids in his mouth.

"We'll see," he said shakily over the intercom. "We'll see, bodysnatcher."

"Why put it in the future, Major?" said the voice of the other. "Why not tell me plainly what you've got against someone working in geriatrics?"

"Nothing," said Jim. "It's nothing to do with me. Let'm all live forever."

"Something wrong with that?"

"I don't see the point of it," said Jim. "You've got the average age up pushing a hundred. What good does it do?" His throat went a little dry. *I shouldn't talk so much*, he thought. But he went on and said it, anyway. "What's the use of it?"

"People are pretty vigorous up through their nineties. If we can push it further. . . . Here's Penard who's over two hundred——"

"And what's the use of it? Vigorous!" said Jim, the words breaking out of him. "Vigorous enough to totter around and sit in the sunlight. What do you think's the retirement age from Frontier duty?"

"I know what it is," said Walt. "It's thirty-two."

"Thirty-two." Jim sneered. "So you've got all these extra vigorous years of life for people, have you? If they're all that vigorous, why can't they ride a Frontier ship after thirty-two? I'll tell you why, bodysnatcher. It's because they're too old— too old physically, too old in the reflexes and the nerves! Snatch all the ancient bodies back from the brink of the grave, but you can't change that. So what good's your extra sixty-eight years?"

"Maybe you ought to ask Raoul Penard that," said Walt, softly.

A dark wave of pain and unhappiness rose inside Jim, so that he had to clench his teeth to hold it back from coming out in words.

"Never mind him." Jim said huskily. For a second it was as if he had been through it himself, all the endless years, refusing to die, beating his ship back toward the Frontier, and the Solar System, at little jumps of ten light-years' length apiece—and home. I'll get him home, thought Jim to himself—I'll get Penard to the home he's been after these two centuries if I have to take him through every Laggi Picket area between here and the Frontier. "Never mind him," Jim said again to Walt, "he was a fighter."

"He still is——" Walt was cut suddenly short by the ringing of the contact alarm. Jim's fingers slapped by reflex down on his bank of buttons and a moment later they swam up beside a dust-scarred cone-shape with the faded legend *La Chasse Gallerie* visible on its side.

In the same moment, the other ships of Wander Section were appearing on other sides of the ancient spaceship. Their magnetic beams licked out and locked—and held, a fraction of a second before *La Chasse Gallerie* buckled like a wild horse and tried to escape by a jump at translight speeds.

The mass of the five other ships held her back.

"Hold—" Jim was whispering into the headpiece of his suit, and circuits were translating his old-fashioned phrases into blinking signal lights beamed at the coneshape ship. "Hold. This is Government Rescue Contingent, title Wander Section. Do not resist. We are taking you in tow—" the unfitness of the ancient word jarred in Jim's mouth as he said it. "We're taking you in tow to return you to Earth Headquarters. Repeat...."

The flashing lights went on spelling the message out, over and over again. *La Chasse Gallerie* ceased fighting and hung docilely in the matching net of magnetic forces. Jim got a talk beam touching on the aged hull.

"... home," a voice was saying, the same voice he had heard recorded in Mollen's office. "Chez moi ..." it broke into a tangle of French that Jim could not follow, and emerged in accented English with the cadence of poetry, "... *Poleon, hees sojer never fight—more brave as dem poor habitants—Chenier, he try for broke de rank—Chenier come dead immediatement ...*"*

"*La Chassee Gallerie. La Chasse Gallerie,*" Jim was saying over and over, while the blinking lights on his hull transformed the words into a ship's code two centuries dead, "can you understand me? Repeat, can you understand me? If so,

---

* From "De Papineau Gun," by William Henry Drummond, in *The Habitant And Other French-Canadian Poems*, copyright 1897 by G. P. Putnam's Sons.

acknowledge. Acknowledge. . . ." There was no response from the dust-scarred hull, slashed by the Laggi weapons. Only the voice, reciting what Jim now recognized as a poem by William Henry Drummond, one of the early poets to write in the French-accented English of the French-Canadian habitant in the late nineteenth century.

". . . *De gun day rattle lak' tonnere*," muttered on the voice, "*just bang, bang, bang! dat's way she go*—" abruptly the voice of Raoul Penard shifted to poetry in the pure French of another poem by a medieval prisoner looking out the tower window of his prison on the springtime. The shift was in perfect cadence and rhyme with the earlier line in dialectical English.

"*Le temps a laissé ton mantau—de vent, de froidure, et de pluie* . . ."

"It's no use," said Walt. "We'll have to get him back to Earth and treatment before you'll be able to get through to him."

"All right," said Jim. "Then we'll head——"

The moan of an interior siren blasted through his suit.

"Bandits," yelped the voice of *Andfriend*. "Five bandits, sector six——"

"Bandits. Two bandits, sector two, fifteen hundred kilometers—" broke in the voice of *Lela*.

Jim swore and slapped his fingers down on the buttons. With all ships locked together, his jump impulse was sorted automatically through the computer center of each one so that they all jumped together in the direction and distance he had programmed. There was the wrench of feeling—and sudden silence.

The siren had cut off. The voices were silent. Automatic dispersal had taken place, and the other four ships were spreading out rapidly to distances up to a thousand kilometers on all sides, their receptors probing the empty space for half a light year in each direction, quivering, seeking.

"Looks like we got away," Walt's voice was eerie in its naturalness, breaking the stillness in Jim's headpiece. "Looks like they lost us."

"The hell they did!" said Jim, savagely. "They'll have unmanned detector probes strung out all the way from here to the Frontier. They know we're not going anyplace else."

"Then we'd better jump again——"

"Not yet! Shut up, will you!" Jim bit the words off hard at

his lips. "The more they collect to hit us with here, the more we leave behind when we jump again. Sit still back there and keep your mouth shut. You're a gunner now, not a talker."

"Yes sir." There was no mockery in Walt's voice. This time Jim did not comment on the "sir."

The seconds moved slowly with the sweep hand of the clock in front of Jim. Inside the headpiece his face was dripping with perspiration. The blood creaked in his ears——.

Moan of siren!

"Bandits!" shouted the *Fair Maid*. "Four bandits——"

"Bandits!" Bandits!"—Suddenly the helmet was full of warning cries from all the ships. The telltale sphere in front of Jim came alive with the green dots of Laggi ships, over and beyond the white dots of his own Section.

They came on, the green dots, with the illusion of seeming to spread apart as they advanced. They came on and——

Suddenly they were gone. They had winked out, disappeared as if they had never been there in the first place.

"Formation Charlie," said Jim tonelessly to the other four ships. They shifted their relative positions. Jim sat silent, sweat dripping off his chin inside his suit. He could feel the growing tension in the man behind him.

"Jump!" It was a whisper torn from a raw throat in Walt. "Why don't you jump?"

"Where to, bodysnatcher?" whispered back Jim. "They'll have planet-based computers the size of small cities working on our probabilities of movement now. Anywhere we jump now in a straight line for the Frontier, they'll be waiting for us."

"Then jump to a side point. Evade!"

"If we do that," whispered Jim, "we'll have to recalculate." He suddenly realized the other's whispering had brought him to lower his own voice to a thread. Deliberately he spoke out loud, but with transmission of the conversation to the other ships of the Section blocked off. "Recalculation takes time. They'll be using that time to find us—and they've got bigger and better equipment for it than the computing centers aboard these little ships."

"But what're we waiting for? Why'd they go away? Shouldn't we go now——"

"No!" snarled Jim. "They went away because they thought there weren't enough of them."

"Not enough? There were twice our number."

"Not enough," said Jim. "They want to kill us all at one swat. They don't want any of us to escape. It's not just *La Chasse Gallerie*. Enemy ships can't be allowed to get this deep into their territory and live. We'd do the same thing if Laggi ships came into our space. We'd have to make an object lesson of them—so they wouldn't try it again."

"But——"

"Bandits—Bandits! Bandits!"

Suddenly the pilots of all the vessels were shouting at once. Jim's hand slammed down on a button and four screens woke to life, showing the interior of the other four ships. The sight and sound of the other pilots and gunners were there before his eyes.

The spherical telltale was alive with green dots, closing in from all sectors of the area, racing to englobe the Wander Section.

"James! Pattern James!" Jim heard his own voice shouting to the other ships. "James. Hit, break out, and check Ten. Check Ten. . . ."

They were driving toward one group of the approaching green lights. *La Chasse Gallerie* was driving with them. Over the shouting back and forth of the Wander Section pilots came the voice of Raoul Penard, shouting, singing—a strange, lugubrious tune but in the cadence and tone of a battle song. As if through the winds of a nightmare, Jim heard him:

*Frainchman, he don't lak to die in de fall!*
*When de mairsh she am so full of de game!*
*An de leetle bool-frog, he's roll veree fat . . .*
*And de leetle mooshrat, he's jus' de same!*

The slow and feeble lasers of the old ship reached out toward the oncoming Laggi lights that were ships, pathetically wide of their mark. Something winked up ahead and suddenly the soft, uncollapsed metal of the point of the primitive, dust-scarred hull was no longer there. Then Wander Section had closed with some eight of the enemy.

The *Fourth Mary* suddenly bucked and screamed. Her internal temperature suddenly shot up momentarily to nearly two hundred degrees as a glancing blow from the light-weapon of one of the Laggi brushed her. There was a moment of insanity. Flame flickered suddenly in the interior of

154

*Fair Maid,* obscuring the screen before Jim, picturing that ship's interior. Then they were past the enemy fifteen and Jim shouted hoarsely "Transmit!" at the same time that he locked his own magnetic beams on the chopped hull of *La Chasse Gallerie* and tried to take her through the jump alone.

It should not have been possible. But some sixth sense in the singing, crazed mind of Raoul Penard seemed to understand what Jim was attempting. The two ships jumped together under the *Fourth Mary*'s control, and suddenly all five ships floated within sight of each other amid the peace and darkness of empty space and the alien stars.

Into this silence came the soft sound of sobbing from one of the screens. Jim looked and saw the charred interior of the *Fair Maid.* Her pilot was out of his seat and half-crouched before the charred barrel-suited figure in the gunner's chair.

*"Fair Maid!"* Jim had to repeat the call, more sharply. *"Fair Maid!* Acknowledge!"

The pilot's headpiece lifted. The sobbing stopped.

*"Fair Maid* here." The voice was thick-tongued, drugged-sounding. "I had to shoot my gunner, Wander Leader. He was burning up inside his suit. I had to shoot my gunner. He was burning up inside his——"

*"Fair Maid!"* snapped Jim. "Can you still compute and jump?"

"Yes . . ." said the drugged voice. "I can compute and jump, Wander Leader."

"All right, *Fair Maid,*" said Jim. "You're to jump wide—angle off outside Laggi territory and then make your own way back to our side of the Frontier. Have you got that? Jump wide, and make your own way back. Jump far enough so that it won't be worth the Laggi's trouble to go after you."

"No!" The voice lost some of its druggedness. "I'm staying, Wander Leader. I'm going to kill some——"

*"Fair Maid!"* Jim heard his own voice snarling into his headpiece. "This Section has a mission—to bring back the ship we've just picked up in Laggi territory. You're no good on that mission—you're no good to this Section without a gunner. Jump wide and go home! Do you hear me? That's an order. Jump wide and go home!"

There was a moment's silence, and then the pilot's figure moved slowly and turned slowly back to sit down before his controls.

"Acknowledge, *Fair Maid!*" snapped Jim.

"Acknowledge," came the lifeless voice of the pilot in the burned interior of the ship. "Jumping wide and going home."

"Out then," said Jim, in a calmer voice. "Good luck getting back. So long, Jerry."

"So long, Wander Leader," came the numb reply. The gloved hands moved on the singed controls. *Fair Maid* vanished.

Jim sat back wearily in his pilot's chair. Hammering into his ears came the voice of Raoul Penard, now crooning another verse of his battle song:

> *... Come all you beeg Canada man*
> *Who want find work on Meeshegan,*
> *Dere's beeg log drive all troo our lan',*
> *You sure fin' work on Meesh——*

In a sudden reflex of rage, Jim's hand slapped down on a button, cutting off in midword the song from *La Chasse Gallerie*.

"Major!"

The word was like a whip cracking across his back. Jim started awake to the fact of his passenger-gunner behind him.

"Well, bodysnatcher!" he said. "Who's been feeding you raw meat?"

"I think I've got my second wind in this race," answered the even, cold voice of Walt. "Meanwhile, how about turning Penard back on? My job's to record everything I can get from him, and I can't do that with the talk beam between us shut off."

"The *Fair Maid*'s gunner just died——"

"*Turn the talk beam on!*"

Jim reached out and turned it on, wondering a little at himself. I should feel like shooting him at this moment, he thought. Why don't I? Penard's voice sang at him once again.

"Look," Jim began. "When a man dies and a ship is lost——"

"Have you looked at Penard's ship, Major?" interrupted the voice of Walt. "Take a look. Then maybe you'll understand why I want the talk beam on just as long as there's any use."

Jim turned and looked at the screen that showed the cone-shaped vessel. He stared.

If *La Chasse Gallerie* had been badly cut up before, she

was a floating chunk of scrap now. She had been slashed deep in half a dozen directions by the light beams of the Laggi ships. And the old-fashioned ceramet material of her hull, built before collapsed metals had been possible, had been opened up like cardboard under the edge of red-hot knives. Jim stared, hearing the voice of Penard singing in his ears, and an icy trickle went down his perspiration-soaked spine.

"He can't be alive," Jim heard himself saying. If a hit that did not even penetrate the collapsed metal hull of the *Fair Maid* could turn that ship's interior into a charred, if workable, area—what must those light weapons of the enemy have done to the interior of the old ship he looked at now? But Raoul still sang from it his song about lumbering in Meeshegan.

"Nobody could be alive in that," Jim said. "I was right. It must be just his semianimate control system parroting him and running the ship. Even at that, it's a miracle it's still working——"

"We don't know," Walt's voice cut in on him. "And until we know we have to assume it's Raoul himself, still alive. After all, his coming back at all is an impossible miracle. If that could happen, it could happen he's still alive in that ship now. Maybe he's picked up some kind of protection we don't know about."

Jim shook his head, forgetting that probably Walt could not see this silent negative. It was not possible that Penard was alive. But—he roused himself back to his duty. He had a job to do.

His fingers began to dance over the black buttons in their ranks before him, working out the situation, planning his next move.

"K formation," he said automatically to the other ships, but did not even glance at the telltale sphere to make sure they obeyed correctly. Slowly, the situation took form. He was down one ship, from five to four of them, and that reduced the number of practical fighting and maneuvering formations by a factor of better than three. And there was something else. . . .

"Walt," he said, slowly.

"Yes, Major?"

"I want your opinion on something," said Jim. "When we jumped out of the fight area just now, it was a jump off the direct route home and to the side of nearly sixty light years. I had to try to pick up *La Chasse Gallerie* and bring her with us. Penard let me do that without fighting me with his own controls. Now, what I want to know is—and it's almost unimaginable that he's got power on that hulk, anyway, but he obviously has—will he let me move him from now on without fighting me, once I slap a magnetic on him? In other words, whether he's a man or a semianimate control, was that a fluke last time, or can I count on it happening again?"

Walt did not answer immediately. Then . . .

"I think you can count on it," he said. "If Raoul Penard is alive in there, the fact he reacted sensibly once should be an indication he'll do it again. And if you're right about it being just a control center driving that ship, then it should react consistently in the same pattern to the same stimulus."

"Yeah . . ." said Jim softly. "But I wonder which it is—is Penard in there, alive or dead? Is it a man we're trying to get out? Or a control center?"

"Does it matter?" said the level voice of Walt.

Jim stiffened.

"Not to you, does it, bodysnatcher?" he said. "But I'm the man that has to order men to kill themselves to get that ship home." Something tightened in his throat. "You know that's what hit me when I first saw you in Mollen's office, but I didn't know what it was. You haven't got guts inside you, you've got statistical tables and a computer."

He could hear his own harsh breathing in the headpiece of his suit as he finished talking.

"You think so?" said Walt's voice, grimly. "And how about you, Major? The accidents of birth and change while you were growing up gave you a one-in-billions set of mind and reflexes. You were born to be a white knight and slay dragons. Now you're in the dragon-slaying business and something's gone wrong with it you can't quite figure out. Something's gone sour, hasn't it?"

"Shut up!" said Jim, sweating. He felt his gloved hand resting on the access flap to his sidearm inside the suit. *I'm within my rights,* the back of his mind told him, crazily, *regulations provide for it. The pilot of a two-man ship is still the captain with the power of life and death in emergency over his crew even if that crew is only one man. If I shot him and gave a good reason, they might suspect, but they couldn't do anything. . . .*

"No," said Walt. "You've been going out of your way ever since you laid eyes on me to provoke this—now listen to it. Your nerves are shot, Major. You've a bad case of combat fatigue, but you won't quit and you're so valuable that people like Mollen won't make you quit."

"Play-party psychiatrist, are you?" demanded Jim through gritted teeth. Walt ignored him.

"You think I didn't have a chance to look at your personal history before I met you?" said Walt. "You know better than to think that. You're a Canadian yourself, and your background is Scotch and French. That's all anyone needs to know to read the signs—and the signs all read the same way. Your ship's named the *Fourth Mary*. And the *Fourth Mary* was the one that died, remember?" Abruptly he quoted from the old Scots ballad: *"Last night there were four Marys— tonight there'll be but three——"*

*"Shut up!"* husked Jim, the words choking in his throat.

"The signs read 'dead,' Major. All of them, including the fact you hate me for being in the business of trying to make people live longer. It was victory over evil you wanted in the first place—like the evil that makes men burn and die in their Frontier ships. Victory, or death. And now that you've been worn down to the conclusion that you can't win that victory, you want death. But you're not built right for suicide. That's the trouble. . . ."

Jim tried to speak, but the strained muscles of his throat let out only a little, wordless rasp of air.

"Death's got to come and take you, Major," said Walt. There was a trace of something like brutality in his voice. "And he's got to take you against the most of your strength, against all your fighting will. He's got to take you in spite of yourself. *And Death can't do it!* That's what's wrong with you, isn't it, Major?" Walt paused. "That's why you don't want to grow old and be forced to leave out here, where Death lives."

Walt's voice broke off. Jim sat, fighting for breath, his gloved fingers trembling on the access flap to the sidearm. After a little, his breath grew deeper again, and he forced himself to turn back to his computations. Aside from the habit-instructed section of his mind that concerned itself with this problem, the rest of him was mindless.

*I've got to do something*, he thought. *I've got to do something.* But nothing would come to mind. Gradually the careening vessel of his mind righted itself, and he came back to a sense of duty—to Wander Section and his mission. Then suddenly a thought woke in him.

"Raoul Penard's got to be dead," he said quite calmly to Walt. "Somehow, what we've been hearing and what we've been watching drive and fight that ship is the semianimate control center. How it got to be another Raoul Penard doesn't matter. The tissue they used kept growing, and no one ever thought to keep one of them in contact with a man twenty-four hours a day for his lifetime. So it's the alter-ego, the control center we've got to bring in. And there's a way to do that."

He paused and waited. There was a second of silence, and then Walt's voice spoke.

"Maybe I underestimated you, Major."

"Maybe you did," said Jim. "At any rate, here it is. In no more than another half hour we're going to be discovered here. Those planet-based big computers have been piling up data on our mission here and on me as Leader of Section, and their picture gets more complete every time we move and they can get new data. If we dodged away from here to hide again, next time they'd find us even faster. And in two more hides they'd hit us almost as soon as we got hid. So there's no choice to it. We've got to go for the Frontier now."

"Yes," said Walt. "I can see we do."

"You can," said Jim. "And the Laggi can. Everybody can. But they also know I know that they've got most of the area from here to the Frontier covered. Almost anywhere we come out they'll be ready to hit us within seconds, with ships that are simply sitting there, ready to make jump to wherever we emerge, their computations to the forty of fifty areas within easy jump of them already computed for them by the big planet-based machines. So, there's only one thing left for me to do, as they see it—go wide."

"Wide?" said Walt. He sounded a trifle startled.

"Sure," said Jim, grinning mirthlessly to himself in the privacy of his suit. "Like I sent *Fair Maid*. But there's a difference between us and *Fair Maid*. We've got *La Chasse Gallerie*. And the Laggi'll follow us. We'll have to keep running—outward until their edge in data lets them catch up with us. And their edge in ship numbers finishes us off. The Laggi ships won't quit on our trail—even if it means they won't get back themselves. As I said a little earlier, enemy ships can't be allowed to get this deep into their territory and get home again."

"So you're going wide," said Walt. "What's the use? It just puts off the time——"

"I'm not going wide." Jim grinned privately and mirthlessly once more. "That's what the Laggi think I'll do, hoping for a miracle to save us. I'm going instead where no one with any sense would go—right under their weapons. I've computed two jumps to the Frontier which is the least we can make it in. We'll lock on and carry *La Chasse Gallerie,* and when we come out of the jump we'll come out shooting. Blind. We'll blast our way through whatever's there and jump again as fast as we can. If one of us survives, that'll be all that's necessary to lock on to *La Chasse Gallerie* and jump her to the Frontier. If none of us does—well, we've done our best."

Once more he paused. Walt said nothing.

"Now," said Jim, grinning like a death's head. "If that was a two-hundred-year-old man aboard that wreck of a ship there, and maybe burned badly or broken up by what he's been through so far, that business of jumping and coming out at fighting accelerations would kill him. But," said Jim, drawing a deep breath. "It's not a man. It's a control center. And a control center ought to be able to take it. . . . Have you got anything to say, Walt?"

"Yes," said Walt, quietly. "Officially I protest your assumption that Rauol Penard is dead, and your choice of an action which might be fatal to him as a result."

Jim felt a kind of awe stir in him.

"By—" he broke off. "Bodysnatcher, you really expect to come out of this alive, don't you?"

"Yes," said Walt, calmly. "I'm not afraid of living—the way you are. You don't know it, Jim, but there's a lot of people like you back home, and I meet them all the time. Ever since we started working toward a longer life for people, they've turned their backs on us. They say there's no sense in living a longer time—but the truth is they're afraid of it. Afraid a long life will show them up as failures, that they won't have death for an excuse for not making a go of life."

"Never mind that!" Jim's throat had gone dry again. "Stand to your guns. We're jumping now—and we'll be coming out shooting." He turned swiftly to punch the data key and inform his four remaining other ships. "Transmitting in five seconds. Five. Four. Three. Two. One. Transmit——"

Disorientation. Nausea. . . .

The stars were different. Acceleration hit like a tree trunk ramming into Jim's chest. His fingers danced on the sublight control buttons. The voice of Raoul Penard was howling his battle-song again:

> *. . . When you come drive de beeg saw log,*
> *You got to jump jus' lak de frog!*
> *De foreman come, he say go sak!*
> *You got in de watair all over your back!*

"Check Ten!" shouted Jim. "All ships check Ten. Transmit in three seconds. Three. Two——"

No Laggi ships in the telltale sphere. . . .

Suddenly the *Fourth Mary* bucked and slammed. Flame flickered for a fraction of a second through the cabin. The telltale was alive with green lights, closing fast.

Fifteen of them or more. . . . Directly ahead of the *Fourth Mary* were three of them in formation, closing on her alone. In Jim's ears rang the wild voice of Penard:

> *P'raps you work on drive, tree-four day—*
> *You find dat drive dat she don' pay.*

"Gunner!" cried Jim, seeing the green lights almost on top of him. It was as desperate as a cry for help. In a moment——

Two of the green lights flared suddenly and disappeared. The third flashed and veered off.

"Bodysnatcher!" yelped Jim, suddenly drunk on battle delight. "You're a gunner! A real gunner!"

"More to the left and up—Sector Ten—" said a thick voice he could hardly recognize as Walt's, in his ear. He veered, saw two more green lights. Saw one flare and vanish—saw suddenly one of his own white lights flare and vanish as the scream of torn metal sounded from one of the screens below him. Glancing at the screens, he saw for the moment the one picturing *Andfriend*'s cabin, showing the cabin split open, emptied and flattened for a second before the screen went dark and blank.

Grief tore at him. And rage.

"Transmit at will!" he howled at the other ships.

"Check Ten! Check Ten——"

He slapped a magnetic on the battered cone shape that fled by a miracle still beside him and punched for the jump——

Disorientation. Nausea. And——

The stars of the Frontier. Jim stared into his screens. They floated in empty space, three gray-white dart shapes and the ravaged cone of *La Chasse Gallerie. Lela* rode level with Jim's ship, but *Swallow* was slowly turning sideways like a dying fish drifting in the ocean currents. Jim stared into the small screen showing the *Swallow's* interior. The two suited figures sat in a blackened cabin, unmoving.

"*Swallow!*" said Jim, hoarsely. "Are you all right? Acknowledge. Acknowledge!"

But there was no answer from the two figures, and the *Swallow* continued to drift, turning, as if she was sliding off some invisible slope into the endless depths of the universe. Jim shook with a cold, inner sickness like a chill. They're just unconscious, he thought. They have to be just unconscious. Otherwise they wouldn't have been able to make the jump to here.

". . . *Brigadier!*" the voice of Penard was singing with strange softness . . .

*. . . repondit Pandore*
*Brigadier! vous avez raison,*
*Brigadier! repondit Pandore*
*Brigadier! vous avez raison!*"

Jim turned slowly to look in to the screen showing *La Chasse Gallerie.* He stared at what he saw. If the old ship had been badly slashed before, she was a ruin now. Nothing could be alive in such a wreck. Nothing. But the voice of Penard sang on.

"No . . ." muttered Jim out loud, unbelievingly. "Not even a semianimate control center could come through that. It couldn't——"

"Identify yourself!" crackled a voice suddenly on Jim's ears. "Identify yourself! This is Picket Six. B Sector, Frontier area."

"Wander Section . . ." muttered Jim, automatically thumbing the communications control, still staring at the tattered cone shape of *La Chasse Gallerie.* Once more he remembered the original legend about the return of the dead voyageurs in their ghost canoe, and a shiver went down his back. "Wander Section, returning from deep probe and rescue mission into Laggi territory. Five ships with two lost and one sent wide and home, separately. Wander Leader speaking."

"Wander Leader!" crackled the voice from Picket Six. "Alert has been passed all along the Frontier for you and your ships and orders issued for your return. Congratulations, Wander Section and welcome back."

"Thanks, Picket Six," said Jim, wearily. "It's good to be back, safe on this side of the Frontier. We had half the Laggi forces breathing down our——"

A siren howled from the control board, cutting him off. Unbelieving, Jim jerked his head about to stare at the telltale sphere. It was filled with the white lights of the ships of Picket Six in formation spread out over a half light-year of distance. But, as he watched, green lights began to wink into existence all about his own battered Section. By sixes, by dozens, they were jumping into the area of Picket Six on the human side of the Frontier.

"Formation B! Formation B!" Jim found himself shouting at the *Lela* and the *Swallow*. But only the *Lela* responded. The *Swallow*, lost to ordinary vision, was still on its long, drowning fall into nothingness still. "Cancel that. *Lela*, follow me. Help me carry *La Chasse*——"

His voice was all but drowned out by transmissions from Picket Six.

"Alert General. Alert General! All Pickets, all Sectors!" Picket Six was calling. "Full fleet Laggi attack. Three wings enemy forces already in this area. We are overmatched! Repeat. We are overmatched! Alert General——"

At maximum normal acceleration, the *Fourth Mary* and *Lela*, with *La Chasse Gallerie* caught in a magnetic grip between them, were running from the enemy ships, while Jim computed frantically for a jump to any safe area, his fingers dancing on the black buttons.

"Alert General! All ships Picket Six hold until relieved. All ships hold! Under fire here at Picket Six. We are under——" the voice of Picket Six went dead. There was a moment's silence and then a new voice broke in.

"——This is Picket Five. Acknowledge, Picket Six. Acknowledge!" Another moment of silence, then the new voice went on. "All ships Picket Six. This is Picket Five taking over. Picket Five taking over. Our ships are on the way to you now, and the ships from other Sectors. Hold until relieved! Hold until relieved——"

Jim fought the black buttons, too busy even to swear.

"Wander Section! Wander Section!" shouted the voice of Picket Five. "Acknowledge!"

"Wander Section. Acknowledging!" grunted Jim.

"Wander Section! Jump for home. Wander Leader, key for data. Key to receive data, and Check Ten. Check Ten."

"Acknowledge!" snapped Jim, dropping his own slow computing. He keyed for data, saw the data light flash and knew he had received into his computing center the information for the jump back to Earth. "Hang on *Lela!*" he shouted. "Here we go. . . ."

He punched for jump——

Disorientation. Nausea. And . . .

Peace.

The *Fourth Mary* lay without moving under the landing lights of a concrete pad in the open, under the nighttime sky and the stars of Earth. The daylight hours had passed while Wander Section had been gone. Next to the *Fourth Mary* lay the dark, torn shape of *La Chasse Gallerie,* and beyond the ancient ship lay *Lela.* Three hundred light-years away the Frontier battle would still be raging. Laggi and men were out there dying, and they would go on dying until the Laggi realized that Wander Section had finally made good its escape. Then the Laggi ships would withdraw from an assault against a Frontier line that two hundred and more years of fighting had taught was unbreachable by either combatant. But how many, thought Jim with a dry and bitter bleakness, would die before the withdrawal was made?

He punched the button to open the port of the *Fourth Mary,* and got clumsily to his feet in the bulky suit. During the hours just past he had forgotten he was wearing it. Now, it was like being swaddled in a mattress. He was as thoroughly wet with sweat as if he had been in swimming with his clothes on.

There was no sound coming from *La Chasse Gallerie.* Had the voice of Raoul Penard finally been silenced? Sodden with weariness, Jim could not summon up the energy even to wonder about it. He turned clumsily around and stumbled back through the ship four steps and out the open port, vaguely hearing Walt Trey rising and following behind him.

He stumped heavy-footed across the concrete toward the lights of the Receiving Section, lifting like an ocean liner out of a sea of night. It seemed to him that he was a long time reaching the door of the Section, but he kept on stolidly, and at last he passed through and into a desuiting room. Then attendants were helping him off with his suit.

In a sort of dream he stripped off his soaked clothing and showered, and put on a fresh jumper suit. The cloth felt strange and harsh against his arms and legs as if his body as well as what was inside him had been rubbed raw by what he had just been through. He walked heavily on into the debriefing room, and dropped heavily into one of the lounge chairs.

A debriefing officer came up to him and sat down in a chair opposite, turning on the little black recorder pickup he wore at his belt. The debriefing officer began asking questions in the safe, quiet monotone that had been found least likely to trigger off emotional outbursts in the returned pilots. Jim answered slowly, too drained for emotion.

". . . No," he said at last. "I didn't see *Swallow* again. She didn't acknowledge when I called for Formation B, and I had to go on without her. No, she never answered after we reached the Frontier."

"Thank you, Major." The debriefing officer got to his feet, clicking off his recorder pickup, and went off. An enlisted man came around with a tray of glasses half filled with brownish whisky. He offered it first to the pilot and the gunner of the *Lela*, who were standing together on the other side of the room with a debriefing officer. The two men took their glasses absent-mindedly and drank from them without reaction, as if the straight liquor had been water. The enlisted man brought his tray over to where Jim sat.

Jim shook his head. The enlisted man hesitated.

"You're supposed to drink it, sir," he said. "Surgeon's orders."

Jim shook his head again. The enlisted man went away. A moment later he came back followed by a major with the caduceus of the Medical Corps on his jacket lapel.

"Here, Major," he said to Jim, taking a glass from the tray and holding it out to Jim. "Down the hatch."

Jim shook his head, rolling the back of it against the top of the chair he sat in.

"It's no good," he said. "It doesn't do any good."

The Medical Corps major put the glass back on the tray and leaned forward. He put his thumb gently under Jim's right eye and lifted the lid with his forefinger. He looked for a second, then let go and turned to the enlisted man.

"That's all right," he said. "You can go on."

The enlisted man took his tray of glasses away. The doctor reached into the inside pocket of his uniform jacket and took out a small silver tube with a button on its side. He rolled up Jim's right sleeve, put the end of the tube against it and pressed the button.

Jim felt what seemed like a cooling spray against the skin of his arm. And something woke in him, after all.

"What're you doing?" he shouted, struggling to his feet. "You can't knock me out now! I've got two ships not in yet. The *Fair Maid* and the *Swallow*—" The room began to tilt around him. "You can't—" his tongue thickened into unintelligibility. The room swung grandly around him and he felt the medical major's arms catching him. And unconsciousness closed upon him like a trap of darkness.

He slept, evidently for a long time, and when he woke he was not in the bed of his own quarters but in the bed of a hospital room. Nor did they let him leave it for the better part of a week, and when he did, it was to go on sixty days' leave. Nonetheless, he had had time, lying there in the peaceful, uneventful hospital bed, to come to an understanding with himself. When he got out he went looking for Walt Trey.

He located the geriatrics man finally on the secret site where *La Chasse Gallerie* was being probed and examined by the Geriatrics Bureau. Walt was at work with the crew that was doing this, and for some little time word could not be gotten to him; and without his authorization, Jim could not be let in to see him.

Jim waited patiently in a shiny, sunlit lounge until a young man came to guide him into the interior of a vast building where *La Chasse Gallerie* lay dwarfed by her surroundings and surrounded by complicated items of equipment. It was apparently a break period for most of the people working on the old ship, for only one or two figures were to be seen doing things with this equipment outside the ship. The young man shouted in through the open port of *La Chasse Gallerie*, and left. Walt came out and shook hands with Jim.

There were dark circles under Walt's eyes and he seemed thinner under the loose shirt and slacks he wore.

"Sorry to hear about *Swallow*," he said.

"Yes," said Jim, a little bleakly, "they think she must have drifted back into Laggi territory. The unmanned probes couldn't locate her, and the Laggi may have taken her in. That's what chews on you, of course, not knowing if her pilot and gunner were dead or not. If they were, then there's nothing to think about. But if they weren't . . . we'll never know what becomes of them—" He broke off that train of thought with a strong effort of will. "*Fair Maid* made it in, safely. Anyway, it wasn't about the Section I came to see you."

"No," Walt looked at him sympathetically. "It was about Raoul Penard you came, wasn't it?"

"I couldn't find out anything. Is it—is he, alive?"

"Yes," said Walt. "He's alive."

"Can you get through to him? What came to me," said Jim, quickly, "while I was resting up in the hospital, was that I finally began to understand the reason behind all his po-etry-quoting, and such. It struck me that he must have started all that deliberately. To remind himself of where he was try-ing to get back to. To make it sharp and clear in his mind so he couldn't forget it."

"Yes," said Walt nodding. "You're right. He wanted insur-ance against quitting, against giving up."

"I thought so. You were right—bodysnatcher," Jim grinned with slight grimness at the other man. "I'd been trying to quit myself. Or find something that could quit me. You were right all the way down the line. I am a dragon-slayer. I was born that way. I'm stuck with it and I can't change it. I want to go through the Laggi, or around them and end this damn mur-derous stalemate. But I can't live long enough. None of us can. And so I wanted to give up."

"And you aren't now?"

"No," said Jim, slowly. "It's still no use, but I'm going to keep hoping—for a miracle."

"Miracles are a matter of time," said Walt. "To make yourself a millionaire in two minutes is just about impossible. To make it in two hundred years is practically a certainty. That's what we're after in the Bureau. If we could all live as long as Penard, all sorts of things would become possible."

"And he's alive!" said Jim, shaking his head slowly. "He's

really alive! I didn't even want to believe it, it was so far-fetched—" Jim broke off. "Is he . . ."

"Sane? No," said Walt. "And I don't think we'll ever be able to make him so. But maybe I'm wrong. As I say, with time, most near-impossibilities become practicabilities." He stepped back from the open port of *La Chasse Gallerie*, and gestured to the interior. "Want to come in?"

Jim hesitated.

"I don't have a Secret clearance for this project—" he began.

"Don't worry about it," interrupted Walt. "That's just to keep the news people off our necks until we decide how to handle this. Come on."

He led the way inside. Jim followed him. Within, the ancient metal corridor leading to the pilot's compartment seemed swept clean and dusted shiny, like some exhibit in a museum. The interior had been hung with magnetic lights, but the gaps and tears made by Laggi weapons let almost as much light in. The pilot's compartment was a shambles that had been tidied and cleaned. The instruments and control panel were all but obliterated and the pilot's chair half gone. A black box stood in the center of the floor, an incongruous piece of modern equipment, connected by a thick gray cable to a bulkhead behind it.

"I wasn't wrong, then," said Jim, looking around him. "No human body could have lived through this. It was the semianimate control center that was running the ship as Penard's alter ego, then, wasn't it? The man isn't really alive?"

"Yes," said Walt, "and no. You were right about the control center somehow absorbing the living personality of Penard. But look again. Could a control center like that, centered in living tissue floating and growing in a nutrient solution with no human hands to care for it—could something like that have survived this, either?"

Jim looked around at the slashed and ruined interior. A coldness crept into him and he thought once more of the legend of the long ghost cargo canoes sailing through the snow-filled skies with their dead crews, home to the New Year's feast of the living.

"No . . ." he said slowly, through stiff lips. "Then . . . where is he?"

"Here!" said Walt, reaching out with his fist to strike the metal bulkhead to which the gray cable was attached. The dull boom of the struck metal reverberated on Jim's ears. Walt looked penetratingly at Jim.

"You were right," said Walt, "when you said that the control center had become Penard—that it *was* Penard, after the man died. Not just a recordful of memories, but something holding the vital, decision-making spark of the living man himself. But that was only half the miracle. Because the tissue living in the heart of the control center had to die, too, and just as the original Penard knew he would die, long before he could get home, the tissue-Penard knew it, too. But their determination, Penard's determination, to do something, solved the problem."

He stopped and stood staring at Jim, as if waiting for some sign that he had been understood.

"Go on," said Jim.

"The control system," said Walt, "was connected to the controls of the ship itself through an intermediate solid-stage element which was the grandfather of the wholly inanimate solid-state computing centers in the ships you drive nowadays. The link was from living tissue through the area of solid-state physics to gross electronic and mechanical controls."

"I know that," said Jim. "Part of our training——"

"The living spark of Raoul Penard, driven by his absolute determination to get home, passed from him into the living tissue of the semianimate controls system," went on Walt, as if Jim had not spoken. "From there it bridged the gap by a sort of neurobiotaxis into the flow of impulse taking place in the solid-state elements. Once there, below all gross levels, there was nothing to stop it infusing every connected solid part of the ship."

Walt swept his hand around the ruined pilot's compartment.

"This," he said, "is Raoul Penard. And this!" Once more he struck the bulkhead above the black box. "The human body died. The tissue activating the control center died. But Raoul came home just as he had been determined to do!"

Walt stopped talking. His voice seemed to echo away into the silence of the compartment.

"And doing it," said Walt, more quietly, "he brought home the key we've been hunting for in the Bureau for over two hundred years. It's pulled the plug on the dam behind which there's been piling up a flood of theory and research.

What we needed to know was that the living human essence could exist independent of the normal human biochemical machinery. Now, we know it. It'll take a little time, but soon it won't be necessary for the vital element in anyone of us to admit extinction."

But Jim was only half listening. Something else had occurred to him, something so poignant it contracted his throat painfully.

"Does he know?" Jim asked. "You said he's insane. But does he know he finally got here? Does he know he made it—home?"

"Yes," said Walt. "We're sure he does. Listen. . . ."

He reached down and turned a control on the black box. And softly the voice of Raoul Penard came out of it, as if the man was talking to himself. But it was a quieter, happier talking to himself than Jim had heard before. Raoul was quoting another of the poems of William Henry Drummond. But this time it was a poem entirely in English and there was no trace of accent in the words at all:

> O, Spirit of the mountain that speaks to us to-night,
> Your voice is sad, yet still recalls past visions of delight,
> When 'mid the grand old Laurentides, old when the earth
> was new,
> With flying feet we followed the moose and caribou.
> And backward rush sweet memories, like fragments of a
> dream,
> We hear the dip of paddles. . . .

Raoul's voice went on, almost whispering contentedly to itself. Jim looked up from listening, and saw Walt's eyes fixed on him with a strange, hard look he had not seen before.

"You didn't seem to follow me, just now," said Walt. "You didn't seem to understand what I meant. You're one of our most valuable lives, the true white knight that all of us dream of being at one time or another, but only one in billions actually succeeds in being born to be."

Jim stared back at him.

"I told you," he said. "I can't help it."

"That's not what I'm talking about," said Walt. "You wanted to go out and fight the dragons, but life was too short. But what about now?"

"Now?" echoed Jim, staring at him. "You mean—me?"

"Yes," said Walt. His face was strange and intense, with the intensity of a crusader, and his voice seemed to float on the soft river of words flowing from the black box. "I mean you. What are you going to be doing—a thousand years from today?"

# MISS PRINKS

Miss Lydia Prinks was somebody's aunt. Not the aunt of several somebodies, but the aunt of one person only and with no other living brothers, sisters, cousins, nephews, or nieces to her name. A sort of singleton aunt. It would be possible to describe her further, but it would not be in good taste. To draw a clearer picture possibly would be to destroy the anonymity that Miss Prinks has, at the cost of a very great sacrifice indeed, maintained. Think of her then as a singleton aunt, and you have a pretty fair picture of her.

She lived on a sort of annuity in a small apartment up three flights of stairs on a certain street in a middle-sized city. The apartment had pale gold curtains of lace, a green carpet, and furniture upholstered in wine red. It had an assortment of good books in the bookcase and good pictures on the wall and a large, fat cat called Solomon on a footstool. It was a very proper sort of apartment for a singleton aunt living on an annuity, and Miss Prinks lived a peaceful, contented sort of life there.

That is to say, she *did* live a peaceful, contented sort of life until one afternoon just after lunch when the grandfather clock in the corner of the living room, having gone from twelve noon through twelve forty-five, went one step farther than it had ever done before, and instead of striking one o'clock, struck thirteen.

"What on earth——" said Miss Prinks, looking up astonished from her current Book-of-the-Month Club selection and staring at the clock. Solomon, the fat cat, also raised his head inquiringly.

173

*"What on earth!"* repeated Miss Prinks, indignantly. She stared hard at the clock, for she was a very ladylike person herself, and the apartment was very ladylike, and there is something nearly bohemian about a clock which, after twenty-eight years of striking correctly, jumps the traces and tolls off an impossible hour like thirteen.

"Now who's responsible for this, I'd like to know?" said Miss Prinks, almost fiercely, addressing the room at large. And then it happened.

Miss Prinks had not really expected an answer to her question. But she got one. For no sooner had the words left her mouth—in fact, while the words were still vibrating in the air—a strange something like a small, busily whirling dust devil began mistily to take form in the middle of the green carpet. At first only a wisp of vapor, it grew rapidly until it was quite solidly visible and the breeze of its rapid rotation fluttered the gold lace curtains.

"I'm afraid," spoke an apologetic voice inside Miss Prinks's head, "that I am responsible, Madam."

Now this was not the sort of answer which would be calculated to calm the fears of an ordinary person who has just discovered that it is thirteen o'clock—a time that never was, and it is profoundly hoped, will never be again. But Miss Prinks was a singleton aunt of great courage and rock-hard convictions. Her personal philosophy started with the incontrovertible fact that she was a lady and went on from there. Starting from this fact, then, and going down the line of natural reasoning, it followed that the miniature dust devil, whatever else it might be, was a *Vandal*—a clock-gimmicking *Vandal*, just as the neighborhood boys who played baseball in the adjoining vacant lot were window-smashing *Vandals*, and the drunken man who on one previous occasion had parked his car up on the apartment building's front lawn was a grass-destroying *Vandal*, and with *Vandals* Miss Prinks took a firm line.

"You're a *Vandal!*" she said angrily, to put the creature in its place and make it realize that she saw it for what it was.

This appeared to disconcert the dust devil somewhat. It paused before replying, by thought-waves, of course.

"I beg your pardon?" it thought. "I don't seem to understand that name you called me. Surely you never saw me before?"

"Perhaps not," retorted Miss Prinks, fiercely. "But I know your type!"

"You do?" The dust devil's thought was clearly astonished. Then it seemed to gather dignity. "Be that as it may," it thought. "Allow me to explain what has happened."

"Very well," said Miss Prinks in the cold, impartial tones of a judge agreeing to hear a case.

"You may know my type," said the dust devil, mentally. "But I am sure you do not know me personally. I am——" he paused, and Miss Prinks felt little light fingers searching for the proper term in her mind, "a scientist of the eighty-third Zanch dimension. I was doing some research into the compressibility of time for a commercial concern in my sector of eighty-third dimensional space. They wished to know whether it would be feasible to package and ship time in wholesale quantities——"

Miss Prinks made an impatient gesture.

"——Anyhow," thought the dust devil hurriedly, "to make a long story short, there was an explosion, and roughly an hour of the time I was experimenting with was blown into your day. Naturally, I am extremely sorry about it, and I'll be only too glad to take the hour back."

"My clock——" said Miss Prinks, coldly.

"I will take care of it," said the dust devil, or Zanch scientist, to refer to him correctly. "I will realign its temporal coordinates and make whatever spatial corrections are necessary." He waited anxiously for Miss Prinks to agree.

Now, to tell the truth, Miss Prinks was beginning to soften inside. The politeness of the Zanch scientist was making a good impression on her in spite of herself. But she did not want to give in too easily.

"Well . . ." she said, hesitantly.

"Ah, but naturally!" cried the Zanch scientist mentally. "You feel yourself entitled to some compensation for the temporal damage done to your day. Don't think another word. I understand completely."

"Well . . ." said Miss Prinks, with a hint of a deprecating smile that in a less ladylike person would have been a simper. "I know nothing at all about business arrangements of that type——"

"Of course," said the Zanch scientist. "Allow me. . . ." Light fingers seemed to touch the surface of Miss Prinks's mind. "Forgive me for saying it, but I have reviewed your

175

condition and notice several improvements that could be made. If you have no objection. . . ?"

Miss Prinks half turned her head away.

"Of course not," she said.

It has often been recorded in history that two people have come to shipwreck upon the mutual misunderstanding of a single word. This was merely one more of those instances. Miss Prinks was a lady, and she thought in ladylike terms. To her, the word *condition* referred to a person's position in the world, and particularly to that aspect of position which is related to the financial by grosser minds. She believed, therefore, that the Zanch scientist was, with the utmost delicacy, offering her monetary damages. Such things were, out of consideration for one another's feelings, referred to in periphrasis. Her sensitivity to the social situation forbade her to do anything as gross as inquiring about the amount.

The Zanch scientist, of course, had no such intention in mind. He was telepathic, but not particularly perceptive, and he knew nothing of human mores. To him, Miss Prinks was an organism with certain mental and physical attributes. Frankly, over a cup of something Zanchly, he was later to admit to a coworker that these were pretty horrible. But such bluntness was reserved for moments of intimacy among his own people. In his way, he also had manners. Therefore he used the thought *condition,* as a manager might refer to his boxer, or, more appositely, as a doctor might refer to a patient in the last stages of a wasting disease.

"Of course not," said Miss Prinks.

"Fine," said the Zanch scientist. There was a sudden shimmer in the air of the apartment living room, and Miss Prinks felt a strange quiver run from the soles of her feet to the tips of her hair. Then the room was empty.

The grandfather clock solemnly tolled two.

"Well!" said Miss Prinks.

Now that the Zanch scientist was actually gone, she found herself of two minds about him. He had undoubtedly been polite, but then he had also as undeniably been in the wrong. However, the important thing was that he was gone. And it was two o'clock.

She had shopping to do. There was a small business center two blocks from where she lived, and when the weather was good it was her practice to visit this early in the afternoon, leaving the latter part of the day for a visit to the public library which was only a block away from the shopping center in another direction. Miss Prinks reached for her purse, which was ready on the table beside her, and arose from her chair.

*Arose* is indeed the best description. With the first effort she exerted to get up from the chair, Miss Prinks shot forward and upward in an arc that carried her across the room, through the gold lace curtains and the window, which was fortunately open, and down three stories to the sidewalk below. She landed on her feet, and, though the sound of her landing was noisy in the drowsy summer afternoon, it did not seem as if the fall had hurt her in any way. In fact, thought Miss Prinks, standing on the sidewalk with a disturbed expression on her face, she had never really felt so well in her life.

Just at that moment, however, she became aware that somebody was calling her name. She turned and recognized her neighbor on the first floor below her apartment—a somewhat mousy little woman with the name of Annabelle LeMer.

"Oooh, Lydia!" cried Annabelle LeMer, as she reached Miss Prinks by the expedient of running frantically out into the street. "I was watering the flowers in my window box and I saw it all. Whatever possessed you to jump out the window?"

There are some times when a lady must take refuge in a complete refusal to discuss a subject. Miss Prinks was quick to realize that this moment was one of those. She drew herself up with queenly dignity.

"I?" she repeated in tones of icy outrage. "I jump out a window? You are having one of your bilious attacks, Annabelle."

"But I saw—" babbled the little woman in desperation.

"Bilious!" snapped Miss Prinks in a tone of voice that brooked no contradiction. She glared at Annabelle with such ferocity that the smaller woman faltered and began to doubt the evidence of her own senses. "I jump out a window! The very idea!"

So convincing was her tone that Annabelle LeMer began to half feel the waves of dizziness that in actual truth preceded one of her bilious attacks. She looked at Miss Prinks and then up at the window with the gold lace curtains three stories above. She looked so long that the blood rushed our of her head and when she returned her gaze to Miss Prinks, the street wavered about her.

"P-perhaps—" stammered Miss LeMer dizzily, "perhaps you're right, Lydia." And, turning away from Miss Prinks's angry gaze, she weaved back into her own apartment, to put cold packs on her forehead and collapse on the bed.

Left alone on the sidewalk, Miss Prinks experimented. She found that by being very, very careful not to exert herself, and by attempting what she felt were tiny steps, she could walk in quite a natural manner. By the time she had this matter straightened out, she found herself at the end of the block and, so strong is habit, decided to keep on going and get her shopping done.

This decision was an excellent one, and one that might well have carried her through the rest of the day without mishap. Unfortunately, fate took a hand, and the manner in which it did so was unexpected.

Now it must be confessed that, while Miss Prinks herself was every inch a lady, her neighborhood was perhaps not quite the best that a lady could live in. Perhaps it was not even the second best. One block away from the apartment building in which Miss Prinks lived, and halfway to the shopping center which she patronized and intended to visit today, there was something which for want of a better pair of words must bluntly be described as railroad tracks. Squarely athwart Miss Prinks's way they lay, and to get over them she was forced to cross a bridge beneath which the tracks lay in dark parallels and under which the trains smoked and thundered.

Usually at the time when Miss Prinks normally went marketing there were no trains, and she was able with ladylike detachment to ignore the fact that they existed. But today, owing to the particular circumstances following lunch she was later than usual and just in time for the early afternoon *Comet,* a crack passenger train possessing great speed and a mighty whistle for blowing at railway crossings and other artifacts of present-day civilization. It was a very distinctive and a very powerful whistle, and to tell the truth, the engineer who usually handled the *Comet* on its early afternoon run liked blowing it whenever the excuse offered.

Just what the excuse was this day, no one will ever know. But it is a fact that the engineer blew the *Comet*'s whistle as he started under the bridge Miss Prinks was on. And he blew it just as she was right in the middle of her crossing.

Miss Prinks, it has been shown, had iron courage. But she also had very ladylike and delicate nerves. So, when the *Comet* shot under her feet and the whistle blasted away practically in her ear, she could not repress a tiny start.

Unfortunately, people in Miss Prinks's made-over condition should never start. For ordinary humans it is all right, but Miss Prinks's start shot her up into the air and into a long arc that dropped her on the tracks some twenty yards in front of the charging *Comet*.

Miss Prinks took one horrified glance at the towering engine rushing down upon her, turned heel, and ran.

"Ulp!" said the engineer, and fainted dead away.

The landscape blurred by Miss Prinks and she felt her breath growing shorter. She risked a quick glance over her shoulder and nearly fainted herself. Behind her, the tracks stretched bare and empty to the horizon. The *Comet* was nowhere in sight.

Nor was the city.

Profoundly shaken, Miss Prinks leaped off the tracks, and, skidding to a stop, sat down heavily on a bank by the side of the tracks.

"Am I dead?" wondered Miss Prinks, in awe. "Did the train run me down?"

Being a practical person, she took her pulse—correctly, with the second finger of her left hand on her right wrist. Her blood pulsed strongly and steadily. That settled it, then, as far as Miss Prinks was concerned. She was alive.

Miss Prinks fanned herself with her purse and began to think. She thought back over the last few hours and she thought and she thought, and suddenly she stopped fanning herself and turned a bright pink with embarrassment.

"*Well!*" she said.

She had just realized what the Zanch scientist had meant when he used the word *condition* and what he had evidently done to her. At the thought of being altered, she blushed again.

However, one cannot go on being embarrassed forever, as Miss Prinks abruptly realized with unusual clarity of mind. She had been changed, the Zanch scientist was gone where she most probably could never reach him, and the thing to do was to investigate herself.

Her shoes caught her attention first. These were, quite literally, in ruined condition. The sole and heel of each was worn to rags. There was, in fact, little left but the tops. Torn edges stuck out over the bare arch of her foot like sad tendrils. Miss Prinks began to get some idea of how fast she had been running when she fled from the express train.

"Oh, my poor feet!" thought Miss Prinks, automatically, and then immediately had to correct herself. Her feet felt fine. In fact, they had never felt so fine, even in the dim past of her childhood when she had been allowed to run barefoot. A suspicion struck her, and she leaned over to check once more. Her bunions were gone.

Modestly, she tucked her soleless shoes under her and went back to considering the situation. She, Miss Prinks, could run faster than a train. Impossible; but here she was and—she looked back along the tracks—the *Comet* was not even in sight. If she could run that fast, how high could she jump?

She glanced quickly around the countryside. It was open and deserted with occasional clumps of trees and farmland stretching out of sight over rolling hills. There was no sign even of a building. Miss Prinks got gingerly to her feet, tucked her purse firmly under one arm, crouched slightly, and sprang.

There was a terrific rush of air, a moment's dizzy sensation and Miss Prinks found herself gasping for oxygen high in the atmosphere. Far below her, laid out in neat little checkerboard squares, the ground from horizon to horizon rocked and swayed.

"Oh my!" thought Miss Prinks in dismay as she reached the limit of her spring, turned over and started head downward toward the Earth. "Now I've done it!"

On the way to the ground, however, she thought of the proprieties and turned herself right side up again, which was, as it turned out, a very prudent move. For instead of landing on ordinary ground and sinking in about ten feet, she had the good luck to land on a large boulder which shattered into fragments beneath the impact of her falling body, but left her quite properly on the surface of the Earth.

Miss Prinks took time out to powder her nose and catch her breath.

It would be foolish to deny that at this point she was becoming somewhat excited about the possibilities inherent in her new self. When she had finished powdering her nose, she tried out a few more tests. She discovered that she was now capable of doing the following things:

180

(a) Felling a tree approximately two feet thick with one punch.

(b) Tying knots in sections of rail from the railway track.

(c) Lifting the largest boulder in sight (which was about ten feet high) and throwing it about eighty feet.

(d) Doing all the above without working up an unladylike perspiration.

But it was not these feats that startled her so much as a quite accidental discovery. She had untied the knots in the steel rails and was replacing them on the railway track, hammering in the spikes with dainty taps of her fist, when a tiny splinter on one of the wooden ties seemed to come to life and walk away on six legs. Earlier that morning, Miss Prinks would never have recognized it, but no sooner had its movement caught her attention than she immediately identified it as *Diapheromera femorata*, or common walking-stick insect of the eastern United States—being somewhat far west considering the present latitude.

For a moment her identification astounded her; and then she remembered reading about this particular insect some years previous, one day in one of those little squibs of general information which are used by editors to fill out columns in the daily newspaper. With letter-perfect recall, the item came back to her. For a moment she was tempted to speculate about the family of the *Phasmidae* in general, but she pushed the temptation from her, and set herself instead to considering the implications of this most recent self-discovery.

So Miss Prinks sat and thought, and, after having thought for a while, she took her way back alongside the railroad tracks at a jog trot in the neighborhood of a hundred miles an hour. On her way she passed the *Comet*.

This time the engineer did not faint. He merely shut his eyes firmly and told himself that he needed glasses.

At the outskirts of town Miss Prinks slowed down to an ordinary human gait, so as not to attract attention, and took a streetcar back to her apartment, where she changed shoes and sallied forth once more—this time to the library three blocks away.

The library was a large, rambling building of brown brick, split up into a number of large rooms, each of which specialized in the supply of some particular class of reading material to the general public. One of these dealt with material on the more abstract branches of science, and it was this one that Miss Prinks, with some trepidation, entered.

She spoke to the woman clerk behind the desk, filled out some slips, and after a due wait was supplied with several books, in particular one rather heavy and impressive-looking volume.

It was this one she opened first. She skimmed through the first few pages, clicked her tongue disapprovingly, and went back to the desk to order several textbooks on mathematics, leading up to and including one on tensor calculus. She returned with these to her seat and flipped through them with amazing rapidity. Then she set them aside with a satisfied air, and returned to her original volume.

She sat reading this for some time, and when she had finally finished it and laid it aside she continued to sit deep in thought for some time.

A new factor had entered into her life. A social, scientific, and for all that, probably a moral and ethical problem as well. It had come as a direct result of what the Zanch scientist had done to her. And because of it she had made a serious discovery.

Mr. Einstein was wrong on several points. Ought she to tell him?

For a long time she sat there at her library table, and her thoughts ranged far and wide over the almost limitless vista that her new abilities had opened up for her.

She was, without doubt, the strongest person in the world. The evidence she had just acquired tended to indicate that she was probably also the most intelligent person in the world. Whatever was she to do then, with all this intelligence and strength? How was she to use it? Why? Where? When? What would people think when she told them she could outrun a train?

Possibly, thought Miss Prinks, she could be useful as a sort of lady traffic policeman chasing reckless drivers. Miss Prinks shuddered a little at the thought. No, that would be too undignified, running down a street in a blue uniform at her age. Perhaps she could become some sort of government scientist. But they would probably put her to work designing some sort of super-weapon. As a member of the SPCA, she simply could not do it. Possibly——

A bell rang through the library, notifying all and sundry

that the seven o'clock closing hour had arrived. Still deep in thought, Miss Prinks rose to her feet, returned her books, and made off in the direction of her apartment.

She had thought away the last hours of the afternoon, and twilight was closing down. In the soft dwindling light, she took her way down the almost deserted street, across the railroad bridge (no train this time, thank goodness), and past the closed shops on her way toward home.

She left the bridge behind her and went on in a careful imitation of her usual walk. She had half a block to go to reach the safety and peace of the green rug, the gold lace curtains, the grandfather clock, and Solomon, the cat.

And it was then that the purse-snatcher got her.

He came diving out of the shadows of the narrow alleyway between the pet shop and the hardware store, seconds after Miss Prinks had inched her way past. A few quick running strides brought him up to her—a tall, heavy youth with a scarred face and breath whistling fiercely through his straining, open mouth. With one sudden twitch, he pulled the purse from her arm, tucked it under his own and was away at a dead run down the block.

Now, of course, with her super-hearing, Miss Prinks should have heard his breathing and the pounding of his heart as he waited for her in the alley. With her super-intelligence, she should have instantly divined that he was after the contents of her purse, and with her super-reactions she should have sidestepped and tripped him up quite neatly.

Unfortunately, just like any ordinary mortal, Miss Prinks had become absorbed in her own thoughts, and the purse-snatcher took her by surprise. In fact it was a good 8.7326 seconds, as she later shamefacedly admitted to herself, before the fact registered on her that she had been robbed. When it *did* register, she reacted without thinking. With one super-leap she overtook the youth and snatched at his jacket.

It ripped away from him like so much tissue paper. Frantic with the thought that he might escape, Miss Prinks grabbed again, this time coming away with half his shirt and undershirt. Her fingers were ripping through the left leg of the purse-snatcher's heavy workpants when sanity returned to her. She gasped, stared once at the half-denuded figure fainting before her, and ran.

So, in a third-story apartment on a certain street, Miss

Prinks still lives. She is still a singleton aunt on a pension, and she still has gold lace curtains on the window, the green carpet in the floor, and wine-colored upholstery on her furniture. The grandfather clock and Solomon are intact and present. She does her housecleaning in the morning, her shopping in the afternoon, and still visits the library late in the day, on nice days.

But she never goes in the science room, and she never requests Mr. Einstein's book again. Sometimes, in the evening when she has finished supper at home, she will sit down in her favorite chair to see what the news is. Then, with hands that are capable of crumpling three-inch steel plate, she picks up the evening paper. From the table beside her chair she picks up glasses and fixes them firmly in front of eyes that can see a fly crawling up a window pane two miles away. And, with a perception that is capable of scanning and memorizing a page at a glance, she plods through the news stories, word by word.

And sometimes she comes across an item on the front page reporting the construction of an atomic airplane, or a new discovery of medical science, or a release on the latest Air Force rocket—or on flying saucers. When this happens she reads it through, then shakes her head a little, then smiles. But that is all. She puts the paper down again and goes to bed.

For Miss Prinks made up her mind in that split second of realization that came to her in the heat of her flurry with the purse-snatcher. For the first time she had put her newly acquired powers to use, and in that moment she realized that it never could be.

For perhaps it would benefit the world to have a Miss Prinks who can outrun an express train, jump over the Empire State Building, or correct the Theory of Relativity. These things might be good and they might not. Miss Prinks does not know.

But there is one thing she does know. And it is the reason the world will never see Miss Prinks doing any of these things.

For Miss Prinks is a lady, and such goings-on are far too dangerous. There is no doubt about it, and you are just wasting your breath if you try to argue with her. For there is too great a risk—far too great a risk (and Miss Prinks blushes at the memory) that such exercise of her powers might lead to another such occasion as that in which she—a lady—suddenly found herself *tearing a man's clothes off on the public street!* Further such doings are not for her.

No indeed! Not for Miss Prinks!

# HOME FROM THE SHORE

*1*

Well, it was about four in the afternoon. You know how it is that time of day at Savannah Stand, with most of the day-charter flyers back in the ranks. All the hanging around and talking and the smell of cigarette smoke in the air, and the water stains drying back to the pale color of the concrete from the flyers that have just been washed down. You know what a good time of day that is.

Well, it was maybe a few minutes after four. Everybody was kidding about how the *Nu-Ark* was just about ready to split apart in the air and her pilot never know the difference. We were talking like that when somebody spotted a fare down at the far end of the ranks. He came up along the line, a big young tourist in a flower-patterned Thousand-Islands shirt hanging outside his pants, walking across the water stains already fading out like the cigarette smoke in the sun and looking into faces under the shadows of the ducted fans as he passed. He came on down and stopped at last by the *Nu-Ark* and hired her. And they took off east out over the ocean.

"One to five, in beers," said the pilot of the *Squarefish* as we watched them shrink down in the distance, "one of the fans comes off before he gets back here."

"That's a bad luck bet," said the pilot of the *Slingalong*. "Don't none of you take him up on that." Nobody did, either.

"You got no sense of humor," said the *Squarefish* pilot.

It was one of those hot-bright days in late July, clear as a bell. About twelve miles offshore aboard the *Nu-Ark* they felt the motors to both fans quit, stutter a moment and then take up their tale again, perhaps not just as smoothly as before. But the pilot said nothing and the passenger said nothing. They had not said a word in each other's direction since leaving the Stand. They had not even looked at each other.

The pilot was sitting by himself up front. The passenger stood in back. They were in different sections of the flyer, which was like a metal shoebox in shape between the fans, and divided up near the front by a steel partition with a narrow doorway in it just back of the pilot seat. The whole flyer had a light, flat-tasting stink of lubricating oil from the fans all through it. It vibrated to the hard working of the fans so that anything touched sent a quiver from the finger ends up to the elbow. Up front of the partition there was just room for the pilot, his control bar, and instruments, and a wide windscreen looking forward. In the bigger part of the box behind was the passenger, six bolted-down seats, and luggage racks in the space behind the seats.

The racks were forest-green like the walls, with a permanent color that had been fused into them. The two side walls had a couple of windows apiece. All the seats, which were overstuffed and with arm and headrests, were covered in an imitation tan leather that still looked as good as the day it had been put on at the factory. Only the brown color of the floor had been scratched and worn clear down to silver streaks of metal by the sand tracked in from the beach, which gritted and squeaked underfoot at every step.

With only an occasional little noise from the sand, the passenger stood by one of the windows looking north in the back section, staring out and down at the sea. To his left, back the way they had come, the shoreline where the land ended and the ocean began was sharp and as definite as if someone had drawn it in sand-colored ink. To his right and northeast, from his height the sea was blue-gray, smoke-colored, corrugated and unmoving, stretching miles without end to the horizon, and lost there. There was no doubt about the shoreline. But the distant horizon line where ocean met sky was no line at all. The still, blue-gray waters lifted to the far emptiness until they were lost in it. No one could have said for sure where the one ended and the other began.

The sky, on the other hand, that went to meet the sea, was a pale thin blue with only a small handful of white clouds about thirty miles off and at twenty thousand feet. Right from the moment of takeoff, the passenger had seen that the pilot of the *Nu-Ark* never looked at the clouds. He kept his eyes only on the indefinite horizon. Glancing over now, the passenger saw by the back of a head showing above the headrest of the pilotseat that the pilot was still at it. It looked to the passenger as if the pilot was so used to the sky that he no longer noticed it. He did not notice the vibration, the faltering of his fans, or the stink of oil. Likewise, he seemed used to the look of the sea. But the far-off and strange part of things that was the horizon drew all the attention of his eyes.

They were brown, his eyes, the passenger remembered. A little bloodshot. Set in a middle-aged tropical face tanned and thickened into squint lines around the corners of the eyes. Just then the pilot spoke, without turning.

"Keep straight on out?" he said.

The passenger went tight at the sound of the voice, jerking his eyes back to the pilotseat. But the black, straight hair of the pilot showed unmoving against the tan imitation leather. The passenger hooked a thumb into the neck opening of his bright-printed sports shirt. With one quick downward jerk of the thumb he unsealed the closure and the shirt fell open.

"Straight on out," he said. He shrugged off the shirt and reached for the belt closure of his green slacks. "Another four or five minutes, this heading."

"Ten, twelve miles," said the pilot. "All right."

The black-haired portion of his head that was showing tilted forward. The passenger could see him finally leaning toward the sea. Looking, no doubt, for a vee of wake, a squat triangle of sail, some dark boat-shape.

"Who do you think's out here now—" he began.

He had started turning his head to look back as he spoke. As his eyes came around to see the passenger undressing, he moved with unexpected quickness, letting go of the control bar and swinging himself and his pilot seat all the way around. The flyer shuddered briefly as it went into autopilot. The passenger ripped off his slacks and stood up straight in only khaki-colored shorts. They looked at each other.

The look on the pilot's face had not changed. But now the

passenger saw the brown eyes come to sharp focus on him. He stood balanced and waited.

The only thing he was afraid of now was that the pilot would not look closely enough. He was afraid the pilot might see only the big young man in his early twenties. A young man with a strong-boned body muscled like a wrestler, but with a square, open, and too easygoing sort of face. Then he saw the pilot's eyes flicker to the three blue dots tattooed on his bare right collarbone, and after that drop to the third finger of his right hand which showed a ring of untanned white about its base. The eyes came back up to his face then. When he saw their expression had still not changed, he knew that that one fear, at least, he could forget.

"I guess," said the pilot, "you know who's out there after all."

"That's right," he said. He continued to stand, leaving the next move up to the pilot. Six inches from the pilot's still left hand was the small, closed door of a map compartment. In there would probably be a knife or a gun. The pilot himself was big-boned and thick-bodied. The years had put a scar above one eyebrow and broken and enlarged three knuckles on his right hand. These were things that had caused the pilot to be picked by him for this taxi-job in the first place. He had trusted a man like the pilot of the *Nu-Ark* not to go off half-cocked.

"So you seen a space bat," said the pilot now, still watching him. The name of the void-dwelling creatures came out sounding odd in the southern accent, but for a moment it hit home and the pilot blurred before his eyes as tears jumped in them. He blinked quickly, but the pilot had not moved. Once again he remembered how slow land people were to cry. The pilot would not have been figuring that advantage.

"We all did," he said.

"Yeh," said the pilot. "Your picture was on the news. Johnny Joya, aren't you?"

"That's right," he said.

"Ringleader, weren't you?"

"No," said Johnny. "There's no ringleaders with us."

"News said so."

"No."

"Well, they did."

189

"They don't know."

The pilot shrugged. He sat still for a second.

"All right," he said. "They still got a reward out for you bigger than any of the rest of the Cadets."

They held still for another little moment, watching each other. The flyer bored on through the air, automatically holding its course. Johnny stood balanced. He was thinking that he had picked this pilot because the man was like him. It might be they were too much alike. It might be that the pilot had too much pride to let himself be forced, in spite of the squint lines and broken knuckles and knowing now what his chances would be with someone like Johnny. If it was that, the pilot would need some excuse, or reason.

Easily, not taking his eyes off the pilot, Johnny reached down and picked up his slacks. From one pocket he searched out something small, circular, and hard. Holding it outstretched in his fingers, he took two steps forward and offered it to the pilot.

"Souvenir," he said.

The pilot looked down at it. It was a steel ring with a crest on it showing what looked like a mailed fist grasping at a star.

Two words—*ad astra*—were cut in under the crest.

"Souvenir," said Johnny again.

The pilot looked it over for a long second, then slowly reached out two of his fingers with the broken knuckles and tweezered it between the ends of them, out of Johnny's grasp. He turned it slowy over, first one way and then the other, looking at it.

He said, "Once I would've wanted one like that." He lifted his eyes to Johnny. "I don't understand. Nobody does."

"It looks that way to us, too," he answered, not moving. "We don't understand Landers."

"Yeah," said the pilot. He turned the ring again. "Well, you was the one that was there. You all go home, all you sea kids?"

"It's not our job," he said. "Fill your Space Academy with your own people."

"Yeah," said the pilot, almost to himself. Slowly he folded in the fingers holding the ring until it was covered and hidden in the grasp of his fist. He put the fist in his pocket and when it came out again he no longer held the ring. "All right. Souvenir." He turned back to the controls. "How much on out?"

"About a mile now."

The pilot took hold of the control bar. The flyer dropped. The surface of the sea came up to meet them, becoming more blue and less gray as it approached. From high up it had looked fixed and unmoving, but now they could see there was motion to it. When they got close they could see how it was furrowed and all in action, so that no part of it was the same as any other, or stayed the same.

Johnny put one palm to the ceiling and pressed upward. He stood braced against the angle of their descent, looking past the bunched-up muscles of his forearms at the jacketed back of the pilot and the approaching sea.

"How can you tell?" asked the pilot, suddenly. "You know where we are now?"

"About eight-one, fifty west," said Johnny, "by about thirty-one, forty north."

The pilot glanced at his instruments.

"Right on," the pilot said. "Or almost. How?"

"Come to sea," he answered. "Your grandchildren'll have it." His eyes blurred suddenly again for a second. "Why the hell you think they wanted us for their Space Program?"

"No," said the pilot, not turning his head, "leave me out of it." A moment later he leaned toward the windscreen. "Something in the top of the water, there."

"That's it," said Johnny. The flyer dropped. It came down on the surface and began to rock and move with the ceaseless motion of the waves. The ducted fans were unexpectedly still. Their thrumming had given way to a strange silence broken by the slapping of the waves against the flyer's underbody and small creakings of metal.

"Well, look there!" said the pilot.

He leaned forward, staring out through the windscreen. The flyer had become surrounded by a gang of stunting dolphin and seal. A great, swollen balloon of a fish—a guasa—floated almost to the surface alongside the flyer and gaped at it with a mouth that opened like a lifting manhole cover. Johnny slipped full-eye contact lenses into place and stripped off the shorts. In only the lenses and an athletic supporter, he picked up the small sealed suitcase he had brought aboard and opened the side door of the flyer, just back of the partition on the right. The pilot turned his seat to watch.

"Here—" he said suddenly. He reached into his pocket,

brought out the Academy ring and held it out to Johnny. Johnny stared at him. "Go ahead, take it. What the hell, it don't mean anything to me!" Slowly, Johnny took it, hesitated, and slid it back on his right third finger to carry it. "Good luck."

"All right," said Johnny. "Thanks." He turned and tossed the suitcase out the door. Several dolphins raced for it, the lead one taking it in his almost beakless mouth. He was larger and somewhat different from the others.

"You going very deep there?" asked the pilot as Johnny stepped down on to the top of the landing steps, whose base was in the waves.

"Twenty . . ." Johnny glanced at the gamboling seacreatures. "No, only about fifteen fathoms."

The pilot looked from him to the dolphins and back again.

"Ninety feet," said the pilot.

Johnny went down a couple of steps and felt the soft warmth of the sun-warmed surface waters roll over his feet. He looked back at the pilot.

"Thanks again," he said. He hesitated and then held out his hand. The pilot got up from his seat, came to the flyer door and shook. In the grip of their hands, Johnny could feel the hard callouses of the man's palm.

"It's what you call Castle-Home, down there?" said the pilot as they let go.

"No," said Johnny. "It's Home." On the last word he felt his vocal cords tighten and he was suddenly in a hurry to be going. "Castle-Home's—something else."

He let go of the doorpost of the flyer and stepped down and out into the ever-moving waves.

## 2

The ones that had come up to meet him—the seals, the dolphins, the guasa—went down with him. He saw the color of the underwaters, green as light behind a leaf-shadowed window. And he spread his arms with the gesture of the first man who ever stood on a hilltop watching the easy soaring of the birds. He swam downward.

The salt water was cool and simple and complete around him after all the chills and sweatings of the land. In the stillness he could feel the slow, strong beating of his own heart driving the salt blood throughout his body. He felt cleansed at last from the dust and dirt of the past four and a half years. He felt free at last from the prison of his clothing.

Down he swam, his heart surging slowly and strongly. Around him a revolving circus art of underwater, freeflying aerialists leaped and danced—ponderous guasa, doe-eyed harp seals, bottle-nosed and common dolphins. And the one large Risso's dolphin, with the suitcase in his mouth, circling closest.

Johnny clicked fingernails and tongue at the Risso's dolphin. It was a message in the dolphin code that the Risso's knew well. *"Baldur . . . Baldur the Beautiful. . . ."* The twelve-foot gray beast rolled almost against him in the water, offering the trailing reins of the harness.

He caught first one rein, then the other, and let himself be towed down, no longer pivot man to the group but a moving part of it.

Seconds later there was light below them, brighter than the light from above. They were coming down into the open hub of a large number of apartments, mostly with transparent walls, sealed together into the shape of a wheel. People poured out of the apartments like birds from an aviary. They clustered around him, swept him down, and pushed him through the magnetic iris of an entrance. His ears popped slightly and he came through, walking into a large, air-filled room surrounding a pool. The dolphins, the seals, and the guasa broke water in the pool in the same second. People crowded in after him, swarmed around him, shouting and laughing.

In a second the room was overfull. There was no spare space. A tall, lean young man, Johnny's age, looking like Johnny, climbed up on a table holding a sort of curved, long-necked banjo. Sitting crosslegged, he flashed fingers over the strings, ringing out wild, shouting music. Voices caught up the tune. A song—one Johnny had never heard before— beat at the walls.

*Hey, Johnny! Hey-a, Johnny!*
*Home, from the shore!*
*Hey-o, Johnny! Hey, Johnny!*
*To high land, go no more!*

*Long away, away, my Johnny!*
*Four long years and more!*
*Hey-o, Johnny! Hey, Johnny!*
*Go high land, no more!*

They were all singing. They sang, shouting it, swaying together, holding together, laughing and crying at the same
time. The tears ran down their clean faces.

Johnny felt the arms of those closest to him, hugging him.
Those who could not reach to hold him, held each other. The
song rose, chanted, wept. It would be one of his lean cousin's
songs, made up for the occasion of his homecoming. He did
not know the words. But as he was handed on, slowly, from
the arms of one relative or friend to the next, he was caught
up, at last, in the music and sang with the rest of them.

He felt the tears running down his own cheeks. The easy
tears of his childhood. There was a great feeling in the room.
It was the *nous-nous* of his people, of the People, the People of
the Sea in all their three generations. He was caught up with
them in the moment now and sang and wept with them. They
were moved together in this moment of his returning, as the
oceans themselves were moved by the great currents that
gave life and movement to the waters. The roadways of the
seal, the dolphin, and now the roadways of his people. The
Liman, the Kuroshio, the Humbolt Current. The Canary, the
Gulf Stream in which they were now this moment drifting
north. The Labrador.

For four years he had been without this feeling. But now
he was Home.

Gradually the great we-feeling of the People in the room
relaxed and settled down into a spirit of celebration. The
song of his homecoming shifted to a humorous ballad—about
an old man who had a harp seal, which wouldn't get out of
his bed. Laughter crackled among them. Long-necked green
pressure bottles and a variety of marinated tidbits of seafood
were passed from hand to hand. The mood of all of them
settled into cheerfulness, swung at last to attention on
Johnny. Quiet welled up and spread around the pool, quen-
ching other talk.

Sitting now on the table that his cousin Patrick with the
banjo had vacated, he noticed their waiting suddenly. He had
his arm around the shoulders of a round-breasted, brown-

haired, slight girl who sat leaning against him on the table, her head in the hollow of his shoulder. He had been looking down at her without talking, trying to see what difference four years had made in her. He saw something, but he could not put his finger on just what it was. Like all the sea-people, she was free; although he wondered if the Landers had appreciated the difference between that and their own legal ways when they had set all the Cadets from the sea down as unmarried. But still, she was free; and he had not even been certain that he would find her still here with his family and friends' Group when he came back.

She sat up and moved aside now, to let him sit up. Her eyes glanced against his for a moment and once more he thought he saw a new difference between her now and the girl he remembered. But what it was still stayed hidden to him. He turned and looked out at the people. They were all quiet now, sitting on chairs or hassocks or crosslegged on the floor and looking at him.

"I suppose you've all heard it on the news," he said.

"Only that it was something about the space bats," said the voice of Patrick beneath him.

Johnny leaned forward and peered over the edge of the table. Patrick sat crosslegged there, the banjo upright between his knees with the long neck sloping over his shoulder, his head leaning against it with the edge pressing into his cheek. He winked up at Johnny. The wink was the same wink Johnny remembered, but it put creases in Patrick's lean face he had never seen there before. Without warning, Patrick's face looked as Johnny had seen it on the jacket of a tape of Patrick's Moho Symphony, in a music department ashore. At the time Johnny had thought the picture was a bad likeness.

He winked back and straightened up.

He said, "The space bats were the final straw. That's all, actually."

"Were they big, Johnny?"

It was a child's voice. Johnny looked and saw a boy seated crosslegged almost at the foot of the table, his eyes full open, his lips a little parted, all his upper body leaning forward. He was one who had evidently been born into the Joya Group since Johnny left. Johnny did not know his name.

"The one I saw would have weighed about six ounces down here on Earth." He spoke to the boy as he would have spoken to any of the rest, regardless of age. "But—it was a good quarter mile across."

The boy drew in so deep a breath his shoulder lifted. When he let it out again his whole body shuddered.

"A quar-ter mile!" he whispered.

"A quarter mile," said Johnny, remembering. "A quarter mile. Like a silver curtain waving in the current of an offshore tide. That's how it looked to me."

"You helped catch it?" said Emil Joya, who was an uncle both to Johnny and his cousin Patrick with the banjo.

Johnny looked up.

"No," he said. "They took the senior class, which was mostly made up of us sea people, out beyond Mars to observe. We just watched." He hesitated a second. "They said it'd be something some of us would be doing some day. Part of a project to find out how the space bats make it between the stars, if they do. And how to duplicate the process."

"I don't quite understand," said Emil, his heavy, gray brows frowning in his square rock of a face.

"The Space Project people think the space bats can give up a secret of a practical way to drive our own ships between the stars at almost the speed of light."

"And you caught this one?" said Patrick, beneath the table.

"We watched," said Johnny. "It didn't try to escape. Men on space scooters walled it about with a net of charged particles. Then, all of a sudden, it seemed to understand. And it died."

"You killed it!" said the boy.

"Nobody killed it," said Johnny. "It died by itself. One minute it was there, waving like a silver curtain, and then the color started to go out of it. It fell in on itself. In just a moment it was nothing but a gray ring in the middle of the net."

He stopped talking. There was a second or two of silence in the small-Home crowded with sea people.

"And seeing that made you leave the Academy?" asked Patrick's voice.

"No," said Johnny. He drew a breath as deep as the boy had drawn. "After we came back from the observation cruise, we had to write reports. We wrote them separately, but afterwards we found we'd all written the same thing, we sea-Cadets. We wrote that the space bats killed themselves when they were captured because they couldn't bear being trapped." He breathed deeply again. "We wrote that it would never work this way. The bats would always die. The project was a blind alley."

"And then?" said Patrick.

"Then the CO commended us for the excellence of our reports." Johnny laughed a little. "And the next week we sea-Cadets were all scheduled for some more of their psychiatric explorative examinations—to determine the causes of our emotional reactions, as they called them, to the capture of the bat."

Once more no one said anything.

"It doesn't make sense," said Patrick at last.

"Not to us, it doesn't," said Johnny. "To a Lander it makes very good sense. They never wanted us sea people as people in the first place. When they asked our third-geneartion men to enlist as Academy Cadets they only wanted those parts of us they could make use of—our faster reaction times, our more stable emotional structure—our gift of reckoning location and distance and the new instincts living in the sea has wakened in us. . . ." Johnny's voice trailed off. He thumped softly on the table by his knee with one knotted fist, staring at the blank wall opposite, until Sara Light, the girl beside him, took his fist gently in her hands and cushioned it to stillness.

"We were like the space bats to them," said Johnny after a bit. "Time and again they'd proved it to us. I called a meeting of the other class representatives—I was Senior Class Rep—Jose Polar was rep for the freshmen sea-Cadets, Martin Connor for the second-year group, Mikros Palamas for the juniors. We decided there was no use trying any longer. We went back and told the men in our own class. The next weekend, when we were allowed passes, we all took our rings off and headed as best we could for our own Homes."

He stopped speaking and sat looking across the unvarying surface of the wall.

They swarmed all over him for a second time. But they quieted down soon, the more so as Patrick's banjo did not join them. When it was still again Patrick spoke from under the table.

"You were the one who called the meeting, Johnny?"

"It was me," said Johnny. "I was Senior Representative."

"That's true," said Patrick. A faint E minor chord sounded

from the strings of his banjo as if he had just happened to shift his grip on the neck of it. "That's why the news has been calling you the ringleader. But you had no choice, I suppose."

"No," said Johnny.

"It'll be a hard thing for them to swallow."

"Perhaps," said Johnny. "I've lived with them over four years, and they swallow different from us, Pat. We see and think different from they do. We have instincts already they don't have—and who knows what the next generations will be like? But they're not ready to admit our difference. And until they do, we can't live on dry land with them."

For a second it seemed as if Patrick would not say anything more. Then they heard a faint chord from his banjo again.

"Maybe," said Patrick, "maybe. But we all started with coming from high land in the beginning. A hundred thousand generations of men ashore, and only three or four in the sea. All the history, the art, the music . . . we can't cut ourselves off from that."

His voice stopped.

"We won't," said Emil. He stood up from the chair in which he was sitting. The rest of the people began to rise, too. "We'll be going to Castle-Home, shortly. And Castle-Home will straighten it out with the Closed Congress ashore, the way they've always done before. After all, we're a free people here in the sea. There's no way they can make us do for them against our will."

The people nearest the exit irises were already slipping out. Beyond the transparent front walls of the small-Home they were leaving. The encompassing waters were already darkening toward opaqueness. By ones and severals, saying good night to Johnny, they melted away toward their own small-Homes in the Joya Group's wheel.

Johnny found himself alone by the pool.

He looked about for Sara, but he could not see her. As he stepped toward the iris leading to the inner part of the small-Home unit, she came out of it. He reached out to her, but she avoided his grasp and took his hand. Puzzled, he let her lead him through the eye-baffling shimmer of the iris.

Beyond it he found not one bedroom, but two. Another iris led to a further sleeping room. But in this first area, a single bed was against a well at the foot of which a small nightlight glowed.

On the bed under a light cover, his face dug sideways into the softness of a pillow, dampened by his open-breathing mouth, was a small interloper. It was the boy who had spoken up earlier to ask about the space bats.

Politeness was for all ages among the sea people. Johnny stepped to the bed and reached down to shake gently a small bare shoulder and wake him to the fact that he was in the wrong small-Home. But Sara caught Johnny's hand, and when he looked down into her face he found it luminous with an emotion he did not know.

"Tomi," she said. "His name's Tomi. He's your son, Johnny."

Johnny stared at her. They had talked to and written each other across the distance between them these last four and a half years, and never once had she mentioned a child. Among the People, this was her right, if she wished. But somehow Johnny had never thought that with him a woman—and particularly Sara—

He forced his gaze away from her watching face, back down to the boy. His son slept the heavy slumber of childhood's exhaustion.

Slowly he sank on his knees by the bedside, drawing his hand out of Sara's grasp. A chill ran through him. He felt the heavy muscles of his stomach contract. In the small white glow of the nightlight reflected from the palely opaque walls, Tomi slumbered as if in a world remote, not only from land and sea and all the reaches of space, but from all things outside this one small room. He breathed without a sound. His chest movements were almost invisible, his skin fine to the point of translucency. The chill in Johnny spread numbness through all his body and limbs, and his neck creaked on stiff tendons.

He reached out slowly. With what seemed an enormous, creased and coarse-skinned fingertip, he traced the slight line of an eyebrow on the boy. The brown, fine hairs were crisp to his touch. An abrupt flush of emotion rushed through him, burning away the chill like a wave of fever. He felt clumsy and helpless, and a wild desire prompted him to gather the boy in his arms and, holding him tightly, snarl above him at all the forces of the universe. Wrung and bewildered, Johnny turned his face up to Sara.

"Sara!" It was almost a wail of despair from his lips.

She knelt down beside him and put her arms around him and the boy, together. He clung to her and the sleeping youngster, and the boy, half-waking, roused and held to them both.

And so they held together, the three of them, there in the glow of the nightlight.

# 3

It was the hurricane season. One big wind had begun its march north on the day Johnny left the Academy. On the fourth day of his return, it hammered the ocean surface above the Joya Home into spume and dark, tall masses of leaning water. It battered Georgia and the North Carolina shore.

The Joya Home slipped down to the twenty fathoms' depth and dwelt there in calm, green-blue silence. No effect of the howling, furious borderland between air and water reached down here to the bright wheel-shaped Home, away up in the middle of the ocean universe. The People of the Joya group hardly thought about what was happening above. In their swimmasks or small-Homes, they breathed the atmosphere made for them out of the water elements. They ate and drank of bounty the living ocean supplied. When they reached Castle-Home would be time enough to think about replacing any of the large, complex items of equipment that only the automatories of Castle-Home could supply. Now they were concerned only with the fact of Johnny's being home, and the planning of a party.

But their laughter and their voices were not the pleasure to Johnny that they thought. He told himself he had been too long away. He thought less of their plans and more of the wind and water storming overhead. He felt an urge to leave them. To put on mask and fins and swim up to the surface and feel it for himself. But he held back—a little ashamed of how it would look, at this time, for him to sneak off from the rest of his people.

He tried his hand at the charts showing the currents at various depths, a work the Joya group traded for credit against other needed things supplied through Castle-Home. But they no longer seemed important. The third generation did not need them, with their new instinct for location and direction. The older generations would be gone in a few years. And the Landers would have all the use of them.

He could not work, and he could not relax. Sara still seemed to him to be holding back something from him, something he should know. They were both older and it was not the same between them. She had never explained not telling him about Tomi, and the boy did not call him Daddy, but Johnny.

On the fourth morning a call came to rescue him. It was a phone call from Chad Ridell, Chief of Staff for one of the four Castle-Homes about the sea-waters of the world. Ridell's Castle-Home was nearest, only about four hundred miles north of where the Joya Home drifted now.

"This time," he said, "we're going to have to form a Council to talk to the Closed Congress." Chad was second generation. His lean, fifty-four-year-old face had lines more suited to someone of the first generation. "They're as worked up ashore about this as they were about the whaling industry. Maybe more. I thought we'd eventually have elections, with each ten Homes electing a representative. But for now, I'm simply bespeaking about twenty or so people I think are pretty sure of being elected."

"Patrick, you mean?" said Johnny.

"For one," said Chad. "Because his music's made him known and respected on shore. You, for one of the representatives of the Cadets."

Johnny nodded.

"You'll come as quickly as you can, Johnny?"

"Yes. Patrick too. I'm sure. All of us, I think," said Johnny.

They broke their phone connection and Johnny went to tell the others. Within an hour, the Joya Home was beginning to break into the small-Home sections that made it up. Each small-Home sent an electric current through its outer shell, and the plastic of that shell "remembered" a different shape, changing into an outline like that of a supersonic aircraft. Together, the altered small-Homes turned north at a speed of ninety knots, under the thrust of individual drive units that used a controlled hydrogen fusion process to produce high-pressure steam jets. They drove through the still waters for Castle-Home.

Five hours later, reunited in wheel-shape, the Joya Home trembled into position and locked down atop a column of nine other previously arrived Homes. Johnny, who was acting pilot for the Home, locked the controls and turned from them.

Tomi said, "Why didn't Mommy wait while you did that?"

Johnny looked down. The small face, in which Johnny often found himself searching for a resemblance to himself, looked up at him across a gulf of years.

"Her own folk's Home may be here," Johnny said. "She wanted to find out."

"Grandpa," said Tomi. "And Grandma Light."

"Yes," Johnny said.

"They're my Grandpa and Grandma. They're not yours." The boy stood with feet apart. "Why didn't *she* take me to see my Grandpa and Grandma Light?"

Johnny looked out the wide transparency before him at the blue waters and the ten-Home upright columns of Castle-Home. "I think she wants us to become better acquainted."

Tomi scowled.

"What's 'acquainted'?"

"We aren't acquainted," said Johnny. He looked back at the boy.

"What," said Tomi, "is *acquaint*-ed, I say!"

"Acquainted," said Johnny. "Acquainted's what you are with your mother."

Tomi looked hard at him.

"She's *my* mother," he said at last.

"And you're my son," Johnny gazed at the boy. He was square-shouldered, solid, and thick. His eyes were not brown like Sara's but blue like Johnny's. But their blueness was as transparent and unreflective as a pane of glass.

Johnny said suddenly, "Did your mother ever take you to see the corral at a Castle-Home?"

"Uhh-uh!" Tomi shook his head slowly from side to side. "She never took me."

"Get your mask and fins on, then," said Johnny. "I'll take you."

Outside the small-Home entrance iris, they found Baldur waiting with Sara's bottle-nosed dolphin, Neta, and Neta's half-grown pup, Tantrums.

"Not now, Tantrums!" Tomi shoved the five-foot pup aside and reached toward Baldur, but Baldur evaded the boy, spiraling up on Johnny's far side. Tomi muttered something and grabbed at the reins of the harness on Neta, who let him take them willingly.

"No," said Johnny. The mutter had barely reached his ears over the underwater radio circuit built into the swim masks. If they had been relying on voice-box communication from mask to mask through the water it would not have reached him at all. But he felt it was time to settle this matter. "Baldur is not your dolphin."

Tomi muttered once more. This time it was truly unintelligible, but Johnny did not need to understand the words in this case.

"Our sea-friends pick us, not we them," said Johnny. "Baldur picked me many years ago. While I was gone he let you use him, but now I'm back. You'll have to let him do what he wants."

Tomi said nothing. Letting the dolphins pull them, they headed across the top of Castle-Home through three fathoms of water to a far area of open water where yellow warning buoys stood balanced at various depths. Neta jerked the reins suddenly from Tomi and, herding Tantrums ruthlessly before her, headed home.

"Bad Neta!" shouted Tomi through his voice-box. "Bad dolphin!"

"No. Careful dolphin," said Johnny. "What do yellow buoys stand for?"

"Danger," muttered Tomi. He glanced at Baldur and grumbled again.

"Don't blame the dolphin," said Johnny. "If Sara were here, Neta wouldn't leave her even for Tantrum's sake. It's nothing against you. Some day you'll have your own dolphin for a sea-friend, and it'll stick with you."

"Won't!" muttered Tomi. "I don't want scared little dolphins! A great, great, big space bat, that's what I'll get!"

"Suit yourself," said Johnny. "Well, that's the corral, beyond the buoys there and for four miles out. Want to go in?"

Tomi's face mask jerked up sharply toward his father.

"Pass the yellow. . . ?"

"As long as I'm with you. Well?"

Tomi kicked himself forward.

"Let's go in, Johnny."

"All right. Stay close now." Johnny led the way. Tomi crowded him. Baldur hesitated, then spurted level with them.

They swam forward for thirty or forty feet. Tomi gradually forged ahead. Then, suddenly, he went into a flurry of movement, flipped around, and swam thrashing back into Johnny.

"Daddy!" He clung to Johnny's right arm and chest. "Killers! *Wild* Killers!"

Johnny put his left arm instinctively around the boy. Holding him, Johnny could feel the abrupt and powerful surge of his own heart and the warmth of blood cresting out through his own body.

"It's all right," Johnny said. "They're muzzled."

Tomi still clung. The warmth racing through Johnny came up against a different, powerful pressure that seemed to spread out and down from behind his ears.

"Look at them," he said. Tomi did not move. The pressure moved farther out and downward. He put his hands around the small waist and overpowered the boy's grip, turning him around. He held his son out, facing the killer whales.

For a second, as he turned him, Tomi had gone rigid through all his body. Now the rigidity began to go out of him. He stared straight at the looming shape of the nearest killer whale with the open basket-weaving of the enormous muzzle covering the huge head. Johnny's fingers pressed about the light arch of childish ribs, but he felt no shiver or tremble. He was aware of Baldur quivering in the water at his back, but between his hands there was only stillness.

The boy relaxed even more. He hung, staring at the great, dim shape just ahead. After a second his hands went to Johnny's hand and he pushed Johnny's grip from his waist. He swam a few strokes forward.

Johnny felt the hard beating of his own heart against the pressure in his brain. He was tense as a strung bow himself, and his heart beat with the hard, proud rhythm of a man forging a sword for his own carrying. Without warning he remembered the striped gold length of a Siberian tiger lying in his cage outdoors at the zoo ashore in San Diego. And the small, dancing figure of a ruby-throated hummingbird which floated from some nearby yellow tulips, in through the gleaming bars of the cage. It had hesitated, then, hovering on the blurred motion of its wings, moved driftingly toward the great head and sleepy eye of the tiger that watched it advancing.

Johnny looked about him.

At first there had been only the one killer to be seen. Now, like long boxcar lengths resolving out of the green dimness, other ponderous, dark-backed shapes were making their appearance without seeming to exert any effort of swimming. It was as if they coalesced, and came drifting close under some magnetic influence. They approached sideways. Through the open-work of the muzzle about the one now drifting, rising toward him on his left, Johnny could see the murderously cheerful mouth, the dark intelligent watching of the eye.

The eye, dark and reflective, approached Johnny, growing as it came. Behind it lay the large cetacean brain, and a mind close to Johnny's own. But that mind was a stranger, self-sufficient. Staring now into the approaching eye, Johnny thought he caught there his own sea-image. And it came to him then that it was for something like this he had advised the Cadets' return. It was for something like this that he had brought his son to the killer's pen.

Very mighty, ignorant of domination, moved by deep instincts to act to an end unseen but surely felt, the reflecting eye of the killer whale looked out on an unending liquid universe where there were no lords, no chains, nor any walls. Through this universe only the dark tides of instinct moved back and forth. For the killer whale as for the people, now, those dark tides spoke with a voice of certainty. To listen to that voice, to follow the path it told of, setting aside all things of the moment, all pity, all fear of life or death—it was this knowledge Johnny saw reflected in the killer's eye. In those dark tides there was neither wife nor child, nor friend nor enemy—but only truth and what the mind desired. First came survival. After that what the individual chose to accept. That was the truth, the secret and the truce of the dark tides.

And that was why, thought Johnny over the strong beating of his heart, that it had been safe to bring his son to this place. His son was of the sea. In this place was the truce of the sea, and in that truce he was safe.

"Daddy!"

Tomi's voice shouted suddenly in Johnny's earphone, in the close confines of the mask and over the sound of the bubbling exhaust valve.

"Daddy! Look at me!"

Johnny jerked around in the water. Twenty feet from him and a little higher in the water, Tomi was violating one of the oldest knowledges of the people—that the quicksilver members of the dolphin family hated to be held or clung to by any but their oldest friends. Like a boy on a Juggernaut, Tomi rode high on the shoulder area of the first killer whale.

"—Tomi," said Johnny. He felt neither beating, nor pressure now. Only a wide, hollow feeling inside him. He kept his voice calm.

"Uh-huh!" Tomi kicked carelessly with the heels of his swim fins against the great swelling sides of the killer. Five feet ahead and below him, the dark eye there looked like a poker player's through an opening in the muzzle. It gazed steadily on Johnny. The great flukes of the killer, capable of smashing clear through the side of a small rowboat, hung still in the water. Johnny thought of the truce, of the primitive sense of fun to be found in all the dolphins, the savage humor of the killer whales.

"Tomi," he said, surprised at his own calmness, "it's time to go home."

"All right." Surprisingly without argument, Tomi kicked free of the twenty-five foot shape and swam down towards his father. For a moment Johnny saw the boy beating by the muzzle where the dark eye watched, and then he was swimming freely toward Johnny.

Johnny turned and they swam together toward the edge of the corral. Baldur shot on ahead.

"Tomi—" said Johnny, and found words did not come easily. He started again. "I should have warned you not to get close to them. Killers aren't like dolphins——"

"He's going to be my sea-friend, I think," said Tomi, kicking vigorously through the water.

"Tomi," said Johnny, "killers don't make friends like dolphins."

"Then why does he keep coming after me, Daddy?"

Johnny's head jerked around to look back over his shoulder. A dozen feet behind them, the basket shape of a killer whale's muzzle was gliding through the water. At that moment the yellow buoys loomed before them, and they passed through. Here the killer should have stopped following. But he came on through with them.

"Tomi," said Johnny quietly. "You see the iris on the wall there?"

"I see it," said Tomi, looking ahead to the side of Castle-Home.

"When I tell you to, in just a minute when we get close, I want you to start swimming for it. And don't look back. You understand? I want you to swim as fast as you can and not stop."

The sudden wild clangor of an alarm bell broke through his words, racketing through the water all around them and over Castle-Home. And a buzzer sounded in the earphones of their mask-radio circuit.

"All bespoke members of the Council, this is Chad Ridell speaking," said the voice of the Chief of Staff of Castle-Home. "Please come to the Conference Room at once. All members . . ." Chad's voice repeated the request twice more.

"Daddy!" said Tomi, as the voice stopped. Johnny turned swiftly to him. "Look, Daddy," Johnny followed the boy's pointing finger and saw the waters behind them empty and still. "My killer's *gone!*"

"Never mind," said Johnny automatically. "We've got to streak for home now." He caught up a rein from Baldur and handed another rein to Tomi.

When the two of them entered their own small-Home again, Sara was back.

"Mommy! Mommy, Listen!" Tomi ripped off his mask. "We went in the corral with the killers. And I made friends with one and rode on his back and he followed us but the bell scared him——"

Sara's face flashed up to stare into Johnny's. Her eyes were wide, her nose pinched, the skin over her cheekbones tight and pale. There was an abruptly white look to her eyes.

"I've got to go——" said Johnny. He pulled on his mask and hurried out of the small-Home.

He saw he was late as he stepped into the Conference Room. About twenty of the People were already there. They were seated in a semicircle near the far end of the green-walled room, around the broadest image of a small, middle-aged man, standing, in gray slacks and Lander jacket. Johnny recognized him. It was Pul Vant, Secretary-Advocate for the Closed Congress, governing body of the grouped nations of the land.

Johnny came up quietly and took a seat. His cousin Patrick was among those already there, as were two other representatives of the ex-Cadets—Mikros Palamas and Tom Loy. Besides these, he recognized Chad Ridell, and Toby Darnley of the Communications Dome, here at Castle-Home. And Anna Marieanna, a dark-haired woman of the second generation, startlingly beautiful still in her forties, in spite of the fact her left hand was gone at the wrist. She smiled at him across the semicircle, and he smiled back briefly.

". . . ringleaders," Pul Vant was saying.

"I tell you," Ridell interrupted. "There are no ringleaders among the People."

"Very well. Setting that aside then—" Vant gestured neatly with his hands as he talked. He had the smooth movements of an actor. "I'm trying to explain to you what the Space Program and the Academy can mean to a frontierless people ashore." He went on talking. It was an old argument, one Johnny had heard before. He looked around the semicircle, noting the difference of his people from this little man of the land. Anna Marieanna was not the only one marked by the sea among the older generations, and in his own generation the very structure of the mind and body was different. Different from the Landers. Already they were starting to use the same words to mean different things on each side. And the dangerous thing was they did not realize the difference was there in their words.

"Now," Vant was saying, "the Congress is ready to make the same offer. To take you in as a full member nation——"

"No," said Chad.

"You understand," Vant said, "we can't have six million people without even a government holding seventy-point-eight percent of the world's surface area. You can't do that."

"We've been doing it," said Chad. "We intend to keep on."

Vant lifted his hands and let them drop.

"I'm sorry," he said. "There's nothing I can do then, I just explain the situation, that's all my job is. You know, historically, the tail's never been let to wag the dog very long." He ran his eyes around the semicircle. They met Johnny's eyes, paused for a second, then passed on. "If the rest of the Cadets'll come back voluntarily—otherwise, public opinion's going to get out of hand." He looked at Chad. "We don't *want* to declare war on you."

"No," said Chad. "You don't want that."

Vant waved an easy hand and disappeared. The people rose and began to shove their chairs back to make a full circle, breaking out at the same time into a clatter of conversation. Johnny found himself next to Chad.

"He talked like they caught some of us," Johnny said. Chad looked at him.

"Yes," he said. "A hundred and twenty-nine didn't make it to the sea. They're holding them at Congress Territory on Manhattan. He said they may be tried as deserters."

"Deserters?" Johnny stopped shoving his chair.

"Why should they?" he heard Toby Darnley, of the Communications Dome of Castle-Home, his slightly shrill voice rising over the others. "Why should they give in at all? We can't give in to them. We can't let them put a leash around our necks. But we can't let them put those boys before a firing squad, either." Glancing across the room, Johnny saw Toby's small, square face was rigid and dark. "What is there we can do?"

Beside Johnny, Chad sat down. The circle was formed now. Johnny saw he was the only one standing. For some reason, following the shock of what he had just heard, he found his mind filled by a memory of the eye of the killer whale, as he had seen it watching through the openings in the muzzle. The dark eye, hidden of meaning, and steady. In the same moment something moved in him. It suddenly seemed to him that he felt the actual presence of the hundred and twenty-nine prisoner Cadets, as he had felt Tomi between his hands.

"We can save them," he said. "We can go rescue our own people."

They all stared at him. The roomful of people were silent. Though the four walls of the room barred all about him he felt the eye of the killer whale through them upon him, steadily watching.

# 4

Only Patrick said no to the idea. But when the rest of the council all voted for it, he said nothing more. He sat without talking, watching Johnny. After a little while he left them to their planning.

The sea people could always move at a moment's notice. In an emergency they could almost dispense with the notice. Three hours later, a spindle-shaped formation of small-Homes in their craft-shape bored due east through the brilliant blueness of the hundred-fathom depth toward the New York shore. Before them, a virbatory weapon on low broadcast power herded the sea-life from their path. Their speed was a hundred and seventy knots.

Piloting the lead craft, Johnny stood alone at the controls. The small-Homes behind held nearly five hundred men, almost every one of the ex-Cadets who had been in Castle-Home at the time. The small-Homes were supplied with automatic controls. The ex-Cadets had explosives, the radio equipment built into their masks and take-apart sonic rifles and vibratory weapons of the sort the People used for seahunting. The element of surprise was on their side, they thought they knew where the prisoners were being held in Congress Territory, and they had a plan.

In the lead craft, along, facing the empty, luminous waters showing through the transparent wall before him, Johnny felt detached from the speed of their movement. All sound was damped out and there were no signposts to gauge by, only the strange blue twilight of a hundred fathoms down that had so fascinated Beebe in his first bathysphere descent a hundred years before. It glowed through the transparent forward wall to wrap Johnny in the unreal feeling of a dream. He, the sea, the ex-Cadets behind him—even the destination to which they were all hurtling—seemed ghostlike and unreal.

The sound of footsteps behind him, in the small-Home where he was supposed to be alone, jerked him around sharply.

"Patrick!" he said.

Patrick, dressed like all the ex-Cadets in black, elastic cold-water skins, swim mask, and fins, came like some shuffling monster out of the rear dimness of the small-Home to stand beside Johnny.

"I stowed away," said Patrick. He was looking out at the blue.

"But why? You were against this, weren't you?" Johnny peered at him. Patrick slowly turned his head, but the apparently brilliant blue was so dim that Johnny could not make out the expression on Patrick's face.

"Yes," said Patrick. "I had to. It's true, you know, Johnny. You're a ringleader."

"Ringleader?" Johnny leaned toward him, but still he could not make out the look on Patrick's face.

"Yes," said Patrick. "Just like you were at the Academy. You decide something on your own. And then you always push it through."

"What did I push through?" Johnny let go the controls. On automatic, independent, the craft bored on, leading the formation.

"This." Pat's voice changed. "Johnny," he said. "Johnny, turn back."

"But we have to do this," said Johnny. "Why can't you see that, Pat? We've already broken off from the Landers. We're different."

"You think you're different," said Patrick.

"I know it. So do all the third generation. You know it, Pat." He peered again, unsuccessfully. "You want to make me personally responsible for all this?"

"Yes," said the blur of Patrick's face. "For a war we can't win."

"It's not war yet," said Johnny.

"It's war. War with the land. I wish I could stop you, Johnny."

Johnny stood for a second.

"If you feel like that, Pat, why'd you come along?"

Pat laughed, a queer, choking sort of laugh. "I knew you wouldn't turn back. I had to ask you, though."

He turned and walked back, away. In the dimness, his outline seemed to melt, rather than go off. Left alone, Johnny felt the blue illumination as if it shone coldly through him.

Once he and Patrick had been as alike in their thoughts as twin brothers. They had gone off on months-long expeditions, alone with their dolphins and sonic rifles, living off the open sea like dolphins themselves. Now, in this new dimness, he could not even call clearly to mind his cousin's face. What he remembered was overlaid by the picture of Patrick that had been on the Moho tape in the music store ashore.

Johnny turned back to the controls, and put his mind to the coming work.

Off Jones Beach, they left the small-Homes. Half of these they put together in a mock-up of one of the large Lander deep-sea subs, resting in the Brooklyn Navy Yard a handful of miles away. This and the smaller ships were sent off on automatic controls, to rendezvous with the expedition later in the East River alongside Congress Territory. Individually, Patrick and Johnny among them, they dispersed and headed shoreward—to emerge at last in the early evening of a hot July day, among the Lander swimmers and skin-divers of the crowded beach.

Johnny bought Lander throw-away clothes and changed into them in a pullman dressing-room above the beach. His disassembled sonic rifle and his swim mask with its radio were tucked in under his belt. He headed in to Manhattan.

The first step toward rescuing the prisoners was so completely without incident it was almost dull. Congress Territory covered a full twenty-block area running south from where the old Queensboro Bridge had been. It was a show place, beautifully terraced and landscaped, and quite open. At midnight, Johnny reached the broad boulevard entrance at the north end and saw Mirkos and Tom Loy come up to him.

"All clear?" Johnny asked.

"All clear," said Mikros. His big face under its black hair was grinning. Tom Loy looked a little pale under the lights of the Manhattan dome, but steady enough. Johnny himself felt a little as he had felt facing the killer whales with Tomi.

"Move everybody in, then," Johnny said. They went in. Half an hour later, without being stopped, they were spread out around the plaza, surrounded by office buildings, that lay before the old UN Secretariat. The pool in the plaza was black and still.

"What if they aren't in the blast shelter under the Secretariat Building?" Tom Loy asked. He had asked it twice before.

"Where else could they hold a hundred and twenty-nine men?" asked Johnny. "But if they aren't, we'll just have to search." He took Tom and a dozen of the ex-Cadets. They went in the Secretariat Building, down the regular escalators, to a special old-fashioned, mechanical elevator in a subbasement. They went down this, and it let them out all at once into a guardroom filled with Closed Congress soldiers, half-dressed and wholly unready to fight.

The soldiers submitted without protest. They were lined up and disarmed. The inner doors to the blast shelter were broken open and the captured ex-Cadets poured out.

"That's good," said Johnny to Tom Loy. "Now, we'll get them upstairs as quickly as we can."

He was turning back to the elevator—when the dull, heavy sound of a sonic explosion from above rattled the elevator in its shaft.

For a second no one moved. Then Johnny snatched his swim mask out of his pocket, thumbed the controls and spoke into his radio mike.

"Mikros?" he said. "What happened?"

Mikros' voice was suddenly blurred by the buzzing of a distorter. "Soldiers up in the buildings!"

"Take charge," said Johnny to Tom Loy. He ran for the elevator, rode it up, then ran up the humming escalators to the ground floor.

The present-day ground floor of the Secretariat was fronted by a conservatory lush with flowers, trees, and other plants. Looking through its foliage, Johnny saw most of the dome lights were out over the place. In the dimness, the sea people had taken cover where they could behind hedges and ornamental trees surrounding the pool. From the buildings on three sides of the plaza military gunfire was reaching for them.

Mike was not to be seen. The springing of the trap had evidently caught him somewhere outside. The ventilation was off, and smoke, drifting out of the building on Johnny's right, was thickening and fogging the air in layers that did not move. Water had been splashed out of the pool, darkening a terrace as if the building itself was bleeding. Otherwise, there was no blood to be seen, for the sonic and vibratory weapons wounded and damaged internally.

The distorter, set going to make any bounce-echo sighting mechanism of a sonic rifle useless, buzzed eerily in the heads of all. It sang in Johnny's inner ear like a noise heard in high fever. As he looked about the plaza he saw, here and there, bodies of the sea people, lying still.

Up toward the front of the conservatory, behind a lemon tree in a wooden tub, one of the ex-Cadets crouched suddenly, putting his forehead to the pavement. Johnny ran and knelt down beside him. But when he put his hand on the boy's shoulder, the other went over on one side and lay still with a little trickle of blood showing at the corner of his mouth. It was one of the freshman class. His eyes were closed and his skin showed nearly as finely transparent as Tomi's

213

had been in his sleep. Johnny stared at him, for he could not even now remember the other's name.

"Johnny—" said someone. He looked up and saw Tom Loy. "We're all upstairs."

"Yes." Johnny climbed automatically to his feet. He glanced along the Secretariat's front to a sort of alley between buildings that led to the East River. No soldiers blocked it yet. "Everybody out. Tell Mike." The smoke was thick around them now. "You come with me."

He led the way in a dash to the corner of the Secretariat Building at the alley's entrance. They knelt there and burrowed with their hands in the soft earth of a flower bed. Tom packed a number of the yellow cubes of explosive jelly that they used for deep-sea mining into the hole. Sea people hurried, staggered by them through the smoke.

"Are they all out?" asked Johnny, setting the radio detonator.

"All out, Mike?" Tom asked in open speech into his radio mike.

"All but me." Johnny, putting on his mask, heard Mikros' voice over the distorter in his earphone. "I'll be along in a——"

The swelling impact of another sonic explosion shuddered through the square. Johnny looked and saw Tom's lips move, but he heard nothing. They were deafened. Johnny waved Tom on toward the river, and Tom leaped up, then ran off through the smoke.

Johnny waited. Mikros did not appear. There was no more time. Johnny turned and ran, pressing the detonator transceiver. Behind him the smoke billowed and swirled in an explosion he could not hear. He ran for the river.

"All over, into the water," he shouted into his mike, but he could not even hear himself. He felt an unexpected fear. If they could not hear him. . . .

But then he reached the balcony, fifty feet above the river, and all was going well. The unhurt ex-Cadets were going over feet-first. The wounded were being slid down escape chutes of plastic. The small-Homes and the imitation Lander sub were waiting in the water below. He could see little of this in the smoke, but he knew it was so. Suddenly he seemed to hook in on a network of awareness. It was as it had been when he had stood in the conference room and felt the hundred and twenty-nine prisoners as if he held them like Tomi, between his hands. In this emergency some new instinct of the third generation was taking over; and they were all a unit.

"Keep moving," he said automatically. He felt they heard him. Then he realized it was his own numbed hearing beginning to clear. A little moving air off the river cleared the smoke from the balcony. Only Tom Loy was standing with him. He motioned Tom over, then turned to go himself. Then he felt one of the People still coming from the direction of the plaza.

"Mike," he said, turning. But then the one coming broke into the clear air of the balcony, and it was not Mikros, but Patrick with a soldier's vibratory rifle in his hands. "You, Pat?" said Johnny, staring. Suddenly it broke on him. "You told them about us!"

Pat stopped a few feet from him. The rifle he held wavered, pointing at Johnny. Then, with a sort of sob, Patrick threw the gun from him, grabbed Johnny, stooped and threw him back over the balcony. Johnny turned instinctively like a cat in the air. And the water smashed hard against him.

He caught himself, readjusting his mask, six feet under. Below him he saw the small-Homes waiting. He turned and swam down to them.

# 5

"Don't hang to your father," said Sara to Tomi, when Johnny was once more back in the small-Home with them.

"But——"

"Not now," Sara said. "They're waiting for him in the Conference Room. Daddy just came by for a minute, and we have to talk. Go swim outside."

Tomi hesitated, standing on one foot, face screwed up.

"You go!" said Sara. Her voice had a hard note in it Johnny had never heard before. Tomi's eyes went wide and he left.

Johnny watched him go numbly. The Lander subs had chased them out into open sea. The decoy they had made out of the small-Homes had drawn the Landers off. On automatic controls, it had led the subs three miles deep to the Atlantic ooze and then blown itself up, taking at least one sub with it. A Lander sub carried over two hundred men. There had been more than a hundred of the ex-Cadets who had not come back.

Riding home after that in the rest of the small-Homes, those that returned had begun to sing *"Hey, Johnny!"* And the song had spread over the radio circuit from ship to ship until they all sang. Johnny had turned his face to the rushing blue beyond the transparent wall of his craft to hide the fact he could not sing along with them.

Patrick's voice had sounded again in his ears. *"You're a ringleader. . . ."*

". . . I've got to talk to you about Tomi," Sara was saying.

"Now?" he said dully. His real reason for detouring by here on his way to the Conference Room was that he had wanted to hide for a few moments. At the sound of his son's name he shivered unexpectedly. The dark eye of the killer whale had come back to his mind. But now it gazed without change and without pity on the still shape of the young ex-Cadet he had seen die in the conservatory, ashore.

"I've never told you why I didn't let you know about your having a son all these years. Do you know why?"

"Why?" He focused on her with difficulty. "No—no, I don't." He became aware, for the first time, that her face was stiff and pale. "Sara, what is it?"

"I didn't tell you," she said as if she were reciting a lesson, "because I didn't want him to be like you."

He thought of Patrick and the men who were now dead.

"Well," he said, "I don't blame you."

"Don't *blame* me!" Without warning she began to cry. It was not the easy, relief-giving sorrow of the People. Her tears were angry. She stood with them running down her cheeks and her fists clenched, facing him. "I knew what you were like when I fell in love with you! I knew you'd always be going and pushing things through. No matter what it cost, no matter who it hurt. You say things and people do them—it's something about you! And you just take it all for granted."

He put his hands on her to soothe her, but she was as hard as a rock.

"But you weren't going to kill my baby!" she thrust at him. "I was going to hide him—keep him safe, so he'd never know what his father was like and want to go and be like him. And go away from me, too, without thinking of anything but what he personally wanted to do, and get himself killed all for nothing."

"Sara—" he said.

"And then you came back. And he told me all about that

216

business in the killer whale corral. And then I knew it was no use. No use at all. Because he was just like you. He was born just like you, and there was nothing I could do to protect him, no matter what I did. My baby—" and with that, at last she broke down. All the hardness went out of her, and he held her to him as she cried.

For a moment or two he thought the crisis was over. But she stiffened again and pulled away from him.

"You've got to make me a promise," she said, wiping her eyes.

"Of course," he said.

"Not of course. You listen to what I want. You make me a promise that if anything happens to me, you'll take care of him. You'll keep him safe. Not the way you would—the way I'd keep him safe. You promise me!"

"Nothing's going to happen to you."

"Promise me!"

"All right," he said. "I promise I'll take care of him the way you would."

She wiped her eyes again. "You'd better go now. They'll be waiting for you. Oh, wait." She turned and hurried from him, back into the bedroom. She came back in a second with a tangle of smashed plastic and dangling wires.

"Patrick left it for you," she said. "He said you'd understand."

Numbly he took the ruined banjo.

When he finally reached the Conference Room, it was full of Council members.

"It's war," said Chad Ridell, looking at him bleakly. "We got their declaration an hour after you landed at Jones Beach. And an hour before one of our gull-cameras picked up this."

He touched a button on his chair. The end of the room blanked out. Johnny saw a gull's-view image of the Atlantic sea-surface in the cold, gray-blue light of early dawn. His sea-instinct recognized the spot as less than a hundred miles south.

"Look," said Chad. There was a flicker in the sky, and a hole yawned suddenly huge and deep in the ocean's face. For a moment the unnatural situation lasted. And then leaping up through the hole moved a fist of water. It lifted toward the paling sky of dawn like a mountain torn from the ocean floor, and a roar like that of some huge, tortured beast burst on the Conference Room.

The fist stretched out into a pillar, broke and disintegrated. A cow biscay whale drifted by on her side, trying to turn over, blood running from the corner of her mouth.

"Sonic explosion," said Johnny. "Big enough for all Castle-Home."

"They meant that declaration of war," said Chad.

"But why bomb empty ocean?" Johnny said.

"Castle-Home was there three hours ago," put in Tom Loy, who was standing close by Chad. "They must have spotted us from a satellite and thought we were still close. We can stay deep from now on, though."

Johnny nodded. Castle-Home had been at a hundred fathoms when the expedition had come back. He remembered what he was carrying.

"No," he said, "even that won't work." He handed the tangle of broken plastic and wires to Chad, who stared at it, blankly.

"It's Patrick's banjo," said Johnny. "Pat went in with us. He was the one who tipped off the Congress soldiers so that they laid that trap in the plaza for us. He's on their side now."

"But Patrick—" Tom Loy stared at him across Chad. "Patrick's third generation! He can find Castle-Home as well as any of us."

"That's right," said Johnny.

"But I don't understand it!" Chad got up abruptly from his chair. He faced Johnny. "Why Patrick—Patrick of all people?"

"I don't know," said Johnny. "He thinks we're wrong to fight the land. It's what he believes, I guess." He shrugged his shoulders unhappily. "Maybe I was wrong."

"You don't believe that," said Tom.

"No, I guess not." Johnny tried to smile at Tom. "At any rate, the only thing that seems to make sense to me, now, is for me and and anyone else who wants to come with me to give ourselves up to them." He glanced at Chad. "If they get what they call ringleaders, maybe——"

Cutting through what he was going to say, came the sudden, brazen shrieking of the alarm bell.

"Missile!" cried a voice from the wall speaker of the room.

"This is the Communications Dome. Missile approaching! Missile——"

A sound too great to be heard folded all around them. Johnny felt himself picked up and carried away at an angle upward. He ducked away from the ceiling, but the ceiling was no longer there. For a second, still moving, he was in a little box of air, with water all around him. Then the water closed in on him, he felt himself seeming to fly apart in all directions, and he lost track abruptly of what was going on.

Some time later when he came back to his senses, he and the world about him were moving very fast. He was rushing through the water in the black suit of cold-water skins he had never taken off, and his mask was over his face, in position. Baldur was with him. He had hold of the dolphin's reins and Baldur was towing him swiftly through debris-strewn water at about the fifteen-fathom depth. They came at last to Johnny's own small-Home, sheared almost in half and floating loggily in the surrounding water.

The pool entrance was missing. Neta, Sara's dolphin, was frantically trying the impossible feat of entering the small-Home through the air-iris, all unmindful of Tantrums beside her. Johnny pushed her aside and dove through himself.

Across the room, beyond the pool, he saw Sara lying on a couch covered by a drape. Tomi was sitting huddled with his knees together on a hassock beside the couch. Johnny ran around the pool and dropped on his knees by the couch.

"My mommy's not feeling good," Tomi said.

Johnny looked at Sara. The world, which had been moving so fast about him, slowed and stopped. All things came to an end, and stopped.

Sara lay still, on her back. There was a little blood dried at the corners of her mouth. Her eyes were not quite closed. They looked from under her eyelids at nothing in particular and her cheeks seemed already sunken in a little under her high, cold cheekbones.

He stared down at her and a slow and terrible chill began to creep gradually through him. He could not take his eyes off her still face. Slowly he began to shiver. The shivers increased until he shuddered through his whole body, and his teeth chattered. He saw Tomi coming toward him with arms outstretched to put them around his father. And suddenly

Johnny broke the spell holding him and shoved the boy back, away from him, so hard he staggered.

"Stay away from me!" Johnny shouted. The room tilted and spun around him. The eye of the killer whale rushed abruptly like death upon him through the wall behind the couch, and he fell forward into roaring nothingness.

When he came back after this, it was to find Tomi clinging to him and sobbing. Johnny awoke as somebody might who had been asleep for a long night. The great gust of feeling that had whirled him into unconsciousness was gone. He felt numbed and coldly clear-headed. Automatically he soothed Tomi. Reflexively he went about the small-Home, pulling out a sea-sled and loading it with clothing, medical supplies, weapons, and other equipment for living off the sea.

When it was loaded he took it outside and left Tomi, now also dressed in cold-water skins, fins, and mask, to harness Baldur to it. He himself went back inside.

He set straight the drape over Sara and stood a little while looking down at her body. Then he detached the governor from the small-Home's heating element and went back outside. Together, he and Tomi watched as the small-Home caught fire inside.

Collapsing inward, as its walls melted, it sank away from them, a flickering light into dark depths, with Neta and her pup circling bewilderedly down after it.

"Where are we going?" said Tomi, as Johnny handed a rein to Tomi and took one himself.

"Where you'll be safe," said Johnny. He put the boy's other hand on a rail of the sled.

"All by ourselves?" said Tomi.

"Yes." Johnny broke off suddenly. Inside Tomi's mask, he saw the boy pale and frowning, the way Sara had used to frown. Something moved in Johnny's guts. "All right," he said, but he did not say it to Tomi.

He touched the radio controls of his mask with his tongue, turning the circle of reception up to full. A roar of conversation sounded like surf in his ears.

"This is Johnny Joya," he said into the mike. "Are there any Council members listening?" The surf-sound of voices roared on, unchanging. "This is Johnny Joya speaking. Are there any Council members who can hear me?"

There seemed no change in the sound coming into his earphone. He turned to Tomi, shrugging. And then the roar began to diminish a little. It slackened. "This is Johnny Joya," he said. "Are there any Council members listening?"

The voices dwindled, faded, and disappeared. Silence roared instead in his earphone. From far away, blurredly, a single voice spoke.

"Johnny? Johnny, is that you? This is Tom Loy. Johnny, we're the only Council members left. I found the room. None of the rest got out." Tom hesitated. "Johnny, can you hear me? Where are you?"

"North of you," said Johnny. "And swimming north." There was a cold, clean, dead feeling in him, like a man might experience after an amputation when the pain was blocked. "I'm taking my son, my dolphin, and sea-camping equipment and I'm heading out."

"Heading out?"

"Yes," said Johnny. He touched the rein and moved it and Baldur began to swim, pulling the sled and the two humans with it. Through the rushing gray-blue water, Johnny saw the young arm and hand of Tomi in its black sleeve clinging to the sled rail; and he remembered Patrick's arm, older and larger, seen in the same position. "The rest of you should do the same thing."

"Head out?" Tom's voice faded for a second in the earphone. "Out into the sea without small-Homes?"

"That's right," said Johnny. He watched Baldur sliding smoothly through the water. "Castle-Home is gone. By this time the other Castle-Homes are probably gone, too. We're Homeless, now. Everybody might as well face that."

"But we're going to have to build new Homes."

"We can't," said Johnny. "With Patrick helping, the Landers'll just go on destroying them."

"But we've got to have Homes!"

"No," said Johnny. A strap on the sled was working loose. He reached forward automatically and unbuckled it. "That's what the Landers think. But they're wrong. Every one of the third generation and lots of the second have lived off the sea without Homes for the fun of it. We can do it permanently. We can take care of the older people, as well, if they want."

"But," Tom's voice came stronger in the earphone for a second, "we'll be nothing but a lot of water-gypsies!" He fell silent, as if he had suddenly run out of words.

"No," said Johnny. He pulled the strap tight and buckled it

221

again. It held well this time. "Our Homes were something we brought to the sea from the land. Sooner or later we were bound to leave them behind and live like true people of the sea. The Land's just pushed us to it a little early." He checked the other straps. They were all tight. "I'm only telling you what I think. That's what I'm doing."

There was a long moment of rushing silence in the earphone. Then Tom's voice called out.

"Johnny! You aren't leaving us?"

"Yes," said Johnny.

"But some day we'll be carrying the fight back to the Landers. We need you to plan for then. We need you——"

"No!" The word came out so harshly that Johnny saw Tomi flinch alongside him and stare in his direction. "I've helped too much already. Get someone else to make your plans!"

He felt Tom's eyes reach into him. He reached himself for calmness. For a moment he had almost come back to life, but now the safe feeling, the cold, clean, dead feeling, took him over once again.

"No," he said, more quietly. "You don't want my help, Tom. And besides, my wife is dead and I made her a promise to keep our boy safe. That's all the job I have now. I wouldn't take any other if I could. If you'll take a last piece of advice, though, you'll all scatter the way I'm doing. Spread out through the seas, we'll be safe." He turned off his mike, then turned it on again. "Good-by, Tom," he said. "Good-by, People. Good luck to you all."

Tom's voice spoke again, but Johnny no longer listened. He picked up the rein and turned Baldur's head a little to the northeast, along the water road to the North Atlantic Current. He shut his mind to all the past.

Baldur responded smoothly. He swam easily and not too fast in the graceful underwater up and down weaving motion of the dolphin that brought him occasionally to the surface to breathe. In the earphone, the perplexed conversations picked up once more.

Johnny did not listen. He felt emptied of all emotion. Of sorrow, of bitterness, of fear, of anger. He looked ahead and northward into a future as wide and empty as the Arctic water. Only the wild wastes of the endless oceans were left now to the People of the Sea. They would gather at Castle-Home no more.

He thought that he had no more feeling left in him, and that this was a good thing. And then, in his earphone, he heard one of the parting People begin to sing:

*Hey, Johnny! Hey-a, Johnny!*
*Home from the shore. . . .*

And the voices of others of the People took it up, joining in. The earphone echoed to a spreading chorus:

*Hey-o, Johnny! Hey, Johnny!*
*To high land go no more!*

The song blended in many voices. It reached through the cold, dead feeling of amputation in him to the awareness that had come as he stood in the Conference Room and felt the beating lives of the hundred and twenty-nine prisoners as if he held them in his hands.

It took hold of him as he had been taken hold of, in the moment of perception that had linked him with the other ex-Cadets as, deafened and smoke-blinded, they made their escape into the East River. He had cut himself loose from his people. But he saw now he could not escape them. No, never could he escape them, any more than a molecule of water, in its long journey by sky and mountain and field and harbor-mouth, could escape its eventual homecoming to the salt sea. And the knowledge of this, discovered at last, brought a sort of sad comfort to him.

He opened his mouth to sing with them, but—as in the small-Home returning from Manhattan Island—he found the words would not come. He held to the sled, listening. About him, three fathoms of water pressed against his passage. Baldur swam strongly to the north. The Atlantic Drift was carrying them east and north and in time they would come to the Irminger Current, swinging north between the Iceland coast and the Greenland shore—he, his son, and his dolphin.

Baldur swam strongly, as if he could sense the purpose of their going. Behind, in his earphone, Johnny could hear the voices of the singers beginning to fade and dwindle as they moved out of range. The number of their voices lessened and became distant.

The sun was going down. The three of them broke surface for a moment and the cloud-heavy sky above was darkening gray. Soon it would be full dark, and somewhere in the black water under the stars they would camp and sleep. Tomi held without a word to the sled. The dolphin swam with strength to the north and east. Behind, the last voices were failing, until only one still sounded, faintly, in the earphone:

*Long away, away, my Johnny!*
*Four long years and more.*
*Hey-o, Johnny! Hey, Johnny!*
*Go to land, no more.*

And still the three of them swam to the north, under a gray sky that was like a road, and forever flowing.